CW00543313

Also by William Andrews

The Dirty Truth

Daughters of the Dragon – A Comfort Woman's Story

The Dragon Queen

THE ESSENTIAL TRUTH © 2015 and 2017 by William Andrews

All rights reserved. No part of this book may be reproduced or transmitted in any form or by any means, electronic or mechanical, including photocopying, recording, or by any information storage and retrieval system without permission in writing from the copyright owner.

Printed in the United States of America.

This is a work of fiction. Names, characters, places and incidents either are the product of the author's imagination or are used fictitiously, and any resemblance to any actual persons, living or dead, events, or locales is entirely coincidental.

Cover design by Doug Novak.

Library of Congress Control Number:		2014900030
ISBN:	Print	978-0-9913958-1-1
	EBook	978-0-9913958-0-4

To order additional copies of this book, contact your on-line retailer or visit:

www.williamandrewsbooks.com

To my wife, Nancy.

Acknowledgements

TO NANCY WHO supported me in this and all my endeavors; to Dennis LeDoux who taught me how to put together a readable novel; to all my family, friends, and colleagues who read the manuscript and provided input; thank you.

THE ESSENTIAL TRUTH

People don't follow leaders, they follow courage.

- John Kotter, Harvard Business School

ONE

As Ben Smith stood in the lobby waiting for the elevator to take him to work at the Jacob & Marin advertising agency, he wondered and worried about what kind of day he would have. Over the weekend, his agency's largest client, Katch Financial, informed him they were letting another agency pitch their account. Ben knew that if Jacob & Marin didn't win the review, they'd probably go out of business and one hundred and forty people, including Ben, would lose their jobs.

The elevator didn't come and Ben shook his head. The ad biz hadn't always been this hard. When Ben first got into the business twenty-five years earlier, it was the end of the Madmen era. Men wore expensive suits, crisp cotton shirts and wingtips. Women wore smart dresses and heels. Many of the old-timers still smoked, creating a permanent blue haze in the wood-paneled bullpen. Mostly men occupied the offices around the outside of the bullpen, but women were starting to claw their way in. The heroes were secretaries who could make last-second corrections and quickly make fifteen perfect Xerox copies collated and stapled, and hand them off to the account team rushing out the door to get to a client meeting on time.

It'd been glorious. Ben and the rest of the agency worked long hours, often staying so late that by the time Ben got home he'd missed the late-night news. Their product was creative ideas, ad campaigns that made their clients' sales soar. After work, they'd hit the bars and talk about business, new campaigns and which of their competitors was doing the best work. They were admen, and increasingly, adwomen. They worked hard, drank hard, fucked hard and every single one of their clients would've traded places with them.

But that era died about the same time the old guard's livers gave out. Agency people didn't go out after work anymore, opting instead to go straight home to catch the early news or attend their kid's lacrosse match. Today, most ad people longed for the safer, easier jobs on the client side. The clients had control and their risk-averse management shoved an agency's campaign through research like grist through a mill until all the life was ground out. The rock-stars today were the nerds who could dissect tiny bits of information from a website, Facebook page or an e-mail campaign and find an infinitesimally small competitive advantage.

Still, there were moments when everything came together and the agency created an extraordinary campaign. If the client didn't force a change based on some obscure research finding, and the campaign ran as designed sending the client's sales through the roof, everyone at the agency got a taste of the good old days. And then, Ben would have a martini at lunch and raise a silent toast to the good old days.

Ben needed one of those magical moments now. He pushed the 'up' button a second time, but still the elevator didn't come. Everet Katch, the CEO of Katch Financial, was the last of the old-time clients who loved edgy campaigns and didn't beat the hell out of the agency with ridiculous demands. He was one of the few clients who 'got it', and Jacob & Marin was lucky to have his account. But now it was up for review and it was Ben's responsibility to save it.

Ben punched the elevator's 'up' button one more time. Only Ben and the agency president, Trevor Marin, knew about the review. The news came from Katch's director of marketing through an e-mail sent yesterday afternoon—Sunday of all days—that Ben had read from his laptop.

Our mutual funds business has fallen sharply over the past year and we need to turn it around quickly, the e-mail had read. *That makes our new ad campaign critically important. We've called an emergency meeting of our board of directors to review agencies. You are to present a new campaign next Wednesday afternoon to the entire board of directors. And you should know, we've invited another agency to submit a campaign.*

If the presentation was to the Board of Directors, mutual funds must be in real trouble and now, so was J&M. And what other agency was presenting next Wednesday? It could be only one: Hanrahan Communications run by Sheldon Hanrahan, the enigmatic billionaire communications mogul who had run all the other old-guard agencies out of business.

Finally, the elevator came and took Ben to his floor. "Morning, Julie," he said as he stepped into J&M's lobby on the renovated warehouse's eighth floor. "Is Tree in yet?"

"Haven't seen Mr. Marin," Julie replied from behind the black marble reception desk. "But Tom Clarey is looking for you." Without looking up, she handed him a pink message slip from Tom that said, "Need to see you ASAP."

As Ben walked to his office among the heavy timber beams and old yellow brick, employees of Jacob & Marin Advertising Agency were already hard at work. They talked on phones or focused on computer screens. A few packed briefcases for client meetings. Others leaned against cubicle walls talking casually over the dividers. They were all blissfully unaware that their jobs were in jeopardy.

Ben kept his head up and his step lively as he went to his office, though he'd rather have stayed in bed this morning. He hadn't slept well the night before. He'd read Doug's e-mail five times during the night, the last at 4:15a.m. After that, he never really went back to sleep. Now, at the office, he had to pretend everything was fine.

As Ben got to his office, Jay Stone slid up to him. Jay was one of Ben's young account executives. He had thick black hair and was wearing gray pleated slacks and a blue shirt.

"Boss, you gotta lose that enviro attitude and stop taking the bus. We got a call from Jim Ross at Bug BeGone. He says the coupon ad didn't run in Detroit."

Ben stopped at his office door. "What?"

"That's what he said. Jim's regional manager checked all editions of the *Free Press*. It wasn't there. He's really pissed off."

Ben stepped into his office and snapped on the light. Two windows cut out of the hundred-year old yellow brick wall opened to the street eight stories below. His desk and worktable were stacked with files and papers. A parched philodendron sat on the end of one of the shelves. On his chair, a printout of a new ad had a yellow Post-It note stuck to it that said, "Must have approval this morning!" 'This morning' was underlined three times.

Ben turned to Jay. "We had front-page position for that ad," he said.

"Yeah. With Valassis," Jay said, his hands thrust in his front slacks pocket.

"I also hear Tom Clarey wants to talk to me."

Jay nodded. "Something must be up with him. He was here before me. Maybe he heard about the coupon ad. Oh, and Gerry Hansen wants to know if you've read the Katch research for our nine o'clock meeting."

"Yeah. I read it last night and again this morning on the bus while I was saving the earth."

Ben cleared the printout from his chair and sat at his desk. He told Jay he'd talk to the media department about Bug BeGone, and that Jay would have to take the Katch research meeting without him. Jay agreed and then Ben asked if Jay had seen Tree yet this morning. Jay said no, he hadn't seen him.

Ben took a deep breath. "Jay, I have something to tell you. Close the door." Jay reached over and swung the door closed. Then, Ben told his young assistant about the email from Katch. "That means, in effect, the account is in review," Ben said.

Jay's eyes widened. "You're kidding?"

"Keep it to yourself. And clear your calendar. Our presentation is next Wednesday and we're behind. I don't need to tell you what it'd mean if we lost Katch."

"Geez-a. Katch up for review," Jay said running his hand through his hair.

"Yeah, well, up for review doesn't mean we've lost it. We have to fight for it. Let's see what Tree says when he gets in. He'll know what to do."

Jay looked at his feet, nodded and then left.

Ben clicked on his computer. Among the thirty-seven new e-mails was one from Jim Ross marked urgent. *Coupon ad didn't run in Detroit!! Call me ASAP!!* Ben rubbed his eyes. What a screw up. They'd timed the coupon for when people bought insect repellent for their summer vacations. It'd be six weeks before another ad could run. By then the repellent buying season would be over and Bug BeGone would be history in Detroit.

He didn't have time for this. He needed to talk to Tree about Katch. But Tree wasn't in yet and the missed coupon insert was a serious problem. Better handle it now, Ben thought, before he had to turn all of his attention to Katch.

He headed down the hall to the media director's office. Lucy Johnson was on the phone when Ben arrived. At six feet tall, she was exactly Ben's height but she outweighed him by forty pounds, most of it Iowa corn-fed muscle. Neatly organized three-ring binders filled her office.

"I can't meet with you next week," she said into the phone. "I'm not meeting with reps right now." Lucy was talking to a media sales representative or 'reptile' as the agency media people called them. The reptile was probably trying to get a meeting with Lucy to present their case to be included in media plan.

"Well, I'm sorry, I can't do it. Goodbye." Lucy hung up and glanced at Ben. She turned to a spreadsheet on her monitor and pretended to work on it. She asked what Ben wanted. He told her about Jim Ross' e-mail about the coupon ad not running and Lucy confirmed that it hadn't. Ben asked why.

"You didn't sign the media order," she said without looking at him. "I couldn't place the ad without one."

"What? That's ridiculous! No one signs media orders."

Lucy shook her head. "Not true. Ginny always signs them, and her media is always placed."

"You've got to be kidding!" Ben said. "Look, Lucy, it was on the media plan you yourself wrote. You had the MO two months ago. You could've told me you needed a signature. I've never had to sign one before. Why now?"

Lucy turned from her monitor. "Look, Ben, I'm sorry. But it's not my responsibility to tell account people how to do their jobs. If you had signed the media order, the ad would've run. It's not my fault," she said and quickly turned back to her monitor.

So that was it. Lucy hadn't placed the ad, even though one of Ben's assistants had delivered the media order over two months ago. It was true there was a place on the MO for the account manager to sign, but with the exception of the always-perfect Ginny Rubenstein, no one ever signed them. Now, because of Lucy's mistake, he'd have to put in extra hours—hours he didn't have—to produce an emergency plan to save the Detroit market for Bug BeGone.

"Okay," said Ben. "I'll accept the blame. But I expect you to put in overtime to help me clean up this mess." Lucy kept her eyes on her monitor and didn't reply.

Ben turned on his heel and marched back to his office. He slumped in his chair. He opened a file drawer and pulled out the Bug BeGone media order. Sure enough, no signature. Now he'd have to call Jim Ross, admit his mistake and promise the agency would do everything it could to minimize the damage and get Bug BeGone back on track.

It wouldn't be a pleasant call, and he wanted to get it over with.

But it would have to wait. He had to talk to Tree about Katch. They needed a plan for the pitch and they needed it fast. He grabbed a pad and pen, went to Tree's office and poked his head inside. The corner office, big as a Beverly Hills living room, was dark.

"Hey, Ben," came a voice from a short distance up the hall. It was Joanne, the executive secretary, at her desk outside Tom Clary's office. "Tom's been looking for you. Can you meet with him now?"

Ben took another glance into Tree's dark, empty office and went over to Joanne. She had hair dyed auburn and an outfit a little too youngish for a middle-aged woman. "Hi, Joanne. Where's Tree?"

"I don't know. It's not like him to be this late. Can you meet with Tom?"

"I've got a lot to do, but I guess..."

Joanne offered Ben water or coffee but he refused both. He went into Tom Clarey's office. Tom was at his desk reading the morning paper. When he saw Ben, he stood and smiled. "Ben! Come in. Come in!"

Tom Clarey had an office twice as large as Ben's and as neat as Ben's was messy. A solid walnut desktop supported by stainless steel legs sat at an angle to a bank of windows overlooking downtown Minneapolis. Off to the side, a matching credenza held a collection of Tom's art—a small Ascalon bronze, a hand-painted African vase, a picture of his blonde, blue-eyed wife in an etched silver frame.

Tom himself was as neat as his office. At 49, he was *GQ* handsome. He had thick, dark hair graying at the temples and fashionable, wire-rimmed glasses. Unlike Ben who wore a blue shirt and khaki dress slacks, Tom Clarey never wore casual clothes to work. Today Tom wore an Italian suit and a tie with an unusual, yet conservative pattern.

Tom Clarey was, as the creative people said, the *perfect suit*. Two years earlier, Tree had recruited him out of McCann in Detroit to take charge of J&M's new business effort. He was reputed to be a top-notch rainmaker but the only rain Tom made for J&M was John's

Underwear for Men and the only reason he was able to land that account was because his wife's uncle was the CEO.

Tom pointed to a black leather couch and told Ben to sit. Tom closed the door and sat across from him. "So, how's the family?" Tom asked. He was still smiling, showing off bleached white teeth.

"Fine, Tom. Just fine."

"Great. Great. How's Nan? Is she still working for Senator Thielen and the Democrats?"

"She's well, and yes, she is." Ben noticed a bit of food stuck between Tom's teeth.

"Well we can forgive her for that," Tom said. "And how old is that little one of yours—what's her name, Janet?"

"Jenny. She's ten. She starts fifth grade in the fall. Tom, I have a ton of work to do. What's this about?"

Tom leaned forward and carefully folded his hands in front of him. He changed his expression from cordial to serious. "Ben, I heard Katch is up for review. Is it true?"

"How did you find out?" Ben asked.

"It doesn't matter. Is it true?"

Ben sighed and nodded. "We got an e-mail from Doug Lewis. They want to look at another agency's campaign for mutual funds when they see ours. To me that means the entire account is in review."

"Well. That's a problem. I'll have to make the pitch my responsibility."

"What? You want to take over the pitch?"

"Of course, you'll still handle the day-to-day. But, I'll be the pitch leader and make the presentation."

"Tom," Ben said, "you can't be serious. Katch is my account."

Tom sat back, took a starched white handkerchief from his pocket and began to clean his glasses. "Ben, I needn't remind you that I am in charge of both account service and new business and therefore should I be responsible for the Katch review. When is it?"

"Next Wednesday," Ben answered.

"Perfect," Tom said, slipping on his glasses. "I'll make the presentation in your place."

Ben searched Tom's face for a clue into what was behind this move. As usual, Tom revealed nothing. "Tom," Ben said, "we'll have to see what Tree says. It's his agency. Let's wait to talk to him. He'll know what to do."

"Mr. Marin isn't in yet," Tom said, carefully tucking his handkerchief back into his pocket. "Anyway, we shouldn't always depend on Tree. Who knows how long he'll continue to lead the agency? He may decide to retire. Or..." Tom paused dramatically and leaned toward Ben. "Tree hasn't looked that good lately, Ben," he said in a half whisper. "I must be in the position to take over the agency if... when it becomes necessary."

"Tom," Ben said moving to the couch's edge, "Katch is our most profitable account. Without it, we wouldn't be anything more than a small-time agency. Just let Tree and me handle the review."

Tom stood, strolled over to the credenza and ran a finger over the Ascalon bronze. "The way I see it," he said, his eyes on the bronze, "the account wouldn't be in review if it had been handled correctly. Anyway, it doesn't matter. I'm the Senior Vice President and you report to me. When Tree comes in, I intend to make my case for leading the pitch. I'll tell him you and I talked and you agreed." He looked up at Ben. "Understand?"

Ben fought for control. It was a joke. Tom, taking over Katch in case Tree retired or got sick? Tree Marin would never retire. The agency had been his baby for over thirty years. He was its heart and soul. He was the one who gave it life and made the place run. And Tree Marin was the most robust sixty-nine-year-old man Ben had ever known. He had more energy than most people half his age. Sure, he was missing a lot of work lately. But if Tree got sick or died, the agency would surely die with him. No one could hold it together without Tree.

Tom's move might be a joke, but it wasn't a surprise. He needed leverage so Tree wouldn't fire him for failing at new business. And the timing was perfect. If J&M lost Katch, Tom could point to Ben as the person responsible. On the other hand, if J&M kept the account, it would look like Tom saved Jacob & Marin's largest account and position him as Tree's successor.

There was a knock on the door. Tom looked over. "Yes?"

The door cracked open and Joanne leaned through. "I... I'm terribly sorry to interrupt," she stammered, "but Mrs. Marin is on the phone and wants to talk to Tom immediately. I wouldn't have bothered you, but she said it was urgent."

"Okay," Tom said. "I'll take it."

Tom went to his desk and picked up the phone. "Sarah, hello!" he said cheerfully. "How can I help you?" As Tom listened, his smile fell and his face turned white.

"Oh, no," he said, his voice barely audible.

It was the first time Ben ever saw Tom show an uncontrolled emotion.

TWO

"JACKSON!" A VOICE barked from an office next to Detective Darren Jackson's desk.

"Yeah?" Jackson answered as he studied the Minneapolis crime report from the night before. The report listed two homicides and a third case, yet to be decided if it was a homicide or not. The big case was a drive-by shooting at 9:38p.m. that killed a twelve-year-old African-American girl named Shauna Tate while she sat at her kitchen table reading a book. Three Latino gunmen emptied more than a hundred 9-millimeter rounds into what they thought was the house of a rival gang member. They had the wrong house. The girl was hit by five bullets, one that struck her squarely in the temple killing her instantly. Jackson had seen photos of the girl on the ten o'clock news. She had colored beads in her braided hair, bright-eyes, and an infectious, innocent smile. The incident happened in an African-American neighborhood so there was a lot of pressure on the police to solve the case quickly and bring the Latino shooters to justice. Jackson's office was in the same building as the police headquarters and it was already crawling with reporters. Jackson new the case would get loud and ugly, fast.

Lieutenant Jake West appeared from around a metal doorframe with his hands on his hips. "Goddamn it, Jackson, when I say 'Jackson', what I mean is, 'Get your ass in here', not that I want to hold a conversation while I'm in here and you're out there. Now get in here." West disappeared back into the office.

"Gimme a minute," Jackson replied. He continued to read the report.

Another homicide was at 10:15p.m. when a 33-year-old construction worker beat his wife to death with a tire iron because she was moving out on him. *Apparently*, thought Jackson, *the wife made her decision a little too late.* At 12:31a.m., the police found the husband in a back booth of a corner bar less than two blocks from the murder. When they arrested him, he was on his tenth beer and chaser and was sloppily pleading for everyone to forgive him for what he'd done. He killed his wife, he said, because he loved her and didn't want her to leave. Unlike the previous case, this one would open and close the same day and unlike the previous case, it would receive no press coverage.

Finally, there was fatal, single car accident on a county road in the Lake Independence Township just west of the Twin Cities. A classic 1967 Porsche Targa traveling at an estimated 125 mph, lost control and smashed into an oak tree sometime around three in the morning. The car caught fire, attracting the attention of a nearby resident who called 911. State troopers and the local fire department arrived, put out the fire, and had the burned and mangled car towed away. They sent the equally burned and mangled body to the Hennepin County morgue.

The driver's license found on the body identified the driver as Trevor C. Marin.

According to the report, Minneapolis Homicide got involved because at 6:25a.m., the city desk received a suspicious call from an unidentified male from Miami Beach. The caller urged the police to investigate because, he said, the crash was not an accident. "How the hell would he know that from Miami Beach?" Jackson said aloud.

"Jackson, damn it!" Lieutenant West roared.

Detective Jackson set the report on a corner of his desk, went in to West's small, windowless office. "Okay, Lieu, waddya want?" The

Lieutenant's knuckly hands clutched the *Twin Cities Times*. Only the top of West's curly blonde hair showed above the paper. A picture of a smiling Shauna Tate dominated the front page.

"What's the skinny on this drive-by, this Tate shooting?" West asked.

"It's gonna be a beaut, Lieu," Jackson replied. "This place is already lousy with reporters, neighborhood groups, the NAACP. Hell, even the honorable Reverend Terrance White has a news conference scheduled this afternoon. Everybody's in on this one. Already two church groups—both claim they're the family's only church, mind you—are plannin' prayer vigils and askin' for donations. Girl's school is stagin' a rally and neighborhood parents are protestin.' I tell ya, it's a zoo."

"Yeah, I'll say. There are three pages in the paper about it." West carefully folded the newspaper and set it on his desk. He was in his late fifties with a thick neck, hazel eyes, and a scar on his chin. He had his tie pulled half way down his shirt. "Good thing the gang unit is handling it," West said, "but we still have to help out. Captain called this morning and said we have to handle all the ongoing cases and any new ones that come in while the rest of the department works on the Tate case."

"We're gonna be busy," Jackson said, sliding into a Naugahyde couch.

"So, what about this domestic?" West asked.

"As good as done, Lieu," Jackson answered. "It'll be turned over to the DA by noon. The guy had four domestic assault charges in the past eighteen months and he confessed, too. It's a lock for sure."

"Yeah, but he was drunk when we brought him in," West said. "His attorney will claim he was incapable of a confession."

"Maybe, but he's sober this mornin,' and he waived his right to counsel."

"Good. We need an easy one." West leaned back and clasped his knuckles behind his head. "What about the car accident? Why are we getting it?"

"It's the phone call. The night guys tried to pass it on to the state once the call came in, but they pushed it right back. Said since the call came to us, it's our case."

"Who made the call?" West asked.

"A male from Miami Beach with an untraceable cell phone—you know, one of those pre-paid, disposable ones. But, he musta known something. I mean, how would he know we had a fatal car crash last night?"

"Yeah, you're right." West smiled, pushing out the scar on his chin. "You're going to be a first-class detective someday, Jackson."

Someday? Jackson already was a first-class detective and everyone, including Lieutenant West knew it. He'd joined homicide less than six years before and from the first day on the job, he realized detective work was what he was born to do. It was something in his personality—he became obsessed. He wasn't smarter than the other dicks on the squad, and he didn't have as much experience either. What made him good was his persistence—he never let anything go. Ever. No matter how thin the evidence or how elusive the clues, he simply had to solved the crime.

"I'm already your best detective and you know it," Jackson said.

Lieutenant West let out a thick laugh. "You keep thinking that, Jackson. What else does the report say?"

"It's all straightforward. Maybe there's somethin' in the medical report. It showed up just before you dragged me in here."

"Already?" West said. "Well, get it. Let's have a look-see."

Jackson went to his desk and retrieved the blue folder that contained the medical examiner's report on Trevor Marin. He opened it as he slid back into the couch. The report indicated the cause of death was massive head trauma and third degree burns over sixty percent of the body. Mrs. Sarah Marin positively identified what was left of the body at the county morgue at 6:10 this morning. They took fingerprints, tissue samples, dental photos, and the medical examiner was retrieving Mr. Marin's dental records for additional identification.

"Nothing much in here either, Lieu."

West raised his palms. "Do we have a reason to think it's a homicide?"

"Maybe it was a suicide," Jackson replied. "Who is this Marin anyway?"

West said, "He's a big-shot advertising guy. The president of that agency, Johnson and Marin or something. Isn't the type to off himself."

"So tell me, Lieu, what he's doing drivin' 125 miles per hour in the middle of the night?"

"It was a Porsche, Jackson," West said. "You probably can't go much over fifty in that old Ford of yours, so you wouldn't know about shit like that."

West looked again at the report and ran a hand over his head. "Well, I guess we have to investigate because of the call. We can't afford to let anything slip through, not with all the attention on us with this Tate case. I want a complete autopsy on this guy."

"We'll have to get the body back from the funeral home," Jackson said. "I hate when we have to do that."

"What?" West said. "County's supposed to hold it twenty-four hours."

"Well, they didn't this time. Body was picked up less than two hours ago."

"Gimme that," West said. Jackson handed the medical examiner's report to West. "Who approved the release?" West flipped to the release form. "What... is this? Chief Daniels? Since when does the chief of police sign morgue releases?"

Jackson read the report over West's shoulder. "Damn, man, it's his signature alright."

West handed the ME report back to Jackson. "The chief must not've known about the call. We have to check it out. We can't have loose ends around here when we're under the microscope. Call the funeral home and get the body to the medical examiner. I want a complete autopsy on it. By the way, who picked up the body?"

Jackson ran a finger to the bottom of the medical examiner's report. "Man, this is gettin' peculiar. Look here. Cecil Adams himself picked it up. Signature's right here. The guy owns—what?—most all the funeral homes across Minnesota and he has time to pick up a body? That's unusual, to say the least."

"Unusual," West said with a look. "I don't like unusual. Find out what's going on."

Jackson headed to the door. "Damn right. I'm on it."

"Darren," West said, "make sure we have all of our bases covered on this one. It can't get screwed up. Not now."

"Like I said, Lieu," Jackson said, "your best detective is on it."

*

Jackson got the phone number for Cecil Adams Mortuary service from a full-page ad in the yellow pages. He dialed and a woman with a soothing voice answered. He asked to talk to Cecil Adams. A few seconds later, Cecil Adams came on the line.

"Detective Jackson, how may I help you?" His voice was as soothing as the woman's.

"Mr. Adams, I have to get Trevor Marin's body back from you. We want to run an autopsy. Can you get it back to the morgue this mornin'?"

There was a pause. Then, "I'm afraid not."

"And why is that?"

"I'm sorry to have to tell you, Detective, Mr. Marin has been cremated."

"What?" Jackson leaned into his desk. "Already? You've had the body only two hours."

"Yes, sir," Adams said, not so soothing anymore. "The police released the body, so we went ahead with the cremation. All the papers are in order."

"Mr. Adams, sorry for sayin' but I don't get it. First, you yourself picked up the body. I bet you haven't done that in thirty years. Then, you cremate it right away? Don't you normally wait on a cremation in case the next of kin changes their mind?"

"Yes, of course. I understand, Detective. Let me explain." Adams had recovered his composure and again sounded as if he were consoling Jackson about a recently deceased loved one. He explained that they received a call early this morning from Mrs. Sarah Marin. Adams knew the deceased was a notable businessman so he decided to handle it himself. He met with Mrs. Marin and she approved the arrangements. After she signed all the papers, Adams took care of the matter for her. Since the body was burned badly, they decided to do the cremation right away.

"And Mrs. Marin would not change her mind, Detective," Adams said. "As I said, the body was badly burned and the papers are in order."

Jackson switched the phone to his other hand and leaned an elbow on his desk. "Mr. Adams, we're keepin' this case open as a possible homicide. I expect your cooperation. I want his wallet, clothes, and anythin' else you have. I'll send a car."

"Yes, sir. I'll send copies of the papers, too."

Jackson hung up and he could feel it again—the obsession. There were too many questions—the call from Miami Beach; the chief of police signing the release; the body picked up and cremated so quickly. The police shrink told Jackson he had an obsessive personality. It was the reason his wife said she couldn't live with him anymore when she filed for divorce. And she was right, of course—his obsessions made him a terrible husband. But it also made him a great detective.

"Jackson!" West barked from the other side of the door.

"Yeah, Lieu," Jackson said.

"Get your ass in here. We have more work to do. I just got off the phone with the captain. He wants our help on another case."

More detective work, thought Jackson. *Good*. It was what he was born to do.

*

His directions were clear. If anything unusual happened, he was to place an Internet phone call from his computer to the URL they made him memorize. He could call any time of the day or night and someone would answer. The call would be untraceable.

He sat at his desk in his office with the door closed, typed in the IP address, clicked on the "call" button, and waited. A faint ringing sound came from his computer. A voice answered.

"Yes?"

"The police are investigating. A Detective Jackson called. He said they're keeping the case open as a possible homicide."

"Homicide? Why?"

"The detective didn't say. I didn't ask."

"What did you tell him?" the voice asked, wheezing.

"Nothing. The body has already been disposed of."

"Good. Don't worry. We'll take care of it."

"Okay, but I thought you said there wouldn't be any problems."

The voice coughed and wheezed again. Then it said, "You'll be fine. Just be sure to follow procedures. Delete this call record and do a clean sweep of your hard drive as you were taught to do."

"Yes, sir."

"Cecil," the voice said, "don't worry. It will be okay."

THREE

THE ANNOUNCEMENT FROM JOANNE came over J&M's paging system. "All J&M employees are required to attend an important agency-wide meeting at 10:30 in the large conference room," she said. "There are no exceptions. Do not be late. Thank you."

After the announcement, the agency erupted with gossip. Janice Esteban, the assistant media planner, told Sheila Green, the creative assistant, the meeting was to announce Tree had decided to retire. "I heard he's quitting," she told Sheila. "He just up and decided not to work anymore. This weekend, he called Tom and Andrew and said, 'You take over. I'm done.'"

Sheila agreed enthusiastically and rushed off to tell others.

Rob Hansen, an assistant account executive, told Dyan Peters, a media buyer who Rob thought had the best body of any woman in the agency, that he knew "for a fact" Tree had negotiated the sale of J&M to a large New York agency. "It's a good move," he said. "The company's value is at its peak while Tree can still run it for a few years. The cost of capital is low right now which, of course, makes the acquisition attractive to the buyer. I don't know who is buying us, but that's what the meeting is about—to tell us who our new owner is."

Dyan nodded as Rob snuck a glance at her chest.

Susan Schroeder in accounting told anyone who'd listen that she'd heard "from a reliable source," that Tree ran off to France with a young model he'd met on a photo shoot, but no one believed her because she thought everyone in management was having an affair.

Ben Smith suspected worse news. Tom Clarey had asked Ben to leave his office before Ben could tell what Sarah Marin had called about. But he'd seen Tom's face, heard the shock in his voice, and knew something terrible had happened. Ben hadn't told anyone what he suspected and he hadn't told anyone about the Katch review either. If not for the call from Sarah Marin, the first thing he would've done after the meeting with Tom was to get hold of Tree about the Katch pitch and Tom's plan to take it over. Of course, Sarah's call made him put that plan on hold. He knew that if something had happened to Tree, the agency would be in very serious trouble.

Until Ben knew what Sarah's call was about, he could do nothing about Katch. So he met with Jay to work out a solution to the Bug BeGone media problem. Soon, they had a rough fallback plan for Bug BeGone that Jay was faxing to Jim Ross. Ben thought he might be able to rescue the situation if he could get Lucy to pull some favors with the media reptiles. But there was still the Katch pitch which he had not been able to work on.

And there was Tom.

And now this meeting about Tree.

A few minutes before 10:30, Ben headed to the conference room. It was already full of employees engaged in low talk. They called the room the Octagon because it was in fact, an eight-sided room. And it was huge. "A small airplane hangar" someone had once said. They built it using the old warehouse's timber columns, beams and yellow brick to their advantage. In the center was a granite table that sat thirty people with enough room for each to spread papers around. Electronic gadgetry was everywhere. Along one wall was a large built-in service area for food and drinks.

The Octagon was one of the few things Tom Clarey and the creative director, Andrew Birk, had ever agreed on. Tom wanted a conference room that would make J&M look like a large international agency when he made new business presentations. Andrew wanted a room that would provide a dramatic backdrop for his creative ideas when he presented them. Together, Tom and Andrew prevailed on Tree to "invest", as they said, in "doing it right." It was rumored the room cost over half million dollars.

When Ben walked in, sitting in the back alone was John Turner, a copywriter who'd worked in the ad biz since the Madmen days. John's old-fashioned, straightforward copywriting style was often at odds with the younger creative staff. Even so, John had a light in his eyes and a quick smile that made people like him.

Ben went over to John. "Mind if I join you?"

"Sure," John replied. "Pull up a chair." John had a look that one art director labeled "tweedy." It was an apt description. He wore a dark green sports coat with a cotton sweater underneath. Gray flecked his brown hair. "So, what do you suppose this little gathering is about?" John asked.

"Who knows?" Ben answered.

More people filed in and the room began to fill. Rows of extra chairs surrounded the conference table and people sat in small groups.

"Quite a collection, eh Ben?" John said. "Did you ever notice how people always sit in their own little clusters? Look over there. The creative cluster. Notice how they all try to look so different from the corporate world."

He was right. The men in the creative cluster wore blue jeans and offbeat shirts and joked among themselves. The senior female in the group, Jean Ash, a mid-fiftyish art director with long hair and a long skirt, looked like a throwback from the sixties. She smiled matronly at the other creatives' antics.

John pointed to a cluster of administrative assistants. "Look there," he said. "They always put on an interesting show."

In one corner, a circle of young women primped themselves for the gathering. Those who wore skirts wore them short. Most had heavy makeup. Sherri Fitzpatrick, the traffic coordinator, was wearing another of her outrageous outfits—a pleated plaid skirt, hiking boots with lug soles and red laces, and earrings cut from actual American Express Gold cards.

Ben looked over at the account group cluster—his group. The men wore dress slacks and cotton shirts with no ties. The women wore casual, yet conservative business outfits. In the center sat Ginny Rubenstein, her black hair pulled back in a neat, business-like tail. Every one of them had a notepad and pen in front of them.

"Interesting, isn't it?" John asked. "Like a three-ring circus. The account people are the ringmasters, the creatives are the clowns, and the secretaries are the showgirls. It works, doesn't it?"

It did. These people—the one hundred and forty employees of Jacob & Marin Advertising—had become like a family to Ben over the previous eight years. Some of them were difficult. The creative people were often prima donnas—especially Andrew Birk. Lucy Johnson could be brusque. Tom Clarey's pomposity was barely tolerable. Everyone had their quirks, but under Tree's leadership, they worked well together to make up the best agency Ben had ever worked for.

As he watched his fellow employees gather for the meeting, Ben felt he should be sitting among them. But he knew two things they didn't know. Well, one for sure—the Katch account review. The other was about to be revealed and Ben worried it would profoundly change the agency. He hated losing friends, the people he worked with, joked with, shared his life with. Sure, they were difficult at times, but Ben couldn't bear the thought of losing them. So he stayed with John, away from them all.

A few minutes after 10:30, Tom and Andrew Birk entered the Octagon. Tom appeared just as he did when Ben first saw him earlier—handsome with his suit coat properly closed with the middle button. The agency women eyed him as he came in. Andrew, on the other hand, looked as if he had just lost a fistfight. His black hair was wild and his clothes wrinkled. He was hunched over and his dark eyes darted around the room.

Tom stepped to the head of the table, raised his hand, and the din died. People turned their chairs to face him. The ringmasters picked up their pens and held them over their pads. The clowns stopped joking around. The showgirls sat straight.

Tom put his fingertips on the black marble table and slowly leaned forward as he gazed around the room like a classical actor about to deliver a soliloquy from a Shakespeare tragedy.

Then he began. "There are moments in life when people must pull together to overcome a crisis," he said. His delivery was slow and deliberate. "A time when they must rise to meet an unexpected challenge. People are called to do this in war or during natural disasters. Winners are the ones who take charge, who overcome adversity."

There was a pin-drop stillness in the room. Tom continued. "Companies face these kinds of challenges too. To survive, a company like ours must count on its people—the people in this room—to do what needs to be done. I'm afraid that sort of challenge is upon us."

Tom stood straight and held the eyes of his audience. "This morning, I received a call from Sarah Marin informing me that Tree was in a terrible car accident." He took a deep breath and said, "I'm sorry to tell you, Tree is dead."

All one hundred-forty people in the room drew in a sharp breath as if they'd been hit with cold water. Someone said, "Oh my God!" Sheila Green began to sob. No one moved.

"Dead?" someone asked.

"Isn't he supposed to be in France?" Susan Schroeder asked. The questions went unanswered and the air in the room turned thick.

"What do we do now?" Rob Hansen finally asked.

Tom lifted his chin. "We'll have to go on without Tree."

"No," Rob replied, "I mean, specifically, what should we do?"

The question made Tom look like he forgot his lines. "Ah, well, I, ah, will meet with the senior staff and we'll come up with a plan. You'll be informed."

There were no more questions. Finally, Tom concluded, "I'm

sorry to have had to break this sad news to you. I'm sure there will be a memorial service. We'll let you know when."

Tom backed away from the table and people began to talk quietly. Sheila Green was no longer the only one crying. People were shaking their heads and others stared blankly. Everyone stayed seated as if they didn't know what to do next.

Tom's words stuck in Ben's head—Tree is dead. He'd heard it right. His mentor, his friend, the agency leader was gone. The pit of his stomach rolled and his chest was tight. He felt vulnerable, left behind by one of the few people he could always count on. Among the swirl of his emotions, one thought emerged. How could the agency go on?

Ben looked at the people in the room who just a few minutes ago had seemed so different and who now were all exactly the same, in shock and disbelief. He was sure he was seeing the beginning of the end of a great advertising agency. He'd suspected something bad had happened when Sarah called Tom, but he didn't expect this.

Ben turned to John. John's eyes were dry but the light in them was gone. They didn't say anything for several minutes.

"Tree Marin," John said finally.

FOUR

EVENTUALLY, SLOWLY, people filed out of the Octagon. Ben and John stayed seated, mute. When the room was nearly empty, Tom, Andrew, and Ginny came over. "We need to talk," Tom said to Ben. "Excuse us, John."

"Sure. I'll see you later," John said. When John had left, Tom, Ginny and Andrew sat near Ben.

Tom was the first to speak. "I have more bad news. I talked with Ben about this earlier. The Katch account has been put up for review."

"What?" Andrew said. "You can't be serious."

Tom conveyed the contents of Doug Lewis' e-mail and told the group the agency had until next Wednesday to put together a pitch to keep the account. "This morning, Ben and I agreed I will lead the pitch," he said.

"Why don't we take things one at a time," Ben interjected. "Does Katch know about Tree?"

Tom unbuttoned his suit coat and said that he'd called Doug Lewis right after he hung up with Sarah. Doug and Everet Katch already knew about Tree and told Tom that since they have the board of directors coming in next week, they still wanted to do the review. Doug had said Katch has some additional information about the review and they wanted to meet with J&M on Wednesday at 10:30.

Ginny shook her head "How are we going to do this without

Tree?"

"As I said," Tom said. "I'm taking over."

"Okay fine," Ginny said. "Then, specifically, what should we do?"

Tom didn't have an answer and the question hung in the air like a bomb about to go off. Ben didn't say anything either. It'd always been easy to let someone else answer difficult questions. For the past eight years, it was Tree. But now Tree was gone and Tom wasn't answering. It was starting to feel like they'd already lost the pitch.

Finally, Ben spoke up. "Well, first we have to tell our clients about Tree before they see it on the news. We should call them right away and let them know there are still people here who can create great advertising for them. Then we'll have to write a press release for the *Times* and the TV stations. I suggest we have John Turner write it. We also need to think about our employees. We need to reassure them we'll be all right."

"We won't be if we lose Katch," Andrew said running his hand through his hair. "Who are we competing against?"

"Hanrahan Communications," Tom said.

"Sheldon Hanrahan," Andrew said shaking his head. "Fucking-a. I can't believe Katch is doing this. It really stinks."

Ben waited for someone to say something. Ginny sat in her chair and drew circles on her writing pad. Andrew shuffled his feet, and Tom stared blankly.

"Yeah it stinks," Ben said finally. He pulled himself straight. "But it's the right thing for them to do. Think about it. Katch has to get this mutual funds campaign right. It's critical for them. And they have to do it now. Tree is gone, and we all feel just horrible. Hell, I don't even know what I feel yet. But Katch can't wait for us. Their campaign needs to launch before all the advertising noise begins around the holidays. And we're the agency to do it, not Hanrahan. We've done great campaigns for Katch for thirty years. They need another one right now. They're challenging us to come up with it. We can do it and we have to do it without Tree."

All eyes were on Ben. "Yeah it stinks, Andrew," Ben said returning Andrew's stare. "It's incredibly bad luck. But we don't have a choice."

There was another long silence. Then Tom said, "The employees will panic when they hear Katch is up for review. We shouldn't tell them yet."

Ben shook his head. "No, we have to be honest with them. We need to pull everyone together and do what we've always done for Tree. That means hard work, long hours. We should meet this afternoon on the research. We'll get additional input from Katch this Wednesday. I'll need to write the creative direction by, say, Thursday morning. Then, we'll turn it over to the creative department."

Ben turned to Ginny, "I'll need your help keeping things on track and I'll want to talk through strategic ideas with you. Okay?"

Ginny stopped tracing the circle and set her pen down. "Of course."

"Great," Tom said. "Thanks."

"Andrew," Ben said, "it'll have to be all hands-on deck. You'll probably need three teams."

"Don't worry about us," Andrew replied.

Ben turned to Tom. "When is Tree's funeral?" he asked.

"Sara said something about Thursday afternoon," Tom said. "I assume it'll be at the Basilica."

Ben sighed. "We'll have to work around it. I imagine we should close the agency on Thursday."

"Yes," Tom said. "We'll close the agency on Thursday. I'll make sure everyone gets the message."

"One more thing," Ben said, "I think John Turner should be the head copywriter on the pitch."

Andrew tapped the table. "That's my department. I make those decisions."

"I know," Ben replied, "but I'm asking if John can take a lead role. I think he'd add a lot."

Andrew glowered. "I'll let you know."

"So, we have to tell our employees about the Katch review right now," Ben said.

Tom pulled on a sleeve. "It's your account. You do it. I'll tell them about our plans for the pitch later."

"Fine. I'll send an e-mail. I'll have to word it carefully but I won't candy coat it. We have to meet on the research this afternoon, say three o'clock." They all nodded.

It was quiet for a bit and then Ben said, "We have to do this for Tree."

Ginny, had her eyes fixed on her pad, "Yeah, we do," she said.

They all stood to leave. As Ben got out of his chair, Tom put out a hand. "Ben, can I talk to you a minute?"

*

When the other two left, Ben sat down and Tom sat next to him. "When I talked to Sarah," he said, "she already knew about the Katch pitch. She's the agency owner now and she won't decide who the agency president will be until after the pitch. So, with Tree gone, I'm the next in command. It's my duty to take over the pitch. I expect your help, but I am taking the lead role. You should know that I've talked with Jeff. He's our chief financial officer and he supports me taking over."

"Tom, why don't we just do the work and see what happens?"

"Yes, do that and keep me fully apprised. Understand?"

Ben felt a surge of indignation. It was just like Tom to issue orders and then do nothing himself to help. "Tom," he said, "you said you were worried about employees panicking. Do you know how to prevent it? Words aren't enough. We have to do the work. We have to show them we're working our butts off to prove that we should be Katch's agency. I guarantee I'll do my part. Will you?"

Tom raised his chin and glared at Ben. "I'll see you later," he said.

He stood, buttoned his suit coat, and left.

Ben sat alone at the table in the huge, empty conference room. The beautiful room with the hundred-year-old timber beams, imported granite table, and state-of-the-art electronics somehow seemed pointless now. Tree was gone and the agency would never be the same. It would never have the spirit Tree gave it. And with the Katch account in doubt and Tom trying to take over, it might not even survive.

But maybe Ben could prevent it. He believed in J&M—their process, their creative product and the hard-working people. But who would lead the company now that Tree was gone? Would it be him? He'd always let others do the hard work of leadership—his father and Tree. His father died before Ben was ready to be the leader of the family. And now Tree had died, too. Was he ready to be a leader now? Did he even want to be?

Maybe he didn't have to. All he had to do was put together a great presentation for Katch. It wasn't the same as being the leader. It was only his job and he would do the best job he could.

He had to do it for his friend, Tree Marin.

FIVE

SHELDON HANRAHAN RESTED his feet on his one-inch thick glass desktop and admired the hard modernism of his office on the 46th floor of the Wells Fargo building. He was into modernism a decade before it became fashionable. In fact, he was always into it. Now, everyone was a modernist, but few liked their modernism hard like he did. To Sheldon, it was the epitome of elegance. But elegance was deceptive. It was, he said, complexity wrapped in simplicity. Most people didn't see the complexity in it, how the sharp angles intersected creating subtle geometric patterns, how the open areas were negative spaces that framed those patterns, how it all came together in one grand expression. Sheldon saw it and even felt it. And elegance, Sheldon knew, was in everything. Vermeer. Chopin. Advertising. Politics. Love.

Elegance. Complexity wrapped in simplicity.

The telephone rang. It was his private line. "This is Sheldon," he answered.

"Is Victor." Victor's Russian accent was clipped and gravely. "Trevor Marin, he is dead."

"I know."

"Now what do we do?"

Sheldon liked Victor. He'd first seen him a decade earlier at an art auction in Paris. Sheldon could tell that Victor was one of the few people in the room who knew what he was doing. So when a seemingly unimportant celadon vase came up for auction that Sheldon knew was a Kangxi from the Seventeenth Century and worth ten times the catalog price, he thought Victor would be a bidder. But Victor stayed quiet and the bidding fell to Sheldon and a Chinese man. Clearly, the Chinese man knew the vase's value too, and bid far more than Sheldon was willing to pay.

After the auction, Victor introduced himself and said he too knew the vase was a Kangxi. He told Sheldon he could get the vase for him if Sheldon would pay him the amount of his last bid. Sheldon agreed and knew better than to ask how Victor would acquire the vase. A month later, the vase was in Sheldon's art collection, and a year after that, Victor was Sheldon's chief of security.

Sheldon ran his fingertips over the cool glass of his desk. "This morning we were invited to pitch the Katch account," he said. "So, we win the pitch and then implement the rest of our plan."

"I see. Maybe you think we should wait until dust settles?"

"No, we do it all *before* the dust settles. That way no one will know what's happening until it's too late."

"But Katch—is nothing. Maybe is risky."

"It's worth the risk. Besides, I want Katch as my client. It's personal. You are in charge of security. Make sure the risk is minimized."

"Of course, of course. So we go ahead for Katch?"

"Yes."

"Okay. I do it."

"Victor. Make sure we get it, no matter what. I'll handle the business side. You handle everything else."

"We will get. Always do."

"Keep me apprised." Sheldon hung up.

Jacob and Marin. Louise Jacob. After thirty years, her name still made his pulse race. He pictured her as she was back then, thick dark hair, intense black eyes, a model's figure, and graceful, delicate, long-fingered hands. And her mind. She was the only woman who thought like him, the only one with the intelligence to match his.

Of course, his money and position could buy any type of female companionship he desired. And he had tried them all from the intimate to the salacious. But none of them fulfilled him like Louise. They could have been happy together.

He knew where she was now—two thousand miles away in Thousand Oaks, California with her husband, a professor of English at Cal Lutheran. Sheldon had hired a top private detective to get photos of Louise and the professor, which he kept locked in his desk at home. Of course, the professor was handsome—she would have to have that. And they looked happy together, at peace. But soon she would have to admit what she did to him was wrong. So would Everet Katch. Tree Marin already knew before he died.

His plans were on schedule. First, he'd win the Katch pitch. Then he'd make sure his man, William Howard, won reelection in the upcoming Senate race. In two years, Sheldon would put Howard in the White House. Then…

First things first. He reached back and cracked opened the vertical blinds just enough to throw a thin ray of light across his desk where a single file folder rested. He removed the large dark glasses he'd worn nearly every daylight hour for the past thirty years. The ray of light, even small as it was, hurt his eyes. He blinked away the pain and opened the folder. Inside were several photos, bank statements, tax returns, a floor plan of a house, and pages and pages of information on Ben Smith.

He pulled out a photograph and examined it. Ben Smith was handsome, just like Louise's English professor. Dark hair, a natural smile. Sheldon set the photo down and reached back to close the blinds.

He put on his dark glasses and his modern office was in the shadows again. *Sorry Mr. Smith. You're in my way.* Even in darkness, everything was all so clear.

SIX

"ARE YOU LISTENING to me?" demanded the business editor from behind her green metal desk. "It's drivel."

In fact, Joel Scheck wasn't listening. He was five years from retirement and needed to keep his job writing the advertising column for the Twin Cities *Times*. He'd been planning his retirement for years. Save five hundred dollars each month, sell his home in North Minneapolis, buy a small cabin on a northern Minnesota lake and retire at age fifty-eight. It would be wonderful. He just needed to keep his job for another five years.

That might not be so easy. Edith DeGroot, sitting in her office in the on the top floor of the aging *Times* building was telling him his latest column was drivel. She had used the word twice. Joel tried not to let it bother him. He knew what Edith was doing. She was trying to get him mad, stir him up. He wasn't going to let her. He'd pretend not to listen and when Edith was done yapping, he'd march out of her office as if he never heard a word. Then he'd check his 401k, look online at a few real estate listings for lake homes. The cabin would have to be on a big lake—at least five-hundred acres. Over a thousand would be better. He wouldn't need a lot of shoreline. A hundred feet would do it, just enough for a boat launch so he could—

"I said are you listening to me, damn it?" Edith shouted. Joel's attention snapped back to his boss. Her green eyes burned behind her oversized glasses and they focused directly on Joel.

"Yeah, yeah, I'm listening," Joel said. "You called my work drivel."

"That's right. Drivel. Have you seen your readership numbers lately? Readership of your little column is off thirty percent from last year. Thirty percent! Apparently, I'm not the only one who thinks your work is drivel."

Joel felt his face redden yet managed to keep himself under control. But she was starting to get to him. He shouldn't have to put up with this. After all, he wrote the goddamn column every week and after thirty years, the goddamn stories didn't come that easily. What did Edith expect, Woodward and Bernstein?

He had little respect for the newspaper's business department anyway. The bony woman sitting across the desk from him ran the department and it was losing readership fast. *Of course, it was losing readership,* Joel thought. *Men are supposed to run newspapers.*

"Look, look at this," Edith said, thrusting a recent *Times* issue toward Joel as if it were a picture of him doing something lewd. "Your column from three weeks ago on how some agency used flowers in their ads. Forty-four column inches on flowers in ads! What is this, the Home and Garden section? You're supposed write stories on the business of advertising, not about how some arsty-fartsy art director likes to use a lot of damn flowers in his ads."

Joel crossed his arms and struggled to stay cool. "The campaign won an award in New York. The flowers were a unique device. They conveyed freshness, newness. They were a visual support to the product." He couldn't remember what the product was. "Anyway, you approved the story."

The skin on Edith's neck turned red and she slammed the paper on her desk. "That's because you didn't have anything else!" she bellowed. "I had no choice. What am I supposed to do, run two columns of blank space? Hell, maybe I should. It couldn't be worse than this drivel."

Drivel. The word struck Joel like a slap. He pushed himself

straight in his chair.

"Damn it Edith, quit insulting me. What do you want from me? I try to make the column appeal to a broad audience. That's your direction. This is a community newspaper, you said. Write for the general public, you said. It can't be too complicated, you said. I do all that, and you piss all over me."

Edith pushed her glasses back up her nose. She looked tired and the stacks of newspapers and file folders in her office seemed to tower over her. "Joel, we need stories with more substance. Yes, it needs to appeal to a broad audience, but it doesn't mean you can't write stories that are more interesting. You're covering an industry where a person can fly higher than a rocket one day and crash and burn the next. There's drama here and it all happens in a glamorous industry full of sex, money, fashion, and media. What more could you ask for? With all of that going for you, I'd think you'd write stories that are more… provocative."

More provocative stories. Sex, money, fashion—maybe he could write like Jackie Collins. *Hollywood Wives*. Joel noticed dirt on the toe of his left shoe and reached to brush it off.

"Look," Edith said sympathetically, "remember the story you did when we were both new reporters? The one about Stein and Conklin when they went belly-up? You know the three-part series. What was the name of that scandal again?"

"Zulugate."

"Yeah, yeah. Zulugate. We need another story like Stein and Conklin. That was a great series, Joel. Well-written. Well done. It had the highest readership score the business section has ever had. That's what I want. That's what your column needs. More drama."

Joel had to admit, it was a great story—the best of his career. He wrote it thirty years earlier when he was just a kid, fresh out of journalism school with high expectations and a drive to succeed. The Stein and Conklin story fell in his lap.

Stein and Conklin was the largest ad agency in Minnesota, headed by the eccentric Patrick Conklin who loved edgy ads and off-color jokes. He'd created the first national advertising agency in Minneapolis in the sixties and was widely recognized as the person who made Minneapolis an advertising industry powerhouse.

One day, a group of Twin Cities businesspeople invited Conklin to give a lunch-hour speech. The speech was about how to create great advertising, and since Patrick gave rousing speeches, the gathering was well attended. Included in the audience was a young, eager *Times* business reporter, Joel Scheck.

Patrick Conklin opened the speech by saying that creating effective advertising was easy enough. You just had to understand that most clients had their heads up their asses. In fact, he said, most were like the boy in this next photograph. He clicked his overhead projector to the first slide of his speech—the slide that caused the esteemed Stein and Conklin advertising agency to go out of business three months later.

On the screen was a photograph of a young African Zulu boy with his head in a cow's ass kissing the animal's genitals to stimulate it to produce milk. The audience gasped and stared in shock. Patrick quickly clicked to the next slide and tried to cover the gaffe by joking that the audience was particularly tough that day. He went on with his speech and received polite, albeit subdued, applause at the end.

The whole Zulu boy incident would have blown over as just an error in judgment by an aging advertising agency executive if not for Joel. The next day he wrote an article about Patrick's opinion of clients and reprinted the offensive photograph. When a radical young black Baptist preacher named Terrance White who was angling to become the spokesperson for the Twin Cities African-American community read the story, he seized on it claiming the incident was evidence that advertising agencies were inherently racist and propagated stereotypes through the advertising they created. He demanded an apology from Patrick Conklin.

The agency would have probably survived with minimal damage

had Patrick Conklin apologized, agreed to be more sensitive to African-Americans in the future and then kept his mouth shut. Instead, when Joel interviewed him days later, an angry and overly proud Patrick Conklin stated that Reverend White should shove *his* head up a cow's ass and ship himself back to Africa where he belonged. When Joel's follow-up story came out, Reverend White had the conflict he needed to thrust him into the spotlight. He went on television calling for African-Americans nationwide to boycott Stein and Conklin clients. African-American leaders across the country took up the cause. Soon the story, which reporters dubbed "Zulugate," was on the front page of not only the *Twin Cities Times,* but also the *New York Times* and the rest of the national press.

Two clients left the first week. Others followed as the pressure from the boycott mounted. A few clients hung on, but after three months they left too and the once venerable Stein and Conklin was forced to shut their doors leaving over five hundred people out of work.

In three articles, Joel, at age twenty-four, was able to cover the ruin of one of the great advertising agencies in America. The story convinced the *Times* editors to let Joel write a regular column on the industry and three decades later he was still at it. But where were the Stein and Conklin stories now? He needed one so he could write his column for another five years, buy his cabin, and quit this rat race.

"Yeah," Joel said. "Stein and Conklin. You liked it because they crashed so badly. Bad news sells papers." *Come to think of it,* thought Joel, *all the stories Edith likes are about companies that fail.*

Edith jumped to her feet. "That's not true! I liked it because… because it was moving. It showed the human side of business. And, yes, I liked it because it got great readership." She shook a finger at Joel. "Don't think for a minute that that's not what we're about here. Damn it, if tragedy sells papers, then tragedy is what we'll write about."

Joel had touched a nerve. He felt a surge of revengeful

satisfaction, but Edith was now clearly pissed.

"Stories like Stein and Conklin don't come along very often," Joel said quickly, "but I'll do what I can. It might take some time."

Edith's eyes filled her oversized glasses. "It better not. The way your readership scores are going, you don't have much time."

She sat and reached for a pad of paper. Without looking up she said, "Keep me apprised.

*

Joel quickly left and went to his gray cubicle alongside a large, open bullpen area. After thirty years, he still had to work in a damn cubicle. Most of the senior staff were in offices ringing the bullpen area. Joel didn't care about having an office anymore. He wanted a cabin on a lake. He wanted out.

Drivel! His writing *was* drivel because nothing was happening. He slumped in his chair and pushed the *Times* morning edition sitting on his desk into the trash can. In his inbox was a four-inch stack of wire service releases and the overnight activities report from the metro area police departments. Today's report began with a shooting in the African-American neighborhood that accidentally killed a teenage girl. This had all the markings of a truly big story that would be on the *Times* front page for several mornings to come. Reverend Terrance White would probably get involved. Joel had to admit, the man knew how to use the press.

Further back in the report were several arrests for disorderly conduct, drunkenness, prostitution and more than the usual number of domestic disturbances. Near the end was a report on a fatal car accident in the middle of the night. The driver's name made Joel stop thumbing through the report. Trevor C. Marin, CEO of Jacob & Marin Advertising, was dead at age sixty-nine.

Joel set the report down. Tree Marin was one of the good guys in the agency business. Unlike most other ad people, he always treated reporters with respect. Whenever Joel needed a comment or an insider's perspective, he could count on Tree. Tree was old school—honest but shrewd—and Joel genuinely liked him. And now, he was gone.

Joel looked at the report on Trevor Marin again. There were two letters—UI—in the report's status box. UI—'under investigation'. "What's this?" Joel said aloud. Under investigation? *A car accident?*

Joel picked up the phone and dialed the police department. When the receptionist answered, Joel asked to speak to the officer handling the Trevor Marin's investigation. A few minutes later he heard, "This is Detective Jackson."

Joel introduced himself and said he'd read about the accident and untimely death of Trevor Marin. He reached into a drawer for a pad of paper and a pen and asked Detective Jackson what he knew about the accident.

"You're a business reporter?" Jackson asked.

"I'm a columnist. I write a column on the industry and as you know, Mr. Marin was an important figure."

"I see."

"Well, I was just wondering about the accident. You've listed it as being under investigation. That's not typical, is it? What can you tell me?"

"Did you know Mr. Marin?" Jackson asked.

"Yes, of course," Joel answered. "As I said, he's a leader in the industry. I've interviewed him a few times, even had lunch with him."

"Tell me about him."

"Well, he was gracious, a good guy. But shrewd. He built a great agency, the second largest in Minnesota. Eight or so good national accounts. Several regional accounts. Very profitable."

"Did he have any enemies?"

"Enemies? You're kidding? No, no. Most everyone liked Tree."

"Most every one?" Jackson asked. "Would anyone want to murder him?"

"Murder?" *Murder?* Joel thought. "Is that what you suspect?"

There was no answer. "Look," Joel continued, "Tree was able to win a lot of accounts over the years so I suppose some people didn't like him for that. But, murder? No way."

"What do you think will happen to his agency now that he's gone?"

This guy's asking all the questions, Joel thought. "Well, there isn't anyone at J&M with the kind of stature Tree has… had. They have a challenge on their hands. I imagine Sheldon Hanrahan—Sheldon owns the biggest agency in town, Hanrahan Communications— anyway, I imagine he'll go after most of J&M's accounts, especially Katch Financial. And then… oh, Christ." Joel paused.

"And then…?" Jackson asked.

Joel clicked his pen several times. "I just remembered the election."

"The election?"

"Yes, yes. The election for the senate this fall. J&M is doing the advertising for Janice Theilen. And Hanrahan handles Senator Howard. Sheldon Hanrahan's done Howard's campaigns since the senator first ran for city council over twenty years ago. It's supposed to be a close race, but if Sheldon puts J&M out of business, it could be devastating for Theilen."

"Do you think Hanrahan will put J&M out of business?"

"Yeah, probably, especially if he gets Katch. Sheldon is very aggressive. He has an uncanny ability to win pitches. I can't remember the last time he lost. He's buried most every other agency in town accept for J&M. Some say he cheats."

"He cheats?"

"Yeah, he does things that aren't legal. Allegedly anyway. There's no proof. It's probably gossip. I'm sure it is. It's just… I mean, how does he win every single pitch?"

"I see."

There was a long pause. Finally, Joel spoke up. "I'm sure he has nothing to do with Tree's accident if that's what you're thinking. He and Tree used to be best friends, but they had a falling out."

"Falling out?"

"Yeah, a long time ago. Nobody knows much about it. I've never even met Hanrahan. I hear that in person he's... different."

"Different?"

"Yeah, different." Joel switched the phone to his other ear. "Look, I don't know any details, okay? So, what can you tell me about the investigation?" He held his pen over his still blank pad of paper.

"I'm not at liberty to disclose any information at this time," Jackson said, coolly. "Everything is in the police report."

"But, I . . ."

"Thanks for your call, Mr. Scheck. Please call anytime. Oh, I might want to call you sometime, if it's all right. When I have questions, that is." Jackson hung up.

"Asshole," Joel said, under his breath, still holding the receiver.

He tossed the pen on the desk. Drivel indeed. This wasn't drivel material at all. He dialed Edith DeGroot's number.

"Edith, I think I have the story we've been looking for," Joel said.

As he explained it to her, Joel thought about asking for a raise. If he got one, he reasoned, he just might be able to afford two-hundred feet of shoreline on his lake home.

SEVEN

BEN KNEW THAT the employees would react to Tree's death in one of two ways. Either they'd use the challenge to find an inner strength or they'd lose hope and give up. Sure enough, after the meeting in the Octagon, half of the employees looked like they were giving up. Then, after Ben's e-mail announcing Katch was up for review, nearly everyone did. Nothing got done and people with mortgages and kids to put through college started to quietly panic. Instead of talking about business in scheduled meetings, they talked softly among themselves. "Who will lead the Katch pitch?" they asked. "How will J&M stay in business without Tree?" No one had answers and the result was a grim paralysis.

Only Ben worked. He couldn't let himself be in shock, not now. Tree's death would certainly cause Jim Collins at Bug BeGone to ease up for the time being and the agency's other accounts would go quiet for a while, too. But only for a while.

And there was still the Katch pitch. The agency had to win the pitch to survive. It would be the most important effort of Ben's career and, without Tree, winning the pitch was almost completely dependent on him. When he stopped to think about it, it scared him. So he worked instead.

He was surprised at how business-like he had become in the meeting in the Octagon. It was as if he'd turned into a machine.

Input: *Tree is dead.*

Output: *Without Tree, someone must take charge.*

Input: *We are up against Sheldon Hanrahan to keep the Katch account.*

Output: *We must put together an outstanding presentation to prove we're the right agency for Katch.*

Input: *The presentation is only a week and a half away.*

Output: *Review the research, meet with the team, do the analysis, and write the creative direction immediately.*

It was coldhearted, goal-oriented action. It's what Tree would have done.

By 1:30, the idea of closing the agency for the day began to circulate through J&M's hallways and cubicles. Tom Clarey immediately championed the idea and called Ben, Lucy, and Andrew to his office to say he had decided to close the agency, "Out of respect for Tree," he said.

As they met, the early afternoon sunlight angled through a bank of windows onto the floor in front of Tom's desk. Tom looked as unruffled as he had before Sarah Marin called. He presented his case for closing the office and when he was done, Ben, sitting in one of Tom's side chairs said, "I don't agree. If you want to honor Tree, keep the agency open. Anyway, we have work to do."

"Work to do? Nobody's getting anything done!" Tom said. "They're just standing around! Sheila Green can't stop crying. Everyone has their doors closed. I bet they're making calls to headhunters already. We should let them go home to get over the shock. I know *I* need some time to absorb this. We'll close today and maybe tomorrow too."

"Tomorrow?" Ben protested. "Look, Tom, it's a rotten thing, Tree's death. Of course, we're all in shock. There isn't a person here who didn't think of Tree like a father. And the Katch account review… well, it's just terrible timing. But these are the cards we've been dealt. We can't just quit for a few days to let people get over it. We have to keep working. We have a business to run and a pitch to prepare. We need to meet this afternoon to discuss the Katch research as we agreed. We only have a week and a half."

Tom shook his head. Ben set his jaw and moved to the edge of his chair. "But that's only a small part of it. The fact is people *need* to work. They need to push themselves through, help save Tree's agency—their agency—from going under. It's the best therapy for everyone right now. It won't be easy but it's the right thing to do."

Tom picked lint off his coat sleeve. "You're asking a lot."

"Yep. And we should ask a lot."

"I think you're wrong. I've consulted with Jeff. He's the CFO and he agrees with me."

"He's not close to the clients or the work, Tom," Ben replied. "He doesn't know."

Tom glared at Ben, then turned to Andrew and Lucy. "What do you guys thing?" he asked.

"I guess I agree with Ben." Lucy gave Ben an approving nod from across Tom's Nagochi coffee table. The hostility of the Bug BeGone fiasco from earlier was gone. "I'd really like to go to the nearest bar and throw back a half dozen cosmopolitans. But that isn't what Tree would do. If he were in our shoes, he'd work extra late tonight."

"Andrew?" Tom said turning to the creative director. "What do you think?"

Andrew stood with his backside on Tom's walnut credenza, his arms folded across his chest, only slightly less disheveled than when Ben first saw him this morning in the Octagon. "Fuck, yeah," he said. "We work,"

"We could make it voluntary," Tom said.

"No, Tom." Ben said. "Lucy is right. It isn't what Tree would do."

"Damn right," Andrew said.

Tom, standing from his walnut desk, said, "Well I don't agree. I'm going to make staying voluntary. I'm the senior officer now. It's my decision and that's what it will be."

"Not for the creative staff," Andrew said. "Creative is still my department, and I agree with Ben. The creative department is staying."

"Fine, do what you want. But the rest of the agency can go home."

"We still need to meet on the Katch research," Ben said.

Tom shook his head. "Like I said, staying is voluntary. If people want to stay for your research meeting, then go ahead, have it. Joanne will make the announcement in five minutes."

Everyone left Tom's office and a few minutes later Joanne's voice came over the paging system announcing anyone who wanted to could go home for the rest of the day. After the announcement, Tom strolled through the halls feigning great concern for everyone and encouraged people to go home. People packed briefcases and filed toward the elevators. Tom was right behind them and, soon, the agency was nearly empty. Even most of the creative department left in spite of Andrew's insistence that they stay.

By one o'clock, the agency was almost dead.

*

Ben stayed and worked. He couldn't do anything about the other employees, but he could do something about keeping the Katch account. Maybe it was hopeless. Maybe the account would go to Hanrahan Communications no matter what anyone did. Maybe the agency would go under. But it wouldn't go under without a fight. Working was Ben's way of regaining control and his way of paying his respects to Tree. As hard as it was, it was his therapy and right now, he needed as much therapy as he could get.

At three o'clock, only a handful of people remained in the agency. Ben set aside his work and went to the account group conference room for the research meeting. When he got there, Jay was waiting. Jay stared at the wall without seeing, and Ben could tell he was worried. Of course, he was worried. Jay's wife was five months pregnant, and they were looking at houses. If Jay lost his job, the house would have to wait and the baby would come home to the cheap apartment that Jay and his wife agreed to live in to save for a down payment.

Ben remembered when he himself was a new agency guy with a new wife and his first mortgage. His heart went out to Jay. "Jay," Ben said. "I don't know how this is going to work out. All I know is we're the right agency for Katch, and if we make a good pitch, then… well then, no matter what happens, we'll be okay."

Jay stopped staring and gave Ben a nod. He started to spread out his files for the meeting.

A few minutes after three o'clock, John Turner stepped into the room. "Hi," he said. "I'm here for Andrew. You know how he hates research. He asked me to take his place. Apparently, I'll be working on the pitch with you."

"I'm glad," Ben said.

Finally, Gerry Hansen, the research director, came in with a stack of reports held together with big black metal clips.

"I'm not staying," Gerry said, his droopy mustache twitching as he talked. "I just stopped by to hand these out and see if you had any top-line questions. Jay, you and I already went through it this morning, and I assume you've seen it too, Ben. These have revisions from this morning." He tossed the thick reports on the table.

"Oh, and you should know, I got a call from Doug Lewis at Katch. He told me to make copies of all our research and send it to Hanrahan Communications. It was picked up by the messenger service an hour ago."

Jay shook his head. "Damn. There goes that advantage."

"Yeah, well, we should have expected it," Ben said. "It's only fair."

"They're getting our work," Jay protested.

"And we were paid for it. Katch owns this research, not us. They can do whatever they want with it. But what Hanrahan doesn't have is our analysis. So, let's do a better job at analyzing this stuff and make *that* our advantage."

"I gotta go," Gerry said under his mustache as he headed to the door. "Let me know if you need anything. I'll be in late tomorrow. Dentist appointment."

John took out his reading glasses. "I guess it's just us three. Hand me one of those reports."

"Jay," Ben said, "you've spent the most time with this. What are your conclusions?" Normally, as the senior manager on the account, Ben would have taken the lead in the meeting. He had studied the research, and had thoughts on it. But Ben knew Jay needed to get his mind on work.

Jay took a deep breath, straightened and reached for one of the reports. "Well, there's a lot here, but when you cut through all the details, a few things come to the surface. I can think of three off the top of my head. First, Katch mutual funds are seen as only being for Midwestern farmers who put a hundred bucks away each month for fifty years and don't bother to follow the fund's performance."

"And after fifty years, those farmers are rich on the money they've invested," Ben injected, "and the so-called sophisticated investor is still trying to catch up from the latest hot investment that went south. So what's the problem?"

"The problem is, slow and steady has fallen out of favor," Jay replied. "Mutual funds are evaluated like individual stocks these days."

John thumbed through a report. "That's true. People have a much shorter time horizon than they used to."

"Exactly," Jay continued. "People look at the monthly—even the daily—returns. If a mutual fund isn't at the top of a list, investors dump it. That's bad for Katch because they are almost never at the top."

"Well, maybe the funds aren't very good if they're never on the top of the list," John said.

"Not necessarily," Ben said. He was in familiar territory—

formulating strategy for a client. It eased his pain about Tree. "What's at the top one year can be at the bottom the next. If you're a long-term investor—which you should be if you're saving for retirement or to put your kid through college—you need to consider returns over five, ten or twenty years. Katch funds are always near the top over a long time horizon."

"Right. And that brings me to the second conclusion," Jay said. "Investors today don't understand the importance of style purity."

John looked over the top of his glasses. "Style purity?"

"Style purity is the concept that a fund will stay true to its investment strategy," Jay answered. "Many mutual funds chase big returns in stocks they have no business owning. When the do that, they aren't being honest to their investors. When a hot sector crashes like, say, technology, these funds get clobbered and investors who should be sheltered from the crash lose big."

"Frankly, I'm surprised more of these fund managers aren't thrown in jail," Ben said. He got out of his chair, stood at the window and leaned on a timber column. Soon, the street below would begin to fill with cars heading home. He wouldn't be among them. "What else, Jay? You said you had three points."

"Yeah. The final one is that today, investors are as confused as ever." Jay flipped to a chart in the back of the report. "It's here on page 47. With the technology bust, energy prices all over the map, corporate scandals, banks behaving like speculators, they aren't comfortable investing. People want to be able to plan better. They want consistency. They want—"

"Stability," John said. "The word is stability."

"Exactly," Ben said. "It used to be mutual funds were where investors turned for stability. They aren't stable anymore, except for Katch. Good old boring Katch funds. So there's the opportunity for Katch. Style purity for the investor who wants stability."

"Funds you can plan on," John said.

A tingle of excitement filled the room. "Jay," Ben said, "this is great work. Your analysis is right on the money. Can you put this into a short write-up for our meeting with Katch this Wednesday in case they ask about it?"

"Of course," Jay said. "I'll do it this afternoon."

"Let me see something in the morning. Whatever you have, no matter how rough. I'll also re-read this report tonight to see if there is anything else we can glean from it."

John tucked his reading glasses into his pocket. "I'll do the same. I know I'm just a creative guy, but I like this research stuff."

"Let me know if I can help you interpret the charts," Ben teased. "It's pretty complicated."

The glimmer in John's eyes had returned. "My boy, I was deciphering charts like these when you were learning how to add. I think I'll do just fine, thank you."

Ben turned to Jay. "I want Ginny's input on this too. She has a good head for strategy."

"I'll get her a report," Jay said. "What about Tom?"

"Put a copy on his desk," Ben answered. "He left already. I'll talk to him about it tomorrow."

"John," Ben continued, "are you going to Katch with us on Wednesday?"

"I'm afraid not. Andrew wants to go. If it's a meeting with Ev Katch, he always wants to be the one to go. I'll brief him on the research before Wednesday. Maybe he'll pay attention. He's the creative director but he really doesn't get involved in a campaign until the creative brief is done."

"Speaking of…," Ben said, "we should meet tomorrow to discuss the creative brief with the team. Then let's see what Katch says on Wednesday and take it from there. We'll need the creative brief by Thursday morning, right Jay?"

"That's the plan."

Ben gathered his papers. "Okay. Thanks, Jay. You've done a great job."

"Thank you, Ben," Jay replied. He shot a smile at Ben, gathered his files and headed for the door. "I'll see you later. I gotta get this report done."

Jay left and the distraction of the meeting was gone. And there it was again—the feeling of doom in the agency that just hours before was abuzz with activity. Tree was dead, and it felt like his agency was dead, too.

Ben turned to John. "I need some coffee," he said.

John nodded. "Yeah, I know how you feel. Let's go to Sadie's. My treat."

EIGHT

"I CAN'T BELIEVE this is happening," Ben said, once they got to the artsy coffee shop. The floors were uneven pine, the ductwork was exposed and painted black. An overhead garage-type door was open in the front. The afternoon air was heavy and warm. "It's almost too much. I haven't really had time to think about Tree. You know, I feel my career didn't really begin until I started working for him."

"I feel the same," John said, sipping his tonic water and lime.

"He was a good man."

"He was a great man."

They'd taken a small round table in the back corner so they could talk in private. Ben had ordered a large black coffee. He still had a lot of work to do and hoped the caffeine would keep him going for a while. He hadn't taken a sip yet and as the weight of all that had happened that day began to descend upon him, he was coming to the conclusion that the coffee wasn't going to help.

He thought about Tree. He hadn't had time to process the news of Tree's death yet. He was too busy dealing with everything else. He wanted to talk to someone and John was willing to listen, but now Ben didn't know what to say.

There was heaviness in his chest. He hadn't felt this way since his father died when he was fourteen and Ben and sister Ellen who had turned twelve just two days earlier were without a father, and his mother was without a husband. At the reception after the funeral, his

Uncle Jim had cornered Ben and told him that he needed to be the man of the family. His uncle, normally a jovial type, had been dead serious. "Be the man of the family," his uncle repeated.

Ben didn't know what, specifically, he was supposed to do. Uncle Jim's directive sounded impossible and ominous, and he didn't want the responsibility. He wanted to play basketball, listen to Springsteen and hang out with his friends after school. Only a week earlier he had kissed a girl for the first time—JoAnne Jensen, in the apple orchard behind her house. He was enjoying being a teenager and wanted to kiss JoAnne again and maybe do more with her someday. But he was somehow supposed to be the man of the family, so he stopped hanging out with his friends after school, did his homework without being told, went to church without complaining, and cut the grass first thing on Saturday morning instead of putting it off until Sunday night. He tried to be a big brother to Ellen, asking about her friends and what she did after school. He offered to help with her homework. His carefree teenage years were over and he'd never play on the high school basketball team or go any further than that one kiss with JoAnne Jensen.

And now it was happening again. The agency needed a leader and it might have to be him. Of course, Tom was making a serious bid for it. He looked the part and was putting on a convincing act. He had the CFO, Jeff Novak, on his side. Tom was certainly trying to build support among others in the agency. He was probably already lobbying Sarah Marin to be CEO. But could Tom really lead the agency? Would his condescending, autocratic style get the best work out of one hundred forty intelligent, creative people? Probably not.

Andrew didn't have it either. Andrew had a brilliant creative mind but he wasn't a leader. The creative staff loved working for Andrew because of his energy and passion. But Andrew couldn't be bothered with the fine points of managing people or for that matter, an entire agency. He was far too emotional. A small problem would send him into fits of anger and a rejected campaign would put him in a deep funk for days. Andrew focused only on campaigns and like most creative people, he was not leadership material.

So, when Ben thought about who would lead the agency now that Tree had died, the only person he could think of was himself. For eight years, he'd managed the agency's largest account. He had a good relationship with his clients, the creative team, and the people who reported to him. Everyone in the agency respected him. It was as if Ben was the reluctant eldest son—the one obligated to assume responsibility after the father died.

Was he ready for it? He had never thought about it before. He never had to because Tree was always there, the one everyone including Ben counted on. But Tree was gone and with him, the security of a strong, confident leader. Ben understood why people went home early. They were scared and had no one to turn to for reassurance. Their fear made them take flight. Tom encouraged it and Andrew couldn't even stop his own people from leaving. Hell, Andrew didn't even stay past three o'clock. However, Jay and most of Ben's other direct reports had stayed and he felt them looking to him for what to do. So he put his head down and worked and they worked alongside him and he could tell they all felt better because of it.

It also surprised Ben how upset he was that Katch put their account up for review. He knew why they did it—it made sense. But he was still angry and hurt. After all, he had done the bulk of the work on Katch for all these years. He and Ginny were the day-to-day contacts. They worked together well and year after year created solid and sometimes great campaigns for Katch. It was widely believed that Katch had the best advertising of any financial services company in the industry.

Ultimately, of course, Tree had been in charge of the account. He and Everet Katch were good friends and Tree had supervised the account for nearly thirty years. But over the past several years, Tree had been giving Ben more and more responsibility. In fact, the upcoming mutual funds campaign, the one that was the focus of the review for the entire Katch account, was all Ben's responsibility. This was his opportunity to prove to everyone, including Everet Katch, that he didn't need Tree to run the account.

Then there was Tom. Tom Clarey had told Ben just this morning—was it only this morning? —that he wanted to take over the Katch pitch. Ben knew Tom couldn't handle it. He didn't know anything about the account and didn't have the work ethic to do the job. But Tom was still Ben's boss—wasn't he? —and he could make things difficult right at the time when they needed to go smoothly.

To succeed, to save the Katch account and ultimately the agency, Ben would have to outmaneuver Tom and prove to everyone that he could handle Katch without Tree. And he had to prove he could do it better than even Sheldon Hanrahan.

Now at Sadie's, Ben cupped his hands around his coffee, trying to sort through his emotions. Eventually, one emotion surfaced. "I'm scared, John," he said.

John's tweed coat hung on the chair next to him. His brown eyes penetrated deep into Ben's. "Of course you are. Being scared is what you should feel."

"Thanks. You're so supportive."

"What's the matter, Ben? You can handle it. Anyway, what choice do you have? You either do it or you don't."

Ben stared into the blackness of his coffee. He could smell the coffee's bitter aroma but didn't take a sip. "It hurts that Katch put the account up for review," he said. "We've always done good work for them."

"Yes we have. And now you have to do it again. Just put together the best campaign you can," John said. "Do your job and the rest will take care of itself."

"I keep telling myself that. But what do I do about Tom? He wants to take over the pitch. You know as well as I do he can't. It would be a disaster."

"Don't let him." John pushed his shirtsleeves halfway up his forearms.

Ben huffed. "Just like that? He's my boss. I suppose he's the head of the agency now. He's got Jeff Novak on his side."

John shook his head. "Sarah Marin is smart, Ben. She won't decide who's in charge until after the Katch pitch. Anyway, Tom's not the agency leader." John set his tonic water on the table and focused on Ben. "Do you know what a leader is?"

"Tree was one."

"Yes, but what made him one? It wasn't just that he was the agency president. Titles mean nothing."

"So what makes a leader?" Ben asked.

"Courage to take on the fight," John answered. "It's just that simple. These people are afraid, Ben. They are afraid for their jobs, their mortgages, their retirement, their dreams. They're afraid they'll have to move to another city to find work or start another career. Will Tom do the work to save Katch? Does he have courage? He told everyone to go home and then he bolted for home too. They won't follow Tom. They'll follow the person who fights for them. If you believe J&M is the right agency for Katch and you fight to keep the account, the rest of the agency will follow. Which makes you...?"

"Yeah. Great," Ben said. "What if I don't want it?"

"It looks to me by the way you've handled the situation so far, you've accepted it," John said.

Ben said nothing. The two remaining Sadie's customers left, making John, Ben, and the purple-haired waitress the only ones in the coffee shop. Rush-hour traffic inched along in the street outside the open garage door.

John took another sip of his tonic water. "Of course, you realize there's a lot more to this than just the Katch account."

"I know," Ben said. "If we lose Katch, HC will be the only big agency left in town. If we don't work for them, after a few years of shuffling around the house in our bathrobes and slippers, our wives leave us, our children will disown us and we'll become derelicts."

"Been there, done that!" John laughed. "That's why for the past twenty years I drink tonic water *without* the gin. No, my friend, there's more to it than just you and me and our little advertising agency. Much more."

"Oh? Like what?"

"Sheldon Hanrahan," John said.

The name gave Ben the shot of energy he was hoping to get from the coffee. The light in John's eyes had turned to fire.

"Explain," Ben said.

John asked what Ben knew about Sheldon Hanrahan and Ben recited what he knew – that Sheldon was very intelligent, aggressive and on the boards of directors of some very large companies. Other than that, Ben said he knew very little about the man they'd be competing against for the Katch account.

"You're not alone," John replied. "No one knows much about him. Yet he's one of the most powerful people in the country. Think about it. HC is the advertising and public relations agency for several *Fortune* 500 companies. He controls their public image. *Their public image*," John said tapping a finger on the table.

John sat back and carefully observed Ben. "Do you ever think about what we do, Ben? Do you ever think about what we're responsible for, what our clients entrust us with?"

"Their image. Yeah, yeah. I know it's important."

"Important? It's critical! Think about the big companies that were worth billions and went bankrupt when they mishandled their image. When consumers and investors no longer believe in a brand, companies fail, plain and simple. We're responsible for managing that."

John continued. "And it's more about image than ever. It's not about products. Products are commodities today. If a company comes out with a unique product, it's copied by a competitor in a matter of months."

"That's cynical," Ben said. "So substance doesn't matter? It's all about image?"

"It's not cynical, Ben. It's the way the business works. Sheldon knows that. And I have news for you, Tree did too. That's why Sheldon sits on the boards of directors of so many companies, and why our friend Tree was on the board of Katch. These companies understand the value of what we do. Sheldon wields an incredible amount of power and he knows how to use it."

"Okay, professor. So what you're saying is we have to win the Katch pitch so Sheldon doesn't take over the business world. Thanks for the added pressure."

"That's only part of the story," John said. "This goes far beyond business. Don't forget, Sheldon and HC handled the election campaigns for both Governor Patrelli and Senator Howard. He's a personal consultant to both. Some say he tells them what to do, and I believe it."

"Come on, John. Aren't you going a little overboard?"

"No, I'm not. You're an advertising guy, you tell me. How important is image to getting elected? How is getting elected any different than marketing a product?"

"I see your point."

The purple-haired waitress came over and pointed at Ben's coffee, "You don't like your coffee? You're not drinking it."

"It's fine," Ben replied.

"You guys want anything else?" she asked. "It's ten to five. We close at five."

"No thanks," Ben said. She slapped a bill on the table and went back behind the counter.

John continued. "In politics—just like business—image is everything. Hell, a president with a terrible image couldn't get reelected if he balanced the budget, eliminated crime and poverty, and peacefully annexed Canada. Politicians know that and that's why they listen to people like Sheldon."

"And Hanrahan Communications is running Howard's reelection

campaign this year," Ben said.

"Right," John replied. "And J&M is doing the advertising for his opponent, Janice Theilen. In the grand scheme of things, our work for Theilen is probably more important than our work for Katch."

"Chances are Howard will win anyway. He's the incumbent."

"He might. Sheldon doesn't like to lose and will do most anything to win. But right now, it's a close race. All Theilen needs to do is put up a good challenge to prevent Howard from running for president in two years. If she doesn't and Howard wins the White House in two years, Sheldon and his cronies would make some very big changes in our country."

Ben stared at his coffee. "Great."

"So, let's review." John leaned forward and drew on the table with his finger. "If HC wins Katch, Sheldon has his claws into an important international financial company. If we lose Katch, we go out of business and Theilen's campaign has to start all over. Howard wins in a landslide propelling him to the White House in two years."

Ben looked up. "You realize that last week my wife Nan agreed to be the new campaign chair for Theilen."

John face grew into a wry grin. Then he threw his head back and let out a laugh. "No, I didn't know. How ironic. It's perfect. You're fighting not only for your job and for the life of our beloved agency and control of the business world and the good old U.S. of A., but also for your fair lady, the lovely Nan Smith. My God, it's practically Shakespearian."

After a long pause, John said, "Well, take it from me, it isn't so bad being a derelict, as long as you have good boots in the winter."

Ben laughed halfheartedly. He was grateful John had been willing to talk. John was always able to get to the heart of the matter. What was at stake was more than Ben had realized and much more than he wanted to be responsible for. He felt even more inadequate than he had before, but at least now, he had the full picture.

"Have you told Nan about Tree?" John asked.

"Yeah, I called her after the meeting in the Octagon. We talked a long time. She didn't even ask how it would affect our work for Theilen. She just wanted to know if I was all right."

"Hang on to her, Ben. She's something special. I suppose we'll have to do something about Theilen's campaign soon. But Nan is right not to worry about it—the Katch pitch is what's important now."

"Yeah, the Katch pitch," Ben said into his coffee.

"Just do the work, Ben, as best as you can. That's all you can do." John picked up the bill, reached over to retrieve his wallet from the inside pocket of his coat.

"Yeah, that's what I told Jay, earlier."

John drank the last of his tonic water. "Take your own advice, my friend. You were right."

Ben nodded and said he had to get back to work. John gave him smiled. As they left the coffee shop, Ben took his untouched coffee to the counter and asked the waitress for a to-go cup for his coffee.

Work to do, indeed. If John was right about all that was at stake, he'd need the caffeine.

NINE

"The story is probably a three-part series," Joel said. Michael Hanley, eating breakfast across the table from him at the oak-paneled Twin Cites Athletic Club didn't look up. "First, there's the story of the pitch," Joel continued. "Yesterday, I learned that Katch, J&M's biggest account, is up for review and Hanrahan Communications is the other agency pitching it. Now *that* will be interesting. Katch is J&M's biggest account by far. And Sheldon Hanrahan wins every pitch. How, I don't know.

"The second part is the inside story of J&M itself. How will the agency survive without Trevor Marin? *Will* it survive? I have my doubts, especially if they lose Katch. It will be great drama. I see this part focusing on the people at J&M. There are one hundred and forty people there."

Joel pushed to the front of his chair. "But finally, there's the real story. The big story. The election. You know, of course, that Sheldon Hanrahan is handling Senator Howard's bid for re-election and that J&M is doing the advertising for Theilen."

Hanley sliced off a section from his eggs Benedict. "Of course, I know," he said. His thick hair was pure white and impeccably trimmed. He'd carefully folded and draped his gray suit coat over the chair next to him. He had his red club tie tucked into a crisp white shirt.

"That's why I wanted to talk with you. You're the political correspondent for the *Times*. What do you know about the election?

For that part of the story."

"I see," Hanley said. Michael Hanley had been with the *Times* for over forty years although he was never actually at the *Times* offices. He preferred to meet at one of the establishments in downtown Minneapolis where *Times* reporters had been hanging out for decades. The Twin Cities Athletic Club was his favorite.

"So, what can you tell me about the election?" Joel had ordered scrambled eggs and an English muffin. He had taken only one bite of the eggs.

"Let me see if I have this correct," Hanley said. "You predict Sheldon Hanrahan will win the pitch for the Katch account which will put J&M out of business?"

"Probably."

"They'll go out of business right as the election heats up, when Theilen needs them the most. Yes, that is indeed interesting."

Joel felt a surge of excitement. He was on an important story, something he hadn't experienced in years. "Yeah. That's why I called you."

Hanley dabbed his mouth with a corner of a frayed white linen napkin. Not a single strand of his white hair was out of place. "What do you know about Sheldon Hanrahan and his campaign for Senator Howard?" Hanley asked.

Joel explained that Sheldon Hanrahan almost always ran negative campaigns for his political clients. In fact, he said, Sheldon's political advertising could get downright mean. Dirty, even. But Joel admitted he didn't know what Sheldon was planning. "I'm just getting started on this story," he said. "Do you think Sheldon wants to run J&M out of business to hurt Theilen?"

"My boy, I'm sure that's the first thing Mr. Hanrahan thought of when he heard Tree Marin had died."

"See, there it is!" Joel exclaimed. "That's what I'm talking about— the angle on this story. A relatively insignificant advertising account pitch with huge implications on the senate election.

"By the way," Joel said pointing at his plate, "does this food taste funny to you? My eggs taste kinda... old."

"My breakfast is fine. I've been eating here for decades."

There was a pause. Then Hanley said, "Maybe I should handle this story."

Joel set down his fork. "Now wait a minute. This is about the advertising agency business. That's my turf."

"Yes, but you just said it has implications on the senate elections. I agree, it does. And political reporting is *my* turf. Politics can get quite complicated. You don't have the knowledge to do it justice."

"But this isn't just about the election," Joel protested. "As I said, it's a three-part series. The election is only one part."

"Uh, huh." Hanley took a sip of coffee.

"Now look. I mean it. I want this story. I need this story, and I can handle it just fine."

"I don't think you know what you're getting into," Hanley said, flatly.

"Then help me. What do I need to know?"

Michael Hanley leaned forward. "Okay," he said. "Here's something you need to know. The senate race between William Howard and Janice Theilen is one of the most important the county has had in a long, long time. In fact, it might be the most important in any state for the past fifty years. Why? Because Howard could be the next president of the Unites States. Howard has built a strong base in Washington and he has a financial war chest bigger than any other potential candidate. If everything plays out right for him, he'll be the leading candidate for the presidency."

"However," Hanley continued, "Howard needs an impressive election this year. A win by anything less than ten points will be a sign of weakness that might derail his presidential bid. Howard has to crush Theilen or there will be no run for president.

"But a presidential bid alone doesn't make it such an important race," Hanley said. "No, it's what a Howard presidency would do to this country if he wins. Hanrahan has some very different views about America."

"You mean *Howard* has some different views."

"No, I mean Hanrahan," Hanley replied. "Look, Howard is nothing. Why? Because he's been handled perfectly behind the scenes, by—"

"Sheldon Hanrahan?" Joel asked.

"Correct. And where do you suppose the senator, a middle-class dentist from Duluth, Minnesota, got all that money in his political war chest? And where do you suppose many of his connections come from? And the organization he needs to win elections? Who do you think is the main architect of his vision for America?"

"Sheldon Hanrahan."

"Correct again."

"It sounds like you don't agree much with their vision for America," Joel said.

"As a reporter, I'm not supposed to care. I'm only supposed to inform the public about it. The problem is, I do care and the information on Hanrahan and his group's political agenda has been so carefully concealed that I've had very little to work with. The only reason I know about it is because they have enemies. Powerful enemies. People who know what Sheldon is up to. People who are determined to stop them at any cost."

"Theilen?"

"She's one of them. There are many others."

"Who?"

Hanley took the last bite of his eggs Benedict and motioned for the waiter. "Fredrick, bring the bill, please." He waited a moment, then glared at Joel. "Do you still want to try to handle this by yourself?"

"Maybe you and I can co-write the story's political part," Joel said, "but the entire series is still mine. There's more to it than just the political angle."

Hanley pulled his tie out of his shirt. "Oh, yes. That's right. There's the story about a pitch for an advertising account and a few people at a local advertising agency who might lose their jobs. By all means, report that story. I'm sure you'll do a good job. But politics is what I am responsible for and therefore this is what we will do. You keep working on your story, but keep me informed. Daily. I want to know what you uncover, especially as it pertains to the election. Any detail might be important. I want to know everything. While you do that, I'll investigate the political story."

"Michael, damn it, this is my story. You don't have the right to take it from me."

The ancient waiter brought the bill and Hanley signed it. He stood, pulled on his suit coat and tugged at his shirtsleeves. "Joel, don't fight me on this. It wouldn't be good for your career." He turned and left the restaurant.

Joel shoved his plate of uneaten scrambled eggs to the side. He'd hoped to get some background information on the story's political angle but now he was fighting for it against the *Times'* most powerful reporter. It was still a story about the advertising agency business— wasn't it? —so Joel had a right to it. If it became bigger, as Hanley claimed it would, then he'd probably have to give that part to Hanley. They'd push Joel aside with a pat on the back and give him a small role as an expert on the agency business.

Joel had never cared much for the power game played by the reporters at the *Times*. When he was younger, he thought it was all about the story, like Stein and Conklin. Soon, he realized they expected him to hang out after work with the senior reporters like Hanley or play golf with the editors. By then, he believed he was doing just fine and he didn't want to socialize because it took away from his time fishing. And when they passed him over for promotions time and again, he protested to no avail.

Now he had this story—a story like Stein and Conklin that would secure his job until he could buy his cabin and retire—and he was being muscled out by Michael Hanley, the *Times* reporter who played the game better than anyone.

TEN

THE CASE DIDN'T MAKE any sense—the type of case that Detective Jackson lived for. It was Tuesday morning and he'd been at the crash site for over half an hour and what he saw—or rather what he didn't see—was puzzling. There were no skid marks indicating Marin hit the brakes to avoid hitting anything like another vehicle or a deer. And why would a mature businessman like Trevor Marin be on this road at three in the morning going 125 miles per hour? Sure, the Porsche was probably a thrill to drive and this stretch of road late at night would be the safest place to test the car's limits. But if it was safe, why did he crash? Sometimes single car accidents were suicides, but that didn't make sense either. Trevor Marin was hardly the kind of person to kill himself. He was wealthy, successful, happily married, well-respected. There were no signs of any problems that would cause him to take his life.

The call, the body being released so soon, a hasty cremation and now an accident scene with too little evidence of what really happened. It just didn't add up and it was exactly the kind of challenge Jackson loved. He *needed* it to be hard. His very existence required clues that were unclear, people who lied, a mystery to solve. It's what made him feel alive. It was his drug.

The crash site on the west side of a two-lane asphalt state highway about twenty-five miles west of Minneapolis hadn't been difficult to find. This was horse country where, among the gently rolling hills and small pot lakes, trim hobby farms raised purebred horses for the riding pleasure of the wives and daughters of rich Twin Cities families.

The state patrol had sent Minneapolis the crash report with pictures that Jackson referred to as he examined the crash site. Off to the road's west side, Jackson had found the tire tracks leading to a freshly burned-out patch of grass in front of a large oak tree. The accident had peeled off big chunks of bark and black burn marks marred the trunk. In the dirt, Jackson saw where the tow truck had pulled the car back onto the road.

Beyond the tree was a run-down farmhouse that the hobby farm set hadn't bought yet. Two dogs barked at Jackson as he poked around the crash site. To the right was a small cornfield.

A brown state cruiser appeared over a hill and rolled to a stop behind Jackson's car. A stocky, young trooper with a crew cut got out. As he stepped toward Jackson, he put on his wide-brimmed hat and pulled it down tight. "Good afternoon, Detective," he said, extending a hand. "I'm Officer Larson. Sorry I'm late. There was an accident on the interstate and I was the nearest unit. I got here quick as I could."

"It's all right, Officer. Thanks for meetin' me. You were the officer on this call Monday mornin'?"

"Yes, sir. I was."

"Quite the crash here."

Larson rested a hand against the oak tree. "Yes, sir. It was a bad one. Amazing how strong these big oak trees are. Two years from now, the bark will be grown over and you won't even know what happened. I can't say the same for the car or the victim, however." Larson sounded as if he were in the military reporting to a senior officer.

"You estimated the car was goin' a hundred twenty-five?"

"Yes, sir. The vehicle had to travel ninety feet through tall grass and dirt before it hit this tree. As you can see from the photos in your hand there, the accident totaled the car. It had to be traveling at an extremely high speed to do that much damage."

Jackson looked at the photos. Larson was right—the Porsche was barely recognizable as a car. The impact had pushed the front end into the passenger compartment. The left front tire was where the driver's side door should be.

Jackson studied the tree. "You'd think there'd be a lot more damage to the tree."

"Well, sir, old Porsches are light cars. That's why they can go so fast. They're also air-cooled. And the engine is in the rear. No radiator or anything in the front to absorb a crash. And, as I said, these oak trees are tough. By the way, if you don't mind my asking, why is Minneapolis homicide investigating this case, especially with all you have going on with the shooting of that girl?"

"We got a call from someone sayin' this was more than just a car accident."

"Really?" The dogs continued to bark in the farmyard.

"Tell me officer," Jackson said, "was there anythin' unusual about this accident? Anythin' that would indicate it was more than just a car accident?"

"No sir, not really. Except the fire. What I mean is, cars don't usually catch fire after an accident, even in accidents as bad as this one. It's not like the movies where cars explode into flames whenever they hit something. This one did. But it was an old car. Sometimes the wiring is exposed. We didn't think anything of it. The fire department didn't say anything about it either."

"Has the car been examined?"

"Not that I know. We took pictures—the ones you have there. The car was towed after the body was removed."

"Where was it towed to?"

"I assume it was towed to the state lot in Saint Cloud. That's standard operating procedure."

"Who was the towin' company?"

Officer Larson took off his hat and ran his hand over his crew cut. "That's a strange one, too, now that I think about it. We normally call our own towing company—we have a contract with services throughout the state. The dispatcher checks to see who's closest and calls them. But we never had to make the call."

"Why's that?"

"Before we called, this tow truck drives up and asks if we need to have the car towed. He said he was monitoring the police radios and was in the vicinity. He just showed up at the right time. I remember saying to myself, 'four in the morning and this guy is cruising for business? He must be desperate.'"

"Which towin' company was it?"

"Douglas."

"Douglas? They're the biggest auto repair chain in the state. I suppose they have a facility close. Officer, do me a favor. Get on your radio and find out which Douglas location towed the car. Get me the address and phone number. I want my guys to inspect the car. Thank you."

Five minutes later, Officer Larson walked back to Jackson, his hat under his arm and a slip of paper in his hand. He told Jackson that there was no report that the car was dropped off at the state's Saint Cloud facility and they didn't know where it was. He gave Jackson the number of the nearest Douglas location and said they'd probably be the ones who handled the tow. "I'll show you how to get there," he said.

*

Jackson headed south on county road 92 to highway 12, turned east and drove three miles to the town of Maple Plain. Douglas Auto Service was on the highway's north side, just east of town. It was a newer, prefabricated building surrounded by a chain-link fence. There were six service bays and a clean customer service area in the front. Jackson went in and asked to speak to the manager. He was introduced to a pudgy man in his mid-forties wearing a smudged gray work shirt with a white patch that read "Greg Snyder—Assistant Manager" in red letters.

Jackson showed his badge and said he wanted to know about the crash on Sunday night.

"Oh, yeah, I heard about that," Snyder said. "The '67 Porsche 911. What a shame. There ain't too many of them cars around no more."

"It was towed by Douglas," Jackson said. "I assume this would be the facility, bein' you're the closest."

Snyder shook his head. "Nah, it wouldn't be towed by Douglas. We don't have a contract with the state. They wouldn't call us."

Jackson raised an eyebrow. "The trooper on the scene said it was Douglas. Said the driver was monitorin' the police radio and was in the area when he heard the call."

"Well, it wasn't us in Maple Plain. We didn't have no one out on Sunday night. No calls. And I was here at seven Monday morning. I'd remember a '67 Porsche if it was towed here. It wasn't."

"Who else from Douglas would have handled the tow?"

"There's a couple-a shops in Saint Cloud. One in Buffalo. A bunch east of here toward the Cities. But I don't think none of them guys woulda done it. I can check to see if there's a record. We got the tows for each branch on the computer. Just a minute."

A few minutes later, Snyder came back scratching his shoulder. "Sorry Detective. It ain't in our computer. No record of it at all. You got the wrong company."

"Are you sure it'd be in the computer?" Jackson asked.

"Yep. HQ is real strict about record keeping. We gotta keep everything up to date every day. If we towed it, it'd be in the computer."

"Who was on call that night?"

"That's the thing," Snyder said cocking his head. "See if someone needed a tow in the middle of the night, the call'd go through HQ in Minneapolis and it'd be in the computer. Then, they'd call me at home and either I'd do it or I'd call one of my guys. As I said, there weren't no calls. We didn't have no trucks out Sunday night."

Jackson nodded and felt a slight grin cross his face. He asked if he could have a list of all of the Douglas locations in and around the Twin Cities. The assistant manager gave him a brochure and pointed to a list on the back page. Then Jackson asked who he could call at headquarters about the tow. Snyder wrote a name on a smudged piece of paper and handed it to him. Jackson thanked him and left.

Jackson drove the twenty-five miles back to Minneapolis dictating into his voice recorder. That afternoon he'd have to make calls to the dozen Douglas shops around Maple Plain to see if anyone had picked up the 1967 Porsche 911. He already knew the answers, but he had to do it anyway. Later, he would drive to the Douglas headquarters in northeast Minneapolis to talk to the person whose name Snyder had given him.

He already knew what that person would say, too. He smiled to himself. Yeah, *this* was a good case.

ELEVEN

"THE ESSENTIAL TRUTH!" Andrew Birk shouted. "What's the essential truth? I have to have it before I'll start ad concepts."

Ben had been working on the mutual funds strategy for months before the fateful e-mail from Katch announcing the review. As usual, he was using Tree's four-part approach. The first part analyzed the company, in this case, Katch Financial. It answered questions like what is their vision and goals? What are their strengths and weaknesses? What is their brand positioning? The second part looked at market factors—the industry trends and an in-depth analysis of the competition. The third part analyzed the all-important consumer. Who is the target market? How do they work and play? What are their values? And what are their needs and concerns with respect to their finances? The fourth part looked at the social factors—what is the media saying about financial services? What's the buzz on social media? What is the zeitgeist and how is Katch positioned against it?

And the culmination of the entire analysis was the essential truth—the simple one-sentence statement that pulled everything together. It was the most difficult part of the strategic work and Ben still hadn't come up with it.

Now, sitting at the creative conference room table with Tom, Ginny and John, Ben had to listen to Andrew complain that Ben wasn't doing his job. There were toys and games on the table to provide stimulus for the creative staff when they met to develop concepts for campaigns. Pinned to one of the huge timber beams were dozens of ads cut from magazines with yellow Post-it notes stuck to them with comments like, "We want a client that will do this kind of advertising!" or "This art director should not be allowed to breed," or simply, "*What the fuck?!?!*" in Andrew's handwriting.

Andrew stood across from Ben in front of a whiteboard bolted into the yellow brick wall. Written on the board was "Katch Mutual Funds Essential Truth." The rest of it was blank.

Ben had been listening to Andrew for the past ten minutes. Andrew's loud voice and physical antics were impossible to compete with, so as usual, people sat, listened and injected a sentence or two when they could.

In spite of Andrew's dramatics, Ben liked him. Sure, Andrew was impatient and moody almost to the point of manic depression. And sometimes he was downright mean to people—especially to the account team. But he was moody and mean because of his passion for great work. And he was always genuinely sorry after he was mean to someone. Now, Andrew's eccentricity—and creativity—was precisely what J&M needed.

"What's so hard about this essential truth?" Andrew demanded.

"It's complicated," Ben said. "It must be understood in context of Katch's overall business condition. We've spent weeks doing a competitive analysis, months doing consumer research—"

Andrew jabbed a finger in the air. "Fuck research!" He had pulled his shirt out of his jeans and his dark hair was going in every direction. "Research never built a good creative campaign," he said. "Ever. It's mental masturbation."

"Damn it, Andrew," Ben said raising a palm. "Have you read the research? Have you even looked at the strategy? There's important information there. I agree we can't just try to develop a campaign directly from research, but it certainly informs the strategies. Anyway, our client spent tens of thousands of dollars on the research so we can't just blow it off."

"Okay, you handle that part of the presentation." Andrew said. "Fine. I just want to know the essential truth so I can get started on the creative. Can anyone tell me?"

Ginny, her dark hair pulled back tight, said, "Let's just take some time and go over Ben's work. Of course, we need to develop an essential truth and we will. But let's understand the strategies first."

Andrew slumped in a chair. "Jesus Christ. What a waste of time."

Ben's blood pressure began to rise as it often did with Andrew.

Tom Clarey, wearing yet another new Italian suit, this one dark olive, leaned forward and cleared his throat. "I have an answer for you, Andrew." He picked up some papers on the table in front of him. "I spent time on this with Gerry from research. Ben, I know you are working on it, but I sensed you needed some help. Gerry and I developed a three-part essential truth. Let me show you." He handed out the papers.

Ginny took a handout. "A *three-part* essential truth?" she asked.

"Yeah, why not?" Tom replied. "Why does it always have to be a single sentence? This is a complicated situation and we don't always need to stick with traditional methods. We should let the situation determine our approach. I propose doing it this way."

"Tom," Ben countered, "the essential truth has to be the campaign premise distilled into one simple sentence. It's like a log line. Tree always said we needed to start campaigns with an essential truth, just like Hemingway started his books with 'one true sentence'. It's hard to do. You need to go through dozens of options before you get it right."

"Who says it needs to be one sentence?" Tom asked, palms raised. "See what I have here? Three parts. The first is about the product. In this case, it's about style purity—Katch mutual funds do what they say they'll do. The second part is about the consumer— Consumers today need stability in their investing. The third is about how the product and consumer come together—Katch Mutual Funds are funds for an unstable world. This works for me. And Gerry liked it too. I say this is what we should use."

Andrew tossed the paper on to the table in front of him, folded his arms across his chest and closed his eyes. Finally, Ben spoke. "This isn't an essential truth, Tom. It's doesn't consolidate the thinking into one sentence. I doubt it gives the creative department much to work with."

"I don't agree," Tom said. "It's all there. Gerry and I developed it. It works. This is what I want to present to Katch."

Ginny looked at Andrew, then at John. "Why don't we ask the creative team what they think? Does this give you what you need?"

"No," Andrew said without opening his eyes.

"I agree with Ben," John added. "It isn't an essential truth."

"It isn't a *typical* essential truth," Tom said, "but I don't see why you shouldn't be able to work with it. Gerry and I—the head of research and the head of account service—both approve it. So it's what we're going with."

Ben felt the control of the meeting—and of the pitch—slipping away. He leaned forward. "Tom, Tree came up with the concept of the essential truth specifically for Katch. We've used this method for every single one of their campaigns. And we've created terrific campaigns with it. The method works, but it needs to be a simple, one sentence strategic statement like it always is. This isn't it."

Tom pulled on a cuff. "Need I remind you, the account is in review? So now is the time to change. If we want to keep this account, we need to adapt."

Andrew shot out of his chair and headed to the door. "I gotta go. Let me know when you get this figured out. It better be soon. I need time for concepting."

"It is figured out," Tom said. "It's right here. It's what I just gave you."

Andrew looked at Ben. "Do you have anything better?"

"Not yet," Ben answered. "That's why we're meeting. To review the research and talk about the creative brief."

Andrew sneered. "Okay, you do that. For the time being, if this is what I have to work with, I'll take it." He grabbed Tom's papers and stomped out of the room.

"Ben," Tom said, "put this with your background and distribute it to the creative team."

"It isn't right," Ben replied. "We shouldn't change how we do things. Not now. Let me work on the essential truth. I'll use what you have as input. But when we present to Katch, we must have a real essential truth."

"We'll use what I have here," Tom said. "Don't argue with me. I'm leading this pitch and this is our essential truth. Is that clear?"

No one responded. Ben stared at Tom and felt Ginny and John watching him. Tom had issued a direct order and he was Ben's boss. Or was he? Maybe not—not with Tree dead and the agency in trouble. Could Tom fire Ben if he disobeyed? Tom had Jeff Novak on his side and the CFO controlled who got paid and who didn't. But J&M's situation was far too precarious and Ben was too important to the Katch pitch for Tom to make that kind of move. John, Ginny, and probably even Andrew would go along with him if he stood up to Tom.

It was a unique position for Ben. During his entire career, he'd always reported to someone. Final decisions on important matters like this had never been his to make. He'd often suggested a decision or direction and sometimes even acted on them without direct approval of his superiors if he had to. But he was never fully responsible. He had felt safe in that. Since Ben came to Jacob & Marin, Tree was ultimately responsible. But now, Tree was gone and there was a serious question about who would—who could—lead the agency. Sarah Marin said she wouldn't decide who to promote until after the Katch pitch, but as the executive vice president, Tom had the title and position, which put him next in line after Tree. His ability to lead—or lack of it—had never been a question while Tree was still alive. Now Tom was assuming control and had made a decision that could cost them the Katch account and put the agency out of business.

It was a decision Ben strongly disagreed with. But by speaking up now, by taking control of the Katch pitch, Ben would be making a bid to take charge of the entire agency. Then all one hundred and forty employees would depend on him to get it right, win the account and save their jobs.

"I asked if I was clear," Tom demanded. The question hung in the air.

Finally, Ben said, "No. I don't agree. I'm going develop a real essential truth. Yours doesn't work."

Tom glared. He usually keep his emotions under control, even in the most difficult situations, but he was clearly losing it now. "Listen to me, Ben. Don't defy me or I will see to it that you are out of here. Do you understand? I am in charge of this pitch. I'm the leader of this agency now. So you will do as I say."

As he gathered his papers Ben, said, "I've already told you what I'm going to do, Tom. You do what you have to. I've got to get back to my office and come up with a real essential truth."

Tom's hands were trembling. "Now you just wait a minute. John, Ginny, I expect you to go with me on this. Ginny, you report to me, just like Ben. I will fire you too if I have to."

Ginny raised a hand. "I think we should cool off a bit here. Let's just give it a few hours."

"I've already made up my mind," Tom replied. "Ben, if you go forward with this, you will be fired. Period. So think about what you're doing."

Ben let a long silence fill the room. He looked straight at Tom. "Tom, I know what I'm doing. You can't fire me or Ginny or anyone else for that matter because, without us, we'll lose the pitch and this agency will go under. And you can't fire me because I won't leave. Simple as that. Excuse me. I've got a pitch to work on."

Ben rose and left the room. "Wait just a minute," Ben heard Tom say behind him. "Get back here!"

Ben kept walking.

*

As Ben walked back to his office, his fellow employees were hard at work, doing their jobs in spite of the adversity facing them. He realized that because of what he'd just done, these people who had been his coworkers and friends for years were now his responsibility. If he failed, they would lose their jobs and have to work for Sheldon Hanrahan or uproot their families and relocate to another city. And what had John said at the coffee shop? Something about Sheldon Hanrahan and the senate election and Howard running for president of the United States in two years.

Ben walked into his office and sat at his desk. He remembered the last time he had this kind of responsibility—when he had to be the man of the family after his father had died. Back then, he tried to do it and thought he was doing just fine. But when Ellen reached her teenage years, she turned rebellious. She dyed her hair jet black and used way too much makeup. She got caught skipping school and when their mother asked her about it, Ellen cursed at her with words even Ben didn't know. She dumped her old friends and started hanging out with people years older than her. Ben and his mother were losing control and Ben's mother was starting to look years older than she was. Ben tried talking to his sister, but she wasn't listening and sunk deeper into her world. Ben no longer wanted the responsibility of being the man of the family. In fact, he'd hated it. But it would never be the way it was before his father died and the agency would never be the way it was before Tree died either.

He turned to his computer and opened to the Katch strategic plan that still needed an essential truth. As he stared at the blank page, Ben prayed that this time, he would succeed.

TWELVE

"WHAT A DAY," thought Ben as the cab pulled up to the front of his house.

It was 10:50p.m. He had worked straight through since Jay grabbed two burritos at the taco truck so they could work over lunch. Dinner wasn't even an option. Too much to do. During the day, when Ben stopped to think about what he'd gotten himself into, it made his head spin. It was best when he just kept working. One thing at a time. Prioritize, work until you finished the highest priority, and then move on to the next one. Repeat until you couldn't do it anymore. Then, take a cab home—the buses had stopped running hours earlier—and try to rest.

Ben paid the cabbie and pushed himself to the front door of his clapboard house in a gentrifying neighborhood in south Minneapolis. He was hungry and exhausted—the type of physical and mental exhaustion that numbed the body. His mind didn't work, and soon his body would quit too. He pushed the door open and there was Nan in a Northwestern University sweatshirt and faded jeans that hugged her slim hips perfectly. Her silky blonde hair gently curled to a stop just at her shoulders. Her blue eyes sparkled. She took his briefcase and kissed him tenderly, and when she did, some of his fatigue lifted.

Nan. Ben had fallen in love with her the first time he saw her on a sunny day on the tennis court at a local fitness club. She was slim and athletic with a wicked backhand and a competitive drive usually reserved for men with too much testosterone. He decided right then to ask her out even though he was no good at the dating game. As she walked to the locker room after winning her match, he approached her and clumsily asked if she'd let him buy her a drink. She smiled sweetly and asked if she could know his name first. Ben, embarrassed, apologized for his boldness and properly introduced himself. She asked him to wait ten minutes while she showered. Less than a year later, they were newlyweds and madly in love.

"How's my hard-working husband?" she asked as they walked arm in arm through the living room into the kitchen.

"I'm tired and hungry," he answered. "How are you?"

"I'm worried about you."

"I'm fine. I've been better, but I'll live. How is Jenny?" he asked as he leaned against the old Formica kitchen counters. They planned to get them replaced with granite soon.

"She's asleep. She wanted to stay up until you got home to tell you she landed an axel in skating class today. She was very excited."

"I wish I could've talked to her about it. To be honest though, I can't tell those darn jumps apart. Salchow, axel, lutze, toe loop—they all look the same to me. Is a Salchow one of the hard ones?"

"Yes it is, my dear," Nan answered, "but she landed an axel, not a Salchow."

"Sorry. Guess I'm more tired than I thought. Well what about an axel, is that hard?"

"It's pretty good to land one at her age. Can I make you something? There's some leftover ham. How about a sandwich?"

"Yeah, thanks," Ben said. "That sounds great. So, is she going to be a skating star?"

Nan stood at the counter slicing some ham. "Probably not. One girl her age is already doing double axels. Still, Jenny is pretty good and she just loves it."

"All the money for skating lessons, eight hundred-dollar skates, and my ten-year-old daughter won't be able to support me when I lose my job. I miss seeing her when I have to work so much. Maybe it'll be okay if I lose my job so I can spend more time with her."

"She misses you too," Nan said. "If you have time, we'll do something this weekend."

"I love you." Ben hugged his wife from behind. Her blonde hair smelled clean and felt soft on his face.

"Does the Master of the Household want this sandwich or would he like something else instead?"

"Master of the Household? Right," laughed Ben, pushing away. "When did Empress Nan anoint me Master of the Household? Anyway, I'm far too tired for anything other than a bite to eat and some sleep." He slumped into a chair at the kitchen table.

Nan turned serious, "How is it going, really? You've been working so hard."

"I think people will get over Tree's death. But it'll take time. It better be soon because the Katch pitch will be a lot of work."

"I'm so sad about Tree," Nan said. "He was such a nice man. What time is the funeral on Thursday? There wasn't anything in the paper about it."

"In the afternoon. Two, I think. I hate funerals."

"I'll have to ask my mother if she can pick up Jenny from soccer." After a pause Nan said, "The Katch pitch. I'm really pissed about it. Why would they do that to you, put the account up for review? It isn't right."

"I know why," Ben said. "They need to know we can do the job without Tree."

Nan set a plate with his sandwich and some chips in front of him. "You guys are perfect for them. There's no reason for a review. The next time I see Everet Katch, I'll tell him so."

"Whoa, tiger!" Ben said. "I'm afraid we're going to have to earn it through this pitch. I don't think anything you say to Everet Katch will help."

Nan sat across from him at the table and smiled gently while he wolfed down his sandwich. Ben could tell she knew how he felt, the pressure he was under, his worries. She knew from a simple look at him what he was thinking or how he was feeling. He could not do the same with her, however. She was a stoic Scandinavian who didn't want to trouble her husband with her own problems. She kept them to herself and it gave her an advantage in their relationship. But she only used her advantage to help him. Now, he'd need her support to take on the biggest challenge of his life. And of course, as usual, she would give it.

"Don't worry, Ben," she said sweetly. "You can do it, my handsome, smart, hard-working husband. I know you will."

Ben nodded. "Yeah, well, things are trending right. After all, I got a promotion here to Master of the Household. That's a good start. Now I just need to write a killer essential truth for a presentation that will beat Sheldon Hanrahan. All the while, I gotta keep Tom Clarey from screwing things up. And I have to get Andrew Birk to focus on strategy and not go off and do one of his weird campaigns. Once I do all of that, I'm hoping you'll promote me to Lord of the Household. But first I have got to get some rest."

"I think you're good for the promotion to Lord," Nan said.

Ben laughed. It was uncanny how this woman could lift his spirits and instill confidence in him that often he couldn't muster on his own. For the first time since he got the e-mail about the review from Katch, his situation didn't seem so overwhelming.

"Thanks," he said. "And what about you? How's Theilen's campaign going? I'm so proud of you—the youngest campaign manager of all the Senate races this year. And I bet the prettiest, too." Ben finished his sandwich and pushed the plate aside.

"That's not hard since I'm one of only two female campaign managers in the entire country. Oh, by the way, sorry to spring this on you now, but my laptop froze on me this evening. All of my work for Theilen's campaign is on it and I have a meeting tomorrow morning. Will you look at it? Please?"

"I don't know. What's it worth to you?"

Nan batted her eyelashes and affected innocence. "I'm willing to do anything for the Master of the Household."

Ben laughed. "Anything?"

"Anything."

"Tell you what," Ben said. "I'll look at it and take a rain check on 'anything'."

Nan retrieved the laptop and set on the kitchen table it in front of Ben. He pressed the 'on' button but nothing happened. "Are the batteries dead?"

"No, it was fully charged when it froze."

"Then I don't know what's wrong," Ben said. "It doesn't even boot. I don't have a clue how to fix it if it won't boot."

"Damn! I need it for a meeting with Theilen tomorrow at ten. What can I do?"

"We can call Dirk," Ben said. "He's only five minutes away and he's a night owl. No one knows computers better than he does."

"If you're not too tired and if you don't think he'd mind, I'd really appreciate it."

"No problem. He owes me a favor. Hand me the phone."

*

Five minutes later, Dirk Anderson, tall, dark, handsome and disheveled as usual, charged through the front door without knocking. He carried a small computer bag. "Yo," he shouted, "here I am! Superman to the rescue!"

"Hey Clark Kent, keep your voice down," Ben said. "Remember we have a kid and only geeks like you don't know how late it is."

"Oh, sorry," Dirk said, only slightly softer, tromping into the kitchen. "Hey, Nan. How ya doing? Ben, dude, you look awful. Hard day?"

"Thanks a lot. Yeah, hard day. I'll tell you about it later. Thanks for coming over. Nan's computer is acting up and she needs files off it for a meeting tomorrow. It won't even boot."

"Let's have a look." Dirk sat in front of the laptop.

Dirk Anderson was the smartest person Ben knew. Ben had met Dirk twenty years earlier after Dursten Advertising promoted Ben to account executive. Dirk took Ben's job in the research department and right away it was clear Dirk had the goods. He was a master at cluster analysis and was experimenting with several other cutting-edge research techniques that no one other than Dirk really understood. Dirk tried to get the agency to buy an expensive computer system so they could run their own analyses instead of paying outside firms to do them. He had thoroughly researched the hardware and software needs and was convinced the agency would quickly pay off the cost of the system and earn a handsome profit from his work. But he was young and only a few years out of MIT and lacked the tact to sell his idea. Six months later, Dirk, frustrated, quit the agency business. Years later, agencies made fortunes doing the analyses that Dirk had proposed for their clients.

After Dursten Advertising, Dirk went to work at an upstart computer security firm named Secure Digital where he quickly became their top system designer. He convinced the company to use their R&D budget to run a promotion offering one million dollars to anyone able to break through his firewall and hack into their computers. The only stipulation was that the hackers had to show how they were trying to hack in. After a year, no one was able to crack Dirk's system and Secure Digital had more information on hacker's tactics than any company in the industry. With that information, they built the best security systems in the world.

Several years later, in the height of the tech era, Secure Digital went public and Dirk cashed out with millions from his stock options. He became a computer security consultant to governments and companies throughout the world. All along, he and Ben stayed good friends.

Dirk reached into his bag for a small screwdriver and removed the bottom panel on Nan's computer. He pulled his own laptop from the bag and connected some wires from it to a circuit board on Nan's laptop. He entered a few keystrokes and waited. Sixty seconds later a window popped up with diagnostic information.

"Jesus," Dirk said.

"What is it?" Ben asked.

"Can you retrieve the files?" Nan asked.

"Gimme another minute," Dirk answered, staring at his screen. He ran another diagnostic program that took longer than the first. Another, more detailed report flashed on his screen.

"What were you doing when it froze, Nan?" Dirk asked.

"I was online, retrieving some census data for Theilen's campaign. It slowed way down and then, after a few minutes, it just went blank."

"You were online?"

"Yes."

"Well, you got hacked," Dirk said. "Big time. And, since I set it up for you, you have one hell of a security system here in the Smith household. I mean, you have better security than most branches of the Federal Government, which isn't saying much. Ben, you haven't taken out the firewall, have you?"

"No way," Ben said. "I wouldn't know how."

"So someone got through the firewall and hacked me while I was on the Internet?" Nan asked.

"The firewall can't be working," Dirk said. "You must have kicked a wire or something." Dirk marched out of the kitchen and into the spare bedroom that Ben and Nan used for an office. They both followed. Under the desk, were several boxes with blinking lights and wires going every which way. Dirk crawled under the desk and examined the system. "Damn," he said. "I can't believe it. It's still on. That's impossible."

"When you say I got hacked," Nan asked, "what exactly do you mean?"

Dirk sat at the desk. "You said your computer started to run slowly and then it went blank, right? Well, someone got past the firewall and into your computer. They probably stole your files. That's what slowed it down. Then, they trashed your hard drive to cover it up. I can get the computer working again but you've lost all your data."

"I've lost my files?" Nan sighed. "All my work was on there! I was going to print it out tomorrow morning. Damn!" Nan paused. "Wait a minute. This could be serious. We are talking about the plans for Congresswoman Theilen's U.S. senate campaign here. You say someone might have stolen it?"

"I wouldn't jump to any conclusions," Dirk said. "Chances are it's a random hacker who tripped across your firewall and wanted a challenge. He crashed your computer to cover his tracks. It's probably nothing more. In fact, he probably left a signature of some kind on your computer."

"Signature?" Ben asked.

"Yeah. Programming code. Like a hacker's fingerprint. These guys leave traces of code, sometimes on purpose to let people know who it was. Let me take your computer and I'll see what I can find. I want the firewall box, too."

Dirk packed Nan's laptop and the firewall into his bag and Ben followed him to the door while Nan cleaned up in the kitchen. "Dirk, is this serious?" Ben whispered.

"The little fuck got through my firewall. That's seri-ass talent, Dude. I mean I could do it but I build firewalls for the Israeli military." Dirk shook his head. "Only a handful of hackers in the world can do this. And you have to ask yourself who'd want to hack Nan's computer. Why this one? I mean if they want a challenge, why not hack the Federal Reserve or the CIA or Al Qaeda, not some random home computer.

"But I wouldn't worry. It's likely what I said, just a very talented hacker taking on a challenge. Give me a few days before you sound any alarms. I'll let you know what I find. And when I do, I'll hack the prick back and crash his system. See how he likes it. It'll be epic."

"Thanks, man. Let me know as soon as you can."

"Will do, Ben. Get some rest."

*

Ten minutes later, Ben fell into bed and Nan cuddled in next to him. She told him she needed to get to sleep because she planned to get up early to rewrite the campaign plans by hand. Ben knew she was worried about Theilen's advertising campaign. Trevor Marin had agreed to have J&M do Theilen's advertising, and now he was dead and the agency's very existence was in jeopardy. If Ben couldn't save the Katch account, if J&M went out of business, Theilen's campaign would probably lose and Nan would be the losing campaign's manager. She hadn't said anything about it—that was her way. But as Ben lay in bed with the warmth of Nan's breasts against his side, he realized that in the grand scheme of things, Theilen's campaign was more important than his problems.

He pulled her closer and she slid a knee over his leg. He felt her flat stomach rise and fall as she breathed and the ache in his body started to melt. He was surprised how tired he was. But sleep would not come easily. His body was a prisoner of his mind and the events of the past two days affected him like a nightmare.

And now this thing with Nan's computer. *You have to ask yourself who would want to hack Nan's computer,* Dirk had said. Was it to steal Theilen's campaign plans? What was it John said in the coffee shop about Sheldon Hanrahan doing anything to win? And there was something about the presidential election in two years...

Nan rolled over and began snoring softly. Ben crawled out of bed and tiptoed down the hall to Jenny's room. Jenny had been in bed before he left this morning and there she was again, with her blanket thrown to one side and a skinny leg thrown over it. She was ten years old, only a year younger than his sister Ellen was when Ben's father died.

As he watched Jenny lying peacefully, anger swelled within him—anger at Tree's sudden death, anger at Katch for putting their account up for review, anger at not being able to help Nan with Theilen's campaign, anger at the goddamn hacker, anger at still having Formica kitchen counters.

Or maybe it was anger at having all this responsibility again.

He pushed the anger aside. *Not now*, he thought. *Now it's my job to sleep or I won't be good for anything.* So he went back to his room, slid into bed next to Nan, and fell hard asleep.

THIRTEEN

SHELDON HANRAHAN DIDN'T hear the first ring of his phone. It was after midnight, and he was doing what he often did at this time of night—driving his Aston Martin around Lake Minnetonka listening to Anton Webern's *Das Augenlicht* on the car's Linn thirteen-speaker audio system. Sheldon's dark glasses lay on the car seat next to him as the music filled the car. Webern was the genius of the twelve-tone movement—a group of early twentieth-century avant-garde composers who invented a musical system based on mathematics that produced highly complex, atonal music. Very few people liked it, even fewer understood it. It was Sheldon's favorite.

Sheldon didn't hear the second ring either. *Das Augenlicht* had put him in a light trance as shadows glided past the sleek automobile's windows. Webern's twelve-tone melodic theme evolved into a new theme and then another and another, building slowly, transforming and turning over and around on itself and cleanly melding with the harmonic theme in a mathematical precision Sheldon clearly heard and could almost see. The music lifted to a crescendo, resolved into a recapitulation of the original theme and the process of building began again with new musical transformations and interpretations. It was perfectly elegant. Complexity wrapped in simplicity.

He heard the third ring, but it was like an out-of-place character in a pleasant dream and he didn't recognize it. He knew why people didn't like twelve-tone music. The rules were different and the weak-minded were uncomfortable when the rules changed because it made them have to think. But thinking was what Sheldon did best, so when the rules changed or when, as he'd had learned so many years ago, there were no rules, it was to his advantage. If weak-minded people didn't make the effort to understand, they would lose and the strong, like Sheldon, would win.

Finally, the fourth ring brought him out of his Webern-induced trance. The Aston Martin's audio display identified the caller as Senator William Howard. Sheldon pressed the system's hands-free phone button, which automatically silenced the audio system and answered the phone.

"You're up late, Senator." Sheldon spoke as if Howard were in the car with him. A small microphone in the steering wheel picked up his voice.

"Actually, I'm up early," Howard replied, his voice clear through the car's audio system. "I just arrived in London. The President asked me to take the Vice President's place at the economic summit here at the last minute. Apparently, our good Vice President is having heart problems again and couldn't make the trip. There's no way he'll be able to run for the presidency in two years with his health."

Sheldon didn't answer. *Das Augenlicht* last theme was still floating in his mind.

"I'm sorry to bother you this late, Sheldon," Howard continued, "but I know you don't sleep much so I thought you'd be up. I didn't wake you, did I?"

"No, Senator. What's on your mind?"

"I got a quick briefing from my office when my plane landed. They told me about Trevor Marin's accident. That's a shame. I didn't know him well, but he seemed like a good man."

"He was," Sheldon replied.

The senator continued. "I was told you might try to run his agency out of business. I'm wondering, is that wise given his agency is doing the advertising for Theilen? It might make us look like bullies."

"I'm not trying to put J&M out of business," Sheldon said. "We were called yesterday and asked to pitch one of their accounts."

"Oh? Which one?"

"Katch Financial."

"Katch Financial." Howard said. "That's one of the biggest private companies in the country. Big account?"

"Yes it is."

"I see. Well, I guess it's okay. I just don't want to look like we are trying to take advantage of Mr. Marin's death."

"You don't want to take advantage of a situation that has been presented to us?" The Aston Martin glided across a bridge over a wide channel connecting two sections of Lake Minnetonka. From the bridge, Sheldon saw the skyline of downtown Minneapolis in the distance. It was his favorite place on the drive. It began to rain lightly and the lights of Minneapolis filtered through it creating a mystical scene. If the Senator had not called, he would have arrived at the bridge just as *Das Augenlicht* reached its twelve-tone climax.

"I just don't want to look bad," Howard said.

"Ah, that's it," Sheldon said. "Well, Senator, you won't look bad because I make you look good. Anyway, you shouldn't worry about the Katch pitch. It has nothing to do with your campaign. We will get the account and it will help make things much easier for us in the long run. But it's small compared to our overall plans."

Sheldon continued. "The President asked you to go to the economic summit. Perfect. We couldn't have choreographed it any better. So your job is to look presidential. Let me worry about your campaign here in Minnesota and let me take care of my business."

"Yeah, yeah," said the senator, irritated. "I know what I need to do here. You don't have to tell me. I'm the one who's running for the Senate, not you. So it's also my job to make sure you're handling things in Minnesota. It's my image we're dealing with here, not yours."

Sheldon did not respond.

"Sheldon? Are you still there?"

"Yes," Sheldon answered. The rain spit against the car windows.

"Look, what I'm saying is I can't just leave it to you. I have to control my own image."

"No, in fact, you do not," Sheldon said. "That's my job, Senator. I've gotten you this far, haven't I? Even in spite of the little incident you had years ago which, I might add, I was able to manage for you. Wouldn't you agree? I would think, after that, you would have more faith in me."

"Fuck you and that little incident," the Senator yelled. "That little *fucking* incident."

"Yes. What a tragedy it was. Lucky you have friends, Bill. Where would you be without them? Probably not in London filling in for the Vice President."

Sheldon heard the senator's breathing hard on the other end of the line. Finally, Howard said, "No, probably not. Thank you for reminding me. Ok, ok. I'm sorry, all right? I know you have it all under control. You always do."

"Thank you, Senator. And don't worry so much. Everything is in place. Everything is going as planned. This business with Mr. Marin's tragic death will only help us. We will get the Katch account without much trouble. And then we'll focus on your elections."

"Fine," the senator said. "I need to go. They're waiting for me. I'll talk to you when I get back to Washington."

"Have a good meeting with the prime minister. Give him my best. Goodbye."

Sheldon pushed the audio system button to disconnect the phone. *Das Augenlicht* started where it left off, but the senator's call had broken his mood and he knew it wouldn't come back. So he turned off the audio system and pointed the Aston Martin toward home.

As he turned the car, he caught a glimpse of his face in the rearview mirror. He quickly looked away. The old rules, the rules everyone else played by, hadn't worked for him so he ignored them, just like Anton Webern and the twelve-tone composers had done in their day. For him, there was only one rule—win or die.

And when he won, they would all know that he was right. Louise Jacob, Everet Katch—everyone. And what he saw in the mirror wouldn't matter anymore.

FOURTEEN

BEN FIRST SAW the raven-haired woman on his way to work when she boarded his bus. He'd never seen her before, but he had a strange feeling he would see her again. It was the way she looked at him, as if she knew him. The gleam in her green eyes and her shy smile signaled trouble and trouble like that didn't just go away.

Ben had taken the early bus because he had a lot of work to do. Anyway, he hadn't slept well. During the night, he'd had a bizarre nightmare about invaders crawling through the wires of his house to snatch Nan and Jenny. His sister Ellen was there and the people in the wires were after her too.

He'd jerked awake and saw the digital clock read 5:47. He felt that Nan wasn't in bed any more. He heard a desk drawer opened and closed in the office downstairs. It was time for him to get up—he had a pitch to put together, an essential truth to write. He dressed, went downstairs, and kissed his wife on the top of her head while she sat at the desk writing on a pad. He went into the kitchen, poured himself a cup of coffee and a bowl of cereal.

Fifteen minutes later he boarded the 6D bus which would take him through the tidy neighborhoods of south Minneapolis to within two blocks of J&M. Bus 6D had a long, winding route through the suburbs of Bloomington and Edina so that when Ben took it at his usual time, he would have to stand or take one of the few seats left in the back where the bus engine was loud and the ride, bumpy. But the early bus was less than half-full and Ben took a seat near the front. He pulled out a draft of the Katch creative direction from his briefcase and began reading what he'd written the day before. He still hadn't found the essential truth.

Outside the bus' windows, the summer sun was just coming over the treetops, and after the much-needed rain from the night before, the city looked and smelled clean. People retrieved newspapers from doorsteps, joggers ran through the parkways, the city was stirring to life. It was a glorious summer morning in Minnesota.

The bus rolled on to Lake Street, past a sparkling Lake Calhoun, and into the chic uptown neighborhood where merchants were sweeping the previous night's debris from the sidewalks in front of their stores and cafés. The bus turned the corner onto Hennepin Avenue and headed north toward downtown. A few blocks later, it stopped at the transfer station where a clutch of riders waited to board.

Whenever the bus stopped, Ben glanced up from his work to see who got on. It was always an interesting mix. Most were business people like him—well-dressed people who carried briefcases and umbrellas in case an afternoon thunderstorm came up on their way home. Others were people for whom the bus provided the only means of transportation. They had shopping bags, strollers and kids in tow.

This morning at the transfer station, she walked onto the bus and into Ben's life. Normally, when a beautiful woman boarded the bus, he would admire her for a moment and return to what he was doing. He was a happily married man and Nan was no slouch when it came to looks. But when this woman got on the bus, the first thing she did was look directly at Ben and smile.

Ben guessed she was in her early thirties. She wasn't tall, but the way she moved made it seem like she was. Her hair was medium long and jet-black and was combed smooth down her shoulders. She wore a red designer business dress that showed off her long, slender legs and full, round breasts. Her leather bag matched her shoes. She looked like she should be getting into a limo instead of a bus.

She paid her fare and took a seat across the aisle one row in front of Ben. As she sat, she glanced at Ben and smiled again. Her smile revealed white teeth perfectly placed, and now that she was closer, Ben saw faint freckles across her nose and delightful smile lines around her eyes. And her eyes—even from a distance, Ben noticed their color. He had seen that color green before—in the forest in Wisconsin after a May rain. As the bus pulled away from the stop, she crossed her legs, placed her hands on her lap, and looked ahead. She had the radiant intelligence and poise of a well-bred woman.

The bus continued north through a seedier section of Hennepin Avenue, stopping every few blocks to pick up more riders. Ben tried to turn his attention back to the Katch creative direction, but the presence of the woman sitting two rows ahead who had smiled at him was distracting. He glanced at her when he could without being obvious about it and got nothing more done on the Katch essential truth.

As the bus rolled into downtown, Ben laughed at himself for his minor infatuation with the woman and knew it would end when he got off the bus. He wasn't the type to chase women, even beautiful ones who smiled at him. Then, several blocks before Ben's stop, she rose to get off. As she slid into the aisle, she turned and approached Ben. She looked straight at him with her bright green eyes, flashed her shy smile again, and handed him a business card. Flustered, he took the card without saying a thing. She got off the bus, turned the corner, and was out of sight.

An older man with a scruffy beard said, "Geez-a, guy. Must be your lucky day!"

"I... I'm married," Ben replied.

A young businessman across the aisle laughed and shook his head. "Riiight," he said.

Ben inspected the card. The name on it was Elizabeth Kelly with no title beneath he name. The company was Klein Attorneys at Law and below the name was a phone number and an e-mail address.

Ben turned the card over. She'd written on the back, "Call me," in elegant cursive handwriting. "Elizabeth."

Ben slid the card in his pocket, got off at the next corner, one block before his regular stop. He looked back to where Elizabeth Kelly had gotten off the bus, but he couldn't see her. He hurried the last several blocks to J&M, and wondered why Elizabeth Kelly, the dark-haired beauty whom he had never seen before, wanted him to call her.

FIFTEEN

BEN HAD NO IDEA what the 10:30 meeting at Katch would be about. Doug Lewis had told Tom Clarey they had "additional information" that Everet wanted to share with them in person. Ben and his team had been working on the new mutual funds campaign for two months, meeting with mutual fund managers, conducting research. They had stacks of information and dozens of opinions on Katch's flagging mutual funds and it had all landed on Ben's desk. He'd put together a plan with everything except the essential truth. However, all of the data, all the analysis was raw without the transforming quality of the essential truth.

Ben walked to Katch for the meeting while Tom, Ginny, and Andrew drove in Tom's Jaguar. The Katch building was ten blocks from J&M at the east end of downtown and Ben could cover the distance in less than twenty minutes. Most J&M employees drove to Katch but not Ben. Walking gave him time to sort through his thoughts both before and after his meetings, and the exercise got his blood moving.

Soon, he saw the forty-five story Katch building. It had a skin of gleaming blue glass held in place by black aluminum frames. At the top, on all four sides, was the word 'Katch Financial' in silver two-story letters. Ben pushed into the building, checked in at the guard desk and got a security pass clearing him for the forty-fifth floor. He was early so instead of going up, he sat in a Le Corbusier lobby chair and waited for the others to arrive. He watched as Katch employees came and went. He saw some people he knew but he didn't greet them. He was there, after all, because his agency was up for review—to see if these people would continue to have a relationship with J&M.

Ben wondered why Katch wanted an agency review. He believed to his core that J&M was the right agency for Katch. The work they did was great. J&M campaigns had helped Katch build a brand worth billions. But apparently, something had changed. He knew he shouldn't take it personally, but he couldn't help it. He genuinely cared about his clients. They were his friends. They were like family. But now it was as if he had to prove that he was worthy of their friendship.

Eventually, the other three arrived. Andrew carried a small art case, Tom and Ginny each carried briefcases. The guards gave them security badges and they took the elevators to the forty-fifth floor. When they walked into the executive suites, they were still a few minutes early so Tom and Ben headed to the men's room. Tree had taught Ben to check his appearance before every client meeting to be sure he'd combed his hair and that his clothes were smooth and straight and he didn't have something between his teeth. "We're in the image business, Ben," Tree would say. "We have to look good."

The executive restroom had black marble walls and three stainless-steel sinks. Ben ran a comb through his hair, did a quick check of his clothes. He was set for the meeting. Meanwhile, Tom primped in front of the mirror. He smoothed his suit coat, pulled at the sleeves of his shirt to make the coat lay flat, and smoothed his suit coat again. After brushing a tiny piece of lint off his shoulder, he carefully combed his hair and slowly rubbed the palms of his hands across his graying temples. He tightened the knot of his tie, adjusting it three times, poking his finger under the knot to make sure he'd properly centered the dimple. Finally, he was happy with his appearance, but something on his shirt collar caught his eye. He leaned over the sink for a closer look. A thread had come loose on the collar button. He picked at the thread. It grew longer, so he picked at it again and the button fell off. Tom tried to catch it, but it fell into the sink and rolled down the drain. "Shit!" he said into the drain. He looked back up in the mirror. The corner of the collar held down by the button was sticking up from his neck like the wing of an airplane.

"Damn it!" Tom said. "This is a three-hundred-fifty dollar Ralph Lauren Purple Label shirt and the button falls off? Now what do I do?" Tom leaned in to the mirror with his head cocked to the side while his fingers worked at the collar. Every time Tom let go, it popped back up and stood straight out and, every time it did, Tom let out a loud, "Damn it!"

"Won't it lie flat?" Ben asked.

"No. It's the collar stay. It's sewn in and it won't bend."

"Tom, we have to go. You know how Everet is about being on time to meetings. Don't worry about the collar. Just pull your suit coat over it."

Tom pulled his coat up but scowled at the result. "It looks terrible! It makes my shoulders look hunched. And I can't hold my suit coat like this for the entire meeting. Goddamn it!" Tom exclaimed as he let go of the suit coat and the collar popped up again. "I can't go into the meeting like this! I look ridiculous! How do I fix it?"

"You can't fix it. Just explain what happened. No one will care except you. It's not that bad. It's just a collar. We have to go."

Tom stared at the collar in the mirror as if he couldn't believe his bad luck. Ben checked his watch. "Tom, look, you have two choices. You go in to the meeting with your collar the way it is and don't let it bother you or you leave. You have to decide right now."

Tom hesitated. He pushed the collar down again but when he let go, it popped up. Then, without taking his eyes off his image in the mirror, he said, "Ben, you have to take this meeting without me."

"Tom, it's not a big deal. Just come to the meeting."

"I can't. I'll lose all credibility. I'm going home to get a new shirt. Tell Everet I had a family emergency. Better yet, tell him I needed to do something with the lawyers on J&M and Tree's estate. Yeah, tell him that."

"Are you sure?" Ben asked.

"Yes, I'm sure. I won't go into a meeting with Everet Katch looking like this. He's too much of a son-of-a-bitch."

"Okay, Tom. Whatever you—"

In one of the stalls, a toilet flushed. Tom and Ben stared at each other wide-eyed. Whoever was there had heard everything. The stall latch clinked, the door opened and out stepped Everet Katch with the morning edition of the *Wall Street Journal* tucked under his arm. He was six feet three with a slight paunch, short blond hair peppered with silver, a similarly colored close-trimmed beard. He wore a dark blue Polo shirt, and Sperry Topsider loafers without socks. He looked like he was stepping off a yacht. He walked toward Tom and Ben and addressed the sink.

"Gentlemen," he said as a greeting.

"Hi, Everet." Ben quickly moved aside to let Everet at the sink. Tom said nothing and stood stiffly in the middle of the restroom, holding down his shirt collar.

As Everet washed his hands, he looked in the mirror at Tom. "Let me see your collar, Tom," he said as he reached for a paper towel. Tom let his hand drop and the collar popped up as if it were saluting.

"Three-hundred-fifty dollar Ralph Lauren Purple Label shirt?" Everet tried to stifle a laugh, but it came out anyway. He continued to laugh heartily as he tossed the paper towel into the trashcan and strolled out of the restroom.

Tom's face was red. "He heard everything I said! I called him a son-of-a-bitch." He brought his hands to his face. "I'm screwed."

Ben was at a loss for words. He didn't know if what he witnessed was hilarious or tragic or both. He was embarrassed for Tom. But Everet was not the type to get upset about such a trivial thing as someone calling him a son-of-a-bitch. Hell, Everet was probably proud of it.

"We have to get to the meeting," Ben moved to the door.

Tom's hands dropped from his face. "I can't go, not now. He was laughing at me."

"You have to go, Tom. After this," Ben motioned to the bathroom stall, "you don't have a choice."

Tom glowered at Ben. "Don't tell me what to do. I'm still in charge. I'm telling you to handle the meeting. I'm going home to get a new shirt." Tom grabbed his briefcase and stomped out of the bathroom toward the elevators all the while holding down his collar. Ben left the bathroom and turned the other way to the meeting room.

SIXTEEN

THE KATCH EXECUTIVE MEETING ROOM was long but not wide. A wall of floor-to-ceiling windows exposed the rooftops of the buildings of downtown Minneapolis. A door led directly into Everet Katch's office. The table was burled maple, the chairs Herman Miller Aeron. Andrew and Ginny had taken seats at one end of the table. Ginny had a pad of paper in front of her. Ben took a chair between them.

"Where's Tom?" Andrew asked.

"He left. I'll tell you about it later."

The door from Everet Katch's office opened and Everet walked in followed by Doug Lewis. Doug was tall and lanky with black glasses perched on a sharp nose. "Good afternoon, J&M." Everet sounded like he was addressing his sailboat crew. "Where's Tom?"

"Um, he had to leave," Ben replied.

"Ah, I see." Everet smiled. "Probably had to deal with the lawyers on Tree's estate."

"Something like that," Ben said, trying not to smile. Andrew shot Ben a questioning look.

Everet sat at the table's head and Doug Lewis took a seat on the other side of Ben. Everet met the eyes of each J&M person and acknowledged them directly. "Ginny. Andrew. Ben. Thanks for coming. I'm sorry about Tree. Your company lost a great man and a brilliant advertising mind. He was a good friend of mine for over thirty years. I'll miss him, as I'm sure you all will. It's an unhappy time." He paused a moment and smiled sadly through his salt-and-pepper beard.

Then he continued. "The purpose of this meeting is to tell you why we put our account up for review. You might be surprised to learn I had no choice. Let me explain."

Everet reminded them that Katch was a privately held company. He was the CEO and largest stockholder, but his position didn't mean he was able to do whatever he wanted. He explained that thirty-eight individuals owned Katch—thirty-seven now that Tree was gone. He said that a group of shareholders wanted to take Katch public to cash in on the company's success. Everet believed the move was shortsighted and was against it. The stock market would force Katch to "jump through fiery hoops" as he said, and meet unrealistic short-term profit expectations. It would hurt the company's ability to do business the way he, Everet, felt they should.

Everet explained that he was the largest shareholder, and until now, he had enough support to fend off the move to go public. But the pressure, he said, was growing—especially with mutual funds performing poorly.

Everet folded his arms across his chest and leaned back. "A week ago, I got a call from a major shareholder," he said. "This shareholder said they'd ease up on the push to go public if we "corrected a problem" as he put it, with the way Katch does business. Specifically, they have a problem with Katch's advertising. He suggested we change agencies. The shareholder's company uses Hanrahan Communications and he wanted Katch to turn the account over to them."

Everet pulled himself to the table. "Well, I'm still the CEO so I refused," he said. "We argued, he made some threats, and we struck a compromise. We agreed to let Hanrahan show us ideas for mutual funds and compare them to yours. We've called an emergency meeting of the nine members of the board of directors a week from today. HC will present in the morning, and you'll present in the afternoon. We'll make the decision on which agency we'll go forward with right after your presentation.

"By the way," Everet said with a nod toward Doug Lewis, "Doug here also has experience with HC. His previous employer had HC as an agency." Ben looked over at Doug who didn't take his eyes off Everet.

"Doug," Everet said pointing at papers Doug had brought to the meeting, "give these good people your documents."

Doug handed each person a thick stack of papers that had "confidential" printed on the cover page. Everet said. "This report contains the latest information on our mutual funds business. In a nutshell, it says we continue to lose market share faster than we expected. As you can imagine, it puts pressure on me to come up with answers. The only way I can stop us from going public is if we can turn mutual funds around fast."

Everet looked at each J&M person squarely. "So, you guys need to make a helluva presentation next Wednesday if you want to keep the account."

"We'll do our best," Ben said. As soon as he said it, he knew it didn't sound reassuring. He wondered what he should have said instead. He wondered what Tree would have said.

Ginny was skimming the document. "Is there anything in here we should pay particularly close attention to?"

"Good question," Everet said. "Yes, the competitive advertising."

"I've seen the new ads for the Opportunity Funds," Andrew said. "They're very good."

"They definitely attract your attention," Everet said, "but I'm not sure what they really say. You need to study them."

"Anything else you can tell us?" Ben asked.

"Yes. There is one more thing. I want you to know that if I can't convince my board to keep the advertising with J&M, if I'm forced to take the company public and to work with Sheldon Hanrahan, I will resign as CEO."

"What?" Doug Lewis asked, his mouth agape.

Everet looked askance at Doug. "You heard me. I won't continue as CEO." He stood and went over to the wall of windows overlooking downtown. "I've been fighting this battle for longer than any of you realize. I'm seventy-one years old, and now would be as good a time as any for me to retire. I've always wanted to sail around Cape Horn. Most treacherous sail on the planet," he grinned. "Anyway, my leaving would make a statement about the direction this company is heading if these idiots take control."

Everet let his words sink in, then turned from the window to face the group. "One more thing. I want you to know I think you guys do good work for Katch. I always have. I think you should stay on as our agency. That's why I fought to keep you in. But, you're going to need to do a very good presentation. You need to think it through and base it on a solid strategy. You need to prove to my board you can handle our account and turn our mutual funds around without Tree. You need to give us something that impresses nine board members. Or at least five," he said with a dry smile.

Then Everet looked straight at Ben. "I'm sure you can do it." Ben nodded. For a split second, he felt a bond between himself and Everet like allies in a great battle. Everet's challenge said, "Help me," and he'd directed his plea at Ben. Ben was humbled, inspired, and scared all at the same time.

"If there are no other questions," Everet continued, "I'll let you get to work. Doug here will be available if you need anything from us. Thank you for coming." He walked back to his office, shut the door and the meeting was over.

*

Since Tom had taken his Jaguar home to get a new shirt, the three of them had to walk back to J&M. Their pace was slow while each of them thought through what Everet had told them. They walked four blocks before Ginny spoke. "I did a quick scan of the information Doug gave us. There really isn't anything new. And there isn't anything about the competitive advertising either. Why do you suppose Everet mentioned it?"

"The meeting wasn't to give us new information," Ben said. "It was to give us a pep talk—and to let us know what's at stake. Everet wants us to win. The meeting was to give us a shot in the arm."

"He said we should pay attention to the competitive advertising," Andrew said. "What was that about?"

"He mentioned it because he wants us to do a campaign radically different from everyone else's. Everet is telling us we have to give him something special."

"Like Tree did for him all those years," Ginny said.

"Yeah, and like the three of us here have been doing as a team for the past several years," Ben said, "only this time we have to do it without Tree."

"Just give me a good creative brief," Andrew said. "If you give me a real essential truth—not the bullshit Tom gave me—I'll give you something special."

"I'm working on it," Ben replied.

As they walked the final three blocks to J&M in silence, Ben wondered if he could do it. He had reviewed all the research, the competitive advertising, the interviews and he still hadn't found the essential truth for the campaign. He needed to sort through his thoughts but too many other things filled his mind. Now he had to force himself to concentrate. Ben needed to finish the creative brief and essential truth as soon as possible so Andrew would have time to develop creative ideas. Everet Katch, the J&M employees, Janice Theilen, Nan… they were all depending on him.

"By the way," Andrew said as they reached their building, "why did Tom leave?"

"Tom?" Ben replied. "Tom made a decision in the bathroom that might take him out of the picture."

"Oh?" asked Ginny. "What happened?"

"His collar button came off and it made his collar stick out." Ben started to smile as he recalled the scene. "Tom refused to go to the meeting with his collar sticking out and told me to lie to Everet about why he couldn't attend. Problem was, Everet was in one of the stalls and heard the entire conversation."

"No shit?" Andrew laughed. Ginny was laughing too.

"Tom's little blunder won't hurt us," Ben said, "but we still have to do a great pitch."

"Yes we do," said Ginny. Andrew turned quiet.

Do a great pitch, thought Ben. *I'm doing the best I can.*

SEVENTEEN

THE MYSTERIOUS call came in to the night receptionist attending the *Twin Cities Times* city desk and the caller said they had "information Joel Scheck would be interested in." It was past the deadline for the next day's paper so most people had gone home. Outside Joel's cubicle, the cleaning crew was in the bullpen area going from desk to desk emptying trashcans, turning off lights. Normally, Joel would have been gone a long time ago, but the Katch pitch story was due in two days and it wasn't coming together like he'd hoped it would.

Joel had just gotten off the phone with someone who had left J&M three years earlier to take a job with DDB in Chicago. She didn't have much for him. He still had a lot of work to do to shape the story into something that would push his readership scores to where his job would be secure. But the information he had so far was only leading to a story about a high-profile pitch for a large account. If HC won, J&M would struggle, jobs would be lost, and it might even go out of business. It would be interesting, but it wasn't nearly as titillating as Stein and Conklin and the Zulu boy story he'd written thirty years before. God, was that long ago? And it was clear if there were implications for the senate election, Michael Hanley would write that part of the story. Still, it'd be something—the mighty Sheldon Hanrahan forcing yet another competitor out of business.

Maybe this call was something that would help. Joel picked up the phone. "Yes?" he said.

"I have important information on the Katch pitch," the caller said simply. Joel knew that promises like this were usually of little use. Important facts and smoking guns were almost always uncovered by probing and digging, not by someone calling in to the *Times* at night. That only happened on TV or in the movies.

"Okay. Tell me what you have," Joel said coolly.

"It's about the Katch pitch. We must meet so I can give you something."

"Why do we have to meet? Just tell me what you have."

"No. We need to meet. Now."

"Look," Joel said, "I should be home by now. Email it to me. Or I'll send a messenger to pick it up."

"Mr. Scheck, meet me at the Crowell construction site in a half an hour. The workers will be gone and the front gate will be open. Go up the stairs to the fourth floor. Be careful, watch your step. Half an hour. You won't be sorry."

"Wait," Joel said. The phone went dead.

"Christ," he said aloud. "Somebody wants to play Deep Throat. Fine." Joel hung up and shoved some papers into his briefcase. He headed to the elevators. He left through the *Times* building front doors into the cool evening air. The sky was getting dark. He found his Jetta in the lot across the street and pointed the car north on Washington Avenue toward the warehouse district and the Crowell condominiums. *This better not be a waste of time*, he said to himself.

*

The Crowell was Minneapolis' latest high-end condominium development. It was going up on an empty lot that only a few years before was home to vagrants living in cardboard boxes. Over the previous seven years, Minneapolis had seen an outbreak of condominium development around the downtown area and the twenty-story Crowell was the most upscale yet. Joel had heard the smaller units started at over one and a half million dollars and the penthouse was selling for a cool seven million.

Joel pulled the Jetta to the front of the construction site and got out. A chain-link fence surrounded the site. Off to one side, Joel saw a gate opened halfway. He went to the gate and slid through. He tramped over the dusty, rutted ground to the building. The glass skin had not gone up so the building was twenty open floors of concrete, exposed wiring and ductwork. Shadows fell deep inside the structure. In the back, Joel spotted a staircase. He went to it and began to climb to the fourth floor. The stairs were dark, but he saw well enough to negotiate them without stumbling.

"This is crazy," he said aloud.

Joel went to the center of the fourth floor. The interior walls weren't up yet, so the floor was open to the outside and the place smelled of construction dust and curing concrete. To his left was a makeshift table assembled from two sawhorses and a sheet of plywood. Sitting in a chair at the table was a man, gazing out at the downtown Minneapolis skyline.

"The city is beautiful this time of night, don't you agree?" the man said without turning from the skyline. "At twilight when all the lights come on but the sky still has that blue-gray afterglow. It's positively magical."

"Yeah, I suppose it is. Who are you?" Joel approached to get a better look, but the man was hidden in the shadows. Joel thought he detected an accent but couldn't place it. There was the smell of tobacco in the air.

"I happen to be someone with information you should have."

"Yeah, you told me over the phone. This is a bit dramatic for just a story about an advertising account pitch, don't you think?"

"Oh, but it isn't just about an advertising account pitch, is it?" The man continued facing the skyline as he talked.

"Okay, so what's it about?"

"I'm afraid you'll have to figure that out on your own," the man said. "Indeed, what I'm about to give you will help. But, before I do, you must agree to strict confidentiality. As far as you're concerned, you've never met me." The man turned. Through the shadows, Joel saw he was talking to a man in his late fifties wearing a dark jacket and shirt. The man took a pull off a curved pipe and the bowl glowed orange.

Joel was beginning to change his opinion about this meeting. "Of course," he said, "I'll keep everything completely confidential if you wish."

The man reached into a leather satchel on the floor next to him, took out a large, plain envelope and pushed it across the plywood table. "This is the information I told you about. You need to use it carefully. Don't just publish it or even reference it without knowing how it fits into the bigger picture. You mustn't let anyone know you have it until you're ready with your story. Do you understand? Not anyone. And keep your eyes open for anything unusual going on in the Katch pitch. It is important that you get this right."

Joel picked up the envelope, turned it over and then back again. "What's in here?"

"You'll have to read it and find out for yourself. But you should know, you have the potential here to uncover something very big."

Joel opened the envelope and looked at the papers inside. It was too dark to read anything. A breeze spun sawdust around in a swirl. He pushed the papers back inside the envelope.

Joel strained to see the man better. "If this information is as important as you say," he said, "I need to know you're a credible source. I need to know who you are."

"That's not necessary. Everything you need is in the envelope. You must read what's inside, keep your eye on the Katch pitch and do your job, Mr. Scheck. You were an excellent reporter once."

Joel let the comment pass. "How can I contact you if I have a question?"

"I'll contact you if and when I have more to give you. I'm hoping it will be soon."

Joel looked at the envelope and then at the man in the chair. He'd come to the Crowell building expecting this meeting to be a waste of time. Now, he was convinced the distinguished-looking man smoking a pipe in front of him knew exactly what he was doing and this meeting was as important as the man said it would be. Joel clutched the envelope. "Well, thank you. I guess I should read this right away."

"You are welcome, and yes you should. Remember, don't let anyone know you have this information. Oh, by the way, please don't try to find out who I am. Understood?"

"Yes, I understand."

"Good night, Mr. Scheck. Mind your step on the way out." The man stayed seated facing downtown and took another pull off of his pipe. He blew upward and the smoke mingled with the lights of downtown.

*

Joel descended the four flights of steps and slipped through the gate back to his car. He drove a few blocks to where the streetlights were bright. He pulled to the curb, and shut off the Jetta. He tried to remember if he'd seen the mysterious man before. It was dark, and he hadn't gotten a good look.

He took the papers out of the envelope and thumbed through them. A large black paperclip held the papers together. The first pages listed accounts Hanrahan Communications had won over the past twenty years. It was an impressive list. There was a value for the gross billings and estimated agency income for each account. This, too, was impressive—especially the agency income. If the dollar amounts were correct, the accounts were worth much more to HC than Joel or anyone else would have guessed.

Another set of papers listed the dates HC acquired each of its accounts and the details of account wins including timelines and key decision makers. A large airline awarded HC their account because the new director of marketing had once worked for HC where, according to the document, the apparently happily married man with three children was a closet homosexual. Shortly after the discovery, the man left HC to take the head marketing job at the airline and two months later, the airline's existing agency, with which it had a thirty-year relationship, was fired and HC was awarded the account without a review.

There was another story about a manufacturing company who awarded HC its account because an engineer whom Sheldon had gone to college with discovered serious EPA rules violations at the company. After a meeting between Sheldon and the CEO, the company gave HC their advertising and public relations business and, the next year, the company tripled its advertising budget. A few years later, Sheldon's engineer friend retired to Florida.

And then there was the CompuSto pitch. Several years earlier Joel had covered the pitch for a rapidly growing computer storage device company located in rural western Wisconsin. At the time, CompuSto was second on *Business Week's* list of the fastest-growing companies and was widely considered to be the next big high-tech business success. An IPO was in the near future, which would make the founders and anyone else on the inside very, very rich.

Three agencies pitched for the account and HC was one of them. HC was considered a long shot and was only included because they were located less than ninety miles from CompuSto headquarters. A large agency from New York without high-tech experience was a surprise entry. The third agency was Ballard, Inc. from Silicon Valley and from the start, they were the front-runner. Ballard had a well-earned reputation for helping high-tech companies position themselves for IPOs. The genius behind Ballard was its CEO, Keith Ballard, a swashbuckling Englishman with thick, dark hair and a penchant for wearing black. He was married to an ex-fashion model and had two young children.

Though Joel had covered the pitch, the papers he was holding gave him information he'd never known before. Apparently, three days before he was to fly to Wisconsin to make his presentation, Keith Ballard had an auto accident. He'd gone to his local watering hole for his usual after-work martini where an attractive woman started a conversation with him. Two hours later, he was driving his BMW-M5 115 miles per hour on the Bayshore Freeway when he lost control and crashed into the guardrail. Thanks to the BMW's state-of-the-art safety system, he and his female companion had only minor injuries. But when the police arrived, they discovered Ballard had a blood–alcohol level twice the legal limit. The Englishman told the police he always had only one martini and couldn't remember anything since he first met the woman whose name he also couldn't remember and who was sitting, scratched and bruised, in the back of an ambulance. The police didn't believe his story and arrested him on the spot.

Somehow, word of the incident got to western Wisconsin, and suddenly Ballard, Inc. was no longer the front-runner. Keith Ballard had to postpone his presentation but when he finally stood in front of CompuSto's review committee, he was no longer the dependable agency executive the committee's conservative members thought he was when they invited him to pitch their account. CompuSto awarded HC their business and two years later, Sheldon was a large shareholder when the company went public.

Keith Ballard was convinced that someone set him up. He hired a top private investigator in California to find the woman from the bar. The investigator discovered the woman had arrived in San Francisco only a few days before the incident and six months earlier, she was a high-priced prostitute plying her trade in, of all places, Minneapolis. The investigator couldn't find the woman and, after spending tens of thousands of dollars of Keith Ballard's money, couldn't uncover evidence of foul play either. The lack of evidence forced Keith Ballard to drop the investigation.

"I can't believe this," Joel said under his breath as he thumbed through the papers. He knew Sheldon had a reputation for playing on the edge of business ethics, that he was ruthless in account pitches. But this? Some facts accused Sheldon of committing a felony. At the very least, if any of it was true, Sheldon should be run out of business.

Joel stuffed the papers back into the envelope and laid it on the seat next to him. He sat in his Jetta and wondered who the mysterious figure was who gave him these documents. Perhaps it was all a ploy to smear Sheldon Hanrahan before the Katch pitch and torpedo Senator Howard's re-election campaign. Or maybe the information was an accurate accounting of what had built one of the largest communications companies in the world.

Either way, the man at the Colwell was right; it was something Joel should investigate. He had allegations, names, dates and figures to verify. It would take days, maybe even weeks. But even if a fraction of the information were true, Joel would have the makings of a story even bigger than Stein and Conklin.

EIGHTEEN

TODAY IS TREE'S FUNERAL, Ben thought when he awoke on Thursday morning. The thought sent spikes of pain into his stomach. It was the same pain he'd had at his father's funeral—jagged and heavy like someone punched him for not paying a debt. At his father's funeral, the pain came at the end of the church service when Ben realized the priest's gentle words meant he would never see his father again. He'd almost vomited during the benediction. Five years later, at his sister's funeral, the pain returned and this time, Ben vomited his breakfast in the church's basement bathroom before mass. The purge enabled him to get through the mass at his mother's side, but it didn't relieve the pain. Though the funeral was still hours away, he had the same spiky pain. He knew work would help, so he pulled on a pair of jeans and a T-shirt and took a suit with him to the agency.

They'd closed J&M for the funeral, and when Ben came through the front doors, the office felt cold and empty and heavy and sad. As he walked among the timber columns to his office, he imagined the employees, his friends and cohorts, staring at him from their cubicles. He pushed away the image, but it shot fresh spikes into his stomach. He went into his office, turned on his computer and opened the plans for Katch.

He still hadn't come up with an essential truth. The presentation to the board of directors was less than a week away and it wasn't coming to him. When he tried to work on it, he'd freeze in front of his computer or stare at a page of research without reading it. When the doubt was strongest, he considered going with Tom's essential truth. Then, if the pitch failed, if J&M lost the Katch account and went out of business, Tom would be blamed, not him.

But Tom had only regurgitated the research findings and had written a weak essential truth. No real thought had been put into it and Ben knew the result would be a flat, uninspired campaign. What had Everet Katch said? *You need to give us something that impresses nine board members.* And then he said directly to Ben, *I'm sure you can do it.*

So Ben worked alone in the lifeless agency and tried to ignore the daggers in his stomach. The essential truth was somewhere waiting for him to discover. It was in the research or the competitive review or the additional information Katch had given them on Wednesday. It was there, Ben just had to find it. When he had worked with Tree, it was only after days, sometimes weeks of work when a simple, straightforward answer would reveal itself. Ben was always surprised he hadn't seen it before, and Tree would laugh and say, "That's the way it works! You don't get to eat until you've gone on the hunt." Ben was still hunting.

He worked all morning in the quiet of the agency. He filled sheets of a notebook with thoughts and ideas. Working helped dull his stomach pain. At 1:15, he still didn't have an essential truth, but he had made progress. So he set his work aside and changed into the suit he brought with him. He left the agency and drove to the Basilica of Saint Mary for Tree's funeral.

*

The Basilica's graceful lines and exact proportions against the bright blue summer sky made the massive building seem like it was floating. Normally, the sight of it lifted Ben's spirits, but not today. Tree's funeral was taking place inside.

Ben had told Nan he would meet her on the front steps at 1:45.

She wouldn't be late—she never was—so he parked the car and hurried to meet her. She was waiting for him halfway up the granite steps, beautiful in a simple, knee-length black dress.

"Hi," she said. She took his hand and turned them toward the church. She brushed something from his shoulder. The church bells rang.

"I'm not sure I can do this," Ben said. "I hate funerals."

"I know," she replied.

"Can you stay for the reception? I hate them just as much."

"No. My mother can't pick up Jenny. Sorry."

"Damn. I'm on my own."

"I'll try to see Sarah before I go," Nan said.

"Okay."

Ben and Nan walked through the enormous Basilica doors into the narthex, through another set of doors into the nave. The nave's dimensions—length to width to height—had been carefully planned so that in spite of its size, it created an inviting space. The stained-glass windows depicted poignant scenes from the Bible. The ornate altar was alabaster white and reached high into the church's great dome.

As Ben and Nan walked down the aisle, soft organ music floated and echoed in the nave. They took a seat in one of the oak pews half way down. Ben felt another stab in his stomach and moved himself and Nan to the end of the pew in case the pain got worse and he'd have to leave. He took a deep breath and forced himself to look around to take his mind off his stomach. The massive church was almost three-quarters full. Most everyone from J&M was there. Andrew Birk sat with his wife on the other side of the aisle. Not far from Andrew were Ginny Rubenstein and her husband wearing a black yarmulke. John sat alone, wearing a tweed jacket and vest. Tom Clarey was there with his wife who had her blonde hair up for the occasion. J&M clients were present, too. The president of Zenith Data and his wife sat next to the CEO of Byron Booksellers and her husband. Everet Katch and his wife sat near the front. There was a famous university business professor, two well-known medical doctors, the state's most famous criminal lawyer and his much-too-young wife. The chief of police, Kenneth Daniels, looked commanding in his formal uniform. Off to one side was Congresswoman Janice Theilen.

At a few minutes before two, Sarah Marin entered from the side wearing a full-length black dress and a small black hat. She was on the arm of a handsome thirty-ish man who Ben assumed was one of her sons. After Sarah had taken her seat, a tall, lanky man slid in from the side and sat on the end of the front pew. It was the funeral director, Cecil Adams.

Everything was ready and the organ music stopped in preparation for the mass. Ben's stomach stabbed him. He looked to the back of the nave for the quickest way out in case his stomach got worse. Then Ben saw him. In the back, sitting in a pew by himself was Sheldon Hanrahan. He wore a black suit, red tie and his large, heavily tinted glasses. The sight of him made Ben forget about his stomach. He turned back to the front, leaned over to Nan, and whispered, "Sheldon Hanrahan is back there. What's he doing here?"

She leaned to him. "He's here for Tree's funeral."

"Why?"

"Out of respect, I suppose."

"Respect?"

"Shhh," Nan whispered. "It's starting."

The service was the epitome of Catholic Church efficiency. The eulogy, delivered by the bishop in full regalia, was short and to the point. The bishop's words painted a picture of a man who was a true leader of his church, family, and profession. Ben had heard similar words about his father in a funeral a lifetime ago.

To his surprise, Ben's stomach pain died during the service. And when the call came for all Catholics to receive Holy Communion, Ben expected he would stay seated with Nan. Nan was a Lutheran so she wouldn't go. And he hadn't received communion in over twenty years.

But Ben felt strangely expectant. So when the usher invited Ben's row to go forward, he turned to Nan and said, "I'm going."

She replied, "I understand."

Approaching the great altar, Ben realized he was compelled to take communion because of something the bishop had said about Tree. It reminded him of the spring before his father died at Ben's confirmation in his hometown church. The priest challenged the confirmed to be like Jesus—the greatest leader in history. Ben believed he could do it back then. Now, he wasn't sure if he could even lead the one-hundred-forty employees of Jacob & Marin.

Ben knelt at the altar and the priest offered the wafer. "The Body of Christ, broken for you." Ben accepted the wafer and thought of Jesus, his father, and Tree.

A second priest offered the cup. "The Blood of Christ, shed for you." Ben sipped from the cup and he saw the faces of his father and Tree. Was he like his father? Could he be like Tree? Did he have what it would take to save J&M? He stayed kneeling at the altar and said a prayer for the deceased—his father, his sister, and Tree. And then he said a prayer for himself and realized that the expectant feeling he had was hope that communion would deliver him from his sins and make everything turn out all right this time.

Ben returned to his seat. He took Nan's hand and held it. He watched the last people receive communion. Sheldon Hanrahan approached the altar, tall and straight. He knelt and bowed his head. The priests offered the wafer, then the cup and Sheldon humbly accepted both. He appeared to say a short prayer and returned to his pew with his head bowed. Sheldon's penance seemed sincere and Ben wondered what kind of man was really behind the large, dark glasses.

At last, the bishop issued a prayer for Tree's soul and the funeral mass was over. Just like Ben's father and his sister, Tree had passed from Ben's life forever. While the organ piped a melancholy recessional, Ben sat with Nan, waiting for the ushers to dismiss his row. And he realized how much he would miss Tree, his friend and mentor, and how much he'd missed his father and his sister over the years. This time, instead of spiny stomach pain, he was overwhelmed with sadness, and tears filled his eyes.

When they called his row, and he and Nan walked out of the great church, he squinted in the bright afternoon sun, breathed the heavy summer air, and was glad to be done with another funeral. He realized that every death was a new beginning for the living and he had a powerful feeling that his life was starting anew. Holy Communion had cleansed him, and the bishop's eulogy had challenged him.

Maybe, just maybe, he could do it this time.

"Are you all right?" Nan asked as they walked down the Basilica's granite steps.

"Yeah, I'm fine."

"I have to pick up Jenny, and I've missed Sarah. I'm so sorry I won't see her."

"She'll understand," Ben said. He gave Nan's hand a squeeze.

"Please give her my sympathy."

"I will," Ben said. "Tell Jenny I'll be home soon. I'm not going to stay long."

"I'm sorry I can't be with you at the reception. At least it's at the Walker." Nan nodded at the silver building down the street. "Are you sure you're okay?"

"I'll be fine," Ben replied. "Really, I am."

NINETEEN

BEN CROSSED THE STREET to the cube-shaped Walker Art Museum. The museum had closed for the afternoon to host the reception because Tree had been a big contributor. Through the glass doors, Ben saw dozens of people in the lobby talking quietly to one another. Waiters in tuxes offered tea and canapés. Sarah Marin, with one of her sons at her side, stood inside greeting people as they entered. "Thank you so much for coming," she said. And to the next person, "Thank you for those kind words," and to the next, "That's a lovely remembrance." She was a picture of grace and her sentiments were genuine.

Ben arrived at the front of the line. Sarah took his hand and held it. "I'm so sorry, Sarah," he said. A lump rose in his throat, and he was afraid he would cry again.

"Thank you. You know, Ben," Sarah said softly, "Tree liked you a lot. He always told me you'd be successful." Then she leaned in, looked past him, and said, whispering, "You remind me of him."

She let go of his hand and smiled, sadly. Ben didn't know if he'd heard her correctly. Had she said, "You remind me of him"? No, it couldn't be. He must have misunderstood. Ben awkwardly turned away and went into the main lobby, trying to understand what Sarah had just told him.

In the middle of the lobby—a three-story atrium with pure white walls set at odd angles—Ben saw a circle of J&M employees, talking quietly. He approached and the circle opened to let him in. The group continued talking.

"He was a great man."

"He was, indeed."

"He was too young."

"That's for sure."

"I feel so sorry for Sarah."

"She seems to be handling it well."

"The bishop gave such a nice eulogy."

"That's why he's a bishop."

"What a perfect afternoon for it."

"Couldn't be more beautiful."

"It's something that the Walker closed for this reception."

"I'll say."

"What kind of tea are they serving?"

"Chamomile, I think."

The group went quiet. Finally, someone asked, "Ben. The agency. What do you think is going to happen to it?"

How should I know? he thought. The people in the group stared at him waiting for his answer.

"I think the agency lost a great leader and we each lost a friend," Ben began. "So we'll have to step up and make the agency work without him. I honestly think we can do it." Ben wondered if his answer was what they needed to hear.

"Do you think we can win the Katch pitch?" someone else asked.

"Well, we're the incumbent," Ben answered. "We know more about their business than HC does. We do great work for them. We're their best choice. If we give a good presentation, we should keep the account."

And then someone asked, "Are you going to be the new president of the agency?"

Ben was dumbfounded. He'd never thought beyond the Katch presentation next week and certainly never considered becoming the agency's president. But someone had asked the question and the very asking of it meant these people had considered it. The question hung in the air as they waited for his answer.

"I… I honestly don't know," he said, finally. And then he added, "All I can say is, I have a job to do on this pitch. I'll do the best I can. If we win, and I become the president, so be it. Right now, all I can do is my job."

Everyone stood and nodded silently. Then, someone said, "That's all Tree ever did, too." Ben looked across the circle and saw the speaker was John.

After another moment of silence, someone asked the group, "How are the canapés?"

Ben pulled out of the circle. He should mingle with others before he left. He stopped briefly in the reception area to talk to a client, then to another. He avoided Everet Katch. He saw Tom had the president of Zenith Data cornered. Andrew leaned against one of the white walls, alone.

After a few minutes, Ben decided he could leave. As he searched for the quickest way to the door, a voice spoke to him from behind.

"Hello Ben," the voice said.

Ben turned and looked into the face of Sheldon Hanrahan. Ben had never seen him up close. He was taller than Ben had expected and his over-sized dark glasses were menacing. It was impossible to see his eyes.

"M… Mister Hanrahan," Ben stammered.

"You can call me Sheldon," Sheldon said with a slow smile.

"I'm surprised to see you here."

"Why?"

"Because…" Ben hung for a moment between frankness and decorum.

Sheldon let him hang. Then he said, "Tree was a great man, Ben.

And an outstanding competitor. I admired him very much. A long time ago, we were best friends. Naturally, I've come to pay my respect."

"Respect?" Ben said. The emotions of the past several days boiled inside him. "Then why are you trying to take the Katch account from his agency?"

"I was invited to pitch the account, Ben," Sheldon answered. "Anyway, that's strictly business. Attending the funeral of an old friend is personal. You should understand that."

"Well, I don't," Ben replied. "Not at all. It would hurt a lot of people if we lost Katch. So for them, business *is* personal."

Sheldon's smile turned cold. "If you lose the account, you don't deserve to have it."

"That's not always the way it works, is it, Mr. Hanrahan?" Ben countered.

Sheldon's smile warmed again. "Ben, I just came over to say you were lucky to work with Tree. And if you lose the account, you're welcome to work for me." He nodded and turned to leave.

As Sheldon started to walk away, Ben thought of all the employees who were depending on him to win the pitch. He thought of how the media would criticize Nan, Theilen's campaign manager, if the congresswoman lost the election because of J&M. He remembered the coffee shop conversation with John about how Sheldon would do anything to win. He remembered how Nan's computer was hacked. All of his emotions crystallized into an icy fury. He took a step toward Sheldon. "I'll never work for you, Mr. Hanrahan," he snarled. "And one more thing. Stay away from my family."

Sheldon turned around and his smile was gone. Ben felt his cold stare behind the dark glasses. "Really now, Mr. Smith." He held his stare for several seconds and then headed to the door.

John ran up to Ben. "What the hell was that about?"

"Mr. Hanrahan was telling me how much he admired Tree."

"I see," John said. "Ben, I need to talk to you about Sheldon."

"Yeah, you've already told me. He's a ruthless competitor and he'll do anything to win."

"I haven't told you everything. It's time you know the whole story."

"Please John, not now," Ben said. "It's been a helluva week. I'm tired and I haven't spent nearly enough time with my daughter. I hate funerals. And I hate funeral receptions. I'm going home."

"Okay, some other time, soon. Just watch yourself, okay?"

"Yeah," Ben said, "I will."

*

On the drive home, the day swirled though Ben's mind—his stomach pain and how it went away when he saw Sheldon Hanrahan; his urge to take communion; the question the employees asked; his talk with Sheldon Hanrahan. It all made him dizzy.

He knew the cure. He had to go home to Nan and Jenny. Jenny would want to play ball with him. Soccer or basketball or tennis or street hockey. She was a jock like her mother, and loved to compete. And Ben found sublime joy in being the one she competed against. Then, when Jenny was asleep, he would spend time with his wife. They would talk for a while, then make love.

After that, Ben would lie in bed and hope that his prayers at the Basilica's great white altar would be answered.

TWENTY

THE TREVOR MARIN CASE was one of those that fed Detective Jackson's obsession like cheap gin feeds an alcoholic. When the answers came, it was a thrill and he wanted more. But just like too much gin leads to a hangover, an answer meant Jackson was one step closer to solving the case, and a solved case meant Jackson didn't have anything to feed his obsession anymore. It was an unhealthy, vicious circle.

When he was at the downside of the circle, when he didn't have a case with a thousand possibilities to sort through, he had to find something to occupy his mind. When he was married to Martha, she took the brunt of his neurosis. Martha was pretty and smart, and her father was a successful Twin Cities surgeon. Jackson, on the other hand, had come from Chicago's south side. And he was insecure. So he'd obsess about her every move. He'd ask endless questions of her—what she'd done that day, who she had done it with, where had they gone and why. Then he'd imagine all the possibilities and focus on the ones that fed his insecurities. And that's when he'd start making notes, chase clues and sit for hours on stakeouts. He didn't know why he did it. He tried to stop, but just like an alcoholic can't lose the bottle, he kept stalking his wife. Poor Martha. Yeah, she was a victim, and that's why she got out.

As he sat at his computer, filling out an update on the case, Jackson was still sober on the Trevor Marin case. He didn't have any answers and he had a powerful thirst to know what had happened. So he carefully filled out his report, rereading and analyzing every detail.

"Jackson!" Lieutenant West yelled from his office.

"Yeah?" Jackson didn't look up from his computer screen.

"Get in here."

"Can't. Workin' on my report on the Marin case."

Lieutenant West's square head appeared from around the doorframe. "Goddamn it Jackson, that's what I want to talk to you about—the Marin case. Get your ass in here. I need an update."

Jackson pushed back from his desk and followed West into his cluttered office. "If you'd let me finish my report you could read what you want to know in about twenty minutes."

"I need to talk to you now. Got a call from the Captain 'cause he got a call from the Chief." West sat at his desk and clasped his thick hands behind his curly blonde head. He'd rolled the sleeves on his shirt half way up his arms.

"The Chief called about the Trevor Marin investigation?" Jackson asked. He sat in the Naugahyde chair in front of West's desk.

West shook his head. "No, no. He called about the Shauna Tate case, the girl who got shot. We haven't made any arrests yet and the African-American community, the papers, the politicians, and that goddamn Reverend White are putting pressure on us. You have to clear your cases to help out. What do you have on the Marin case?"

"Well, Lieu, I gotta tell ya. A lotta strange things on this one."

"Do tell, Detective," West said.

"Well, first there's the call. The timin' of it, a few hours after the accident. And the call came from Florida, for crissake, two thousand miles away."

"Who did Marin know in Florida?"

"Marin knew people from all over the world. Could be anyone."

"What else?"

"There's the body. It was ash two hours after they picked it up. That ain't the way it's done, Lieu. They're supposed to hold it at least a day."

Jackson hunched forward and rested his elbows on his knees. "And then the car. I can't find who took it, where it is, nothin' about it. It's a 1967 Porsche, all crunched up and burned. You think someone would remember it if they picked it up. No one saw it."

Jackson shook his head. "See what I mean, Lieu? It doesn't add up. The call, the body, the car."

"And then there's the chief releasing the body so soon," West said with a look.

"I might understand about the chief," Jackson replied. "I talked to Mrs. Marin. She said she called Daniels first thing. If he was a friend, he'd help her out. Still, with the Shauna Tate case blowin' up at the same time, I kinda wonder about that, too."

"Okay, so what's your theory?"

"Don't have one," Jackson said with his palms raised. "Maybe the call was a prank. Or maybe someone didn't like Mr. Marin much. I dunno. I gotta be honest with you Lieu, we need to do more work. We just don't have anythin' to go on without the body and the car. Shoot, Lieu, we don't even know if it was Trevor Marin in the car. We gotta dig more. I think we should start talkin' to his employees, business associates, friends. I'll need help."

"Can't do that," Lieutenant West said. He went to his office door and shut it. He went back to his old desk and half sat on the edge of it in front of Jackson. "I told you I got a call from the Captain and he got a call from Chief Daniels. They want you on the Tate case. In fact, they want you to take the lead. You're to drop your other cases and report to the captain this morning."

"They want me on lead? Why?"

"As I said, we haven't made any arrests yet and the African-American community is pressuring us."

"Oh, I see," Jackson said with an exaggerated nod. "I get to be the department's token African-American to relieve the pressure."

"Don't give me that shit, Jackson." West returned to his chair He

136

shook his head. "You know how it works. That asshole Reverend Terrance White is on the news every day, claiming the police don't care about African-Americans. He doesn't give a damn about Shauna Tate. Truth is, he doesn't want us to solve this case. He wants to continue getting his fat face on television. He's playing us and making it impossible to do our job. You can help. You're a good detective, Darren, and right now, the department needs you. Yeah, it's probably because you're black. But it's also because you're good at what you do."

"There are other black detectives who can handle it."

"The Captain asked for you, specifically."

"Me, specifically?" Jackson asked.

"Yep," West answered.

"Great. So you want me to turn over the Marin case to someone?"

"I was told to check into it, and if there was, as the Captain put it, 'no conclusive evidence of foul play,' I was told to close the case. And from what I can see, that's what we should do."

"What?" Jackson said. "We were given direct orders to close the case? I'm surprised the Captain even knows about it."

West looked straight at Jackson. "I got the impression the order came from the Chief."

"The Chief." Jackson stifled a sneer. "I see. The Chief who released the body too soon. This doesn't seem strange to you, Lieu?"

"The case is closed, Detective Jackson. I'll take care of the paperwork. You report to the Captain. He's waiting for you." West picked up some papers and started reading them, signaling the meeting was over. Jackson returned to his desk and stared at the open Marin case file on his computer monitor. The facts, dates and his notes stared back at him. Finally, he forced himself to close the file and log off the computer.

But it wasn't over for him. There were too many unanswered questions and that was something he just couldn't have. If he didn't take care of it, his thirst to know would get worse and worse until it kept him up all night. Even though they had officially closed the case, even though the department had strict rules about working on closed cases, even though the Shauna Tate case would consume him, Jackson had to have answers before he'd forget about it. If he got his answers, then maybe he would let it go.

But only if he got answers.

TWENTY-ONE

BEN SAT AT HIS OFFICE COMPUTER and knew what he had to do. But he couldn't make himself do it. The essential truth for Katch was in front of him on the computer screen. All he needed to do was paste it in the creative direction and turn it over to Andrew. Then it would be done. He was already two days late with it. He promised Andrew he'd have it on Wednesday. Now it was Friday morning and Ben still hadn't finished the creative brief because he couldn't decide which essential truth to use.

He knew why he couldn't decide. As soon as he chose an essential truth, it would be official. Andrew would certainly go with his instead of Tom's, and then everyone would know Ben was in charge of the pitch—and the unofficial leader of the agency. He probably was anyway. Tom had fled from the meeting at Katch because of his shirt collar and had lost all credibility with Everet Katch. Everet was depending on Ben to take charge of J&M and give him the campaign that would convince his board of directors to keep the account with J&M.

Outside Ben's office, the agency was returning to normal. Tom Clarey arrived late, Andrew was ranting and raving as usual, and people in the media department were once again complaining about the noise Andrew made. There were clients to take care of, campaigns to get out, and a major pitch to put together. J&M was back at work.

It wasn't the same for Ben, however. The day before, at Tree's funeral, someone had asked him if he was going to be the agency president. He didn't have an answer. He'd never thought about it before. He didn't even realize he was a candidate. But the J&M employees had asked him the question, and it had changed him. This morning when he arrived at work, he felt everyone watching him, sizing him up. Outwardly, they all seemed the same, rushing off to meetings, busily working at their desks, talking on their phones. But Ben felt the pressure of one-hundred-forty sets of eyes on him.

One thing Ben knew for certain was that a leader set a good example. So he'd worked long hours over the past week. He still had to finish cleaning up the Bug BeGone fiasco from Monday. He also promised Andrew he'd have the Katch creative brief and the essential truth to him by noon today. Jay and the rest of his staff was doing everything Ben asked of them. Ginny had written comments on an early draft of the creative direction that were helpful, even insightful.

As Ben stared at his computer, Tom Clarey came into Ben's office. "Good morning, Ben." He flashed an ivory smile. His suit today was navy blue with thin white pinstripes. His tie was gold.

"Hello Tom," Ben said.

Tom pointed to a chair. "May I?"

"Sure."

"Andrew tells me you're rewriting the creative direction," Tom said.

"I'm working on it now," Ben pointed at his monitor.

"May I see what you have?"

"Why?" Ben asked.

"Because I'm asking, that's why." Tom pulled on the knot of his tie to straighten it.

Ben faced Tom. "The other day you tried to fire me if I didn't accept your essential truth. Now you want to see what *I* have?"

"We're all under stress, Ben," Tom said. "I'm sorry I threatened you. I was caught up in the emotions. Now I'd like to see what you have."

"Are you abandoning your essential truth?"

"No. It's just…" Tom fidgeted. "Andrew says he can't work with it. He says he's waiting for yours. I thought I could work with you on it. Maybe we could combine the two."

"I'm almost done," Ben said, "and I don't need your help. I'm turning it over to Andrew this morning." Ben turned back to his monitor.

"I'd like to see it when you're done, before you give it to Andrew." Tom started to leave. "Okay?"

"Just a minute, Tom," Ben said abruptly turning from his monitor. He knew what Tom was up to. Tom's move to take over the pitch had failed. They didn't need him anymore and he was trying to use Ben to get himself involved.

Ben folded his arms across his chest. "I've been working on this for nearly a week," he said. "I've spent early mornings and late nights on it. I worked all day Monday after you went home and yesterday morning when the agency was closed. I've poured over the research and the competitive review. I've analyzed the information Katch gave us on Wednesday. I've agonized over at least three dozen essential truths. Jay and Ginny have put in long hours too. So has John. And now you want to jump on board after all the work is done?"

"I'm the senior vice president," Tom said tugging on a sleeve. "Katch expects me to be involved."

"Bull," Ben replied. "Katch only wants people involved who'll give them a campaign that will save mutual funds. I've done the work to get them that campaign. If the Katch board members ask difficult questions, who will answer? I will. If they need an in-depth explanation of our thinking, who will give it? I will. I will because I've done the work, Tom, not you. Katch doesn't want you or anyone else involved on their account who isn't working for them, no matter what their title is."

Tom started to reply but Ben cut him off. "And don't think for a minute that you can fake it. The board members are too smart for that. They'll see right through you. No, Tom, you can't have my work."

Tom stiffened. "Don't forget, Ben, I'm still your boss."

Ben laughed aloud. "Right. Go ahead, fire me. Or try. It won't mean a thing because you're not in charge here. Sarah Marin said she isn't making any decisions until after the Katch pitch. And the people out there," Ben pointed out the door, "will follow the person doing the most to save their jobs. And that's me, not you."

There was an awkward silence, then Tom slumped back into the chair. In his slick Italian suit and expensive cotton shirt, Tom looked like a little boy dressed up in his father's Sunday suit. Ben saw by the angle of his shoulders that Tom knew he'd lost his bid to take over the pitch.

"Ben," Tom said, finally, "I need to be involved in this. I want you to include me."

"Tom," Ben answered, "to be perfectly honest, I can't think of a single thing for you to do."

Tom looked beseechingly at Ben. "I need something. I'm the senior vice president. The senior vice president!" Ben didn't reply and finally, Tom pulled himself up and left Ben's office. As Ben watched him leave, he sensed something had changed. It was clear Tom was no longer his boss, and with Tree gone, it meant that for the first time in his career, Ben had no boss at all. He had to make decisions on his own.

A decision like which essential truth was right for Katch. Andrew was complaining about how little time they were giving him to develop creative ideas, and he was right. Ben had taken too long. Just like Tree had said it would, thinking through all the options hurt his head. Yesterday before the funeral, he'd narrowed his choices to three and decided to let it rest for a day. The right one would surface, as it usually did.

He opened the Word document where he had put the three

essential truth statements. Ben read each statement again. He had to choose the right one. Sometimes, the account team would decide on an essential truth that wasn't quite right. When that happened, the creative ideas came out flat or completely wrong. The agency couldn't afford to let that happen this time.

Finally, from some place he couldn't name, one idea rose to the surface and floated above the others. He sensed that it was the right one. He clicked it and read it again for the hundredth time. *Yeah. This is it,* he thought. He pasted it into the creative direction and clicked save.

*

As he was about to send the file to Andrew, he noticed an instant messaging box blinking on and off in the bottom right corner of his computer screen. It must be Nan—no one else knew his username. They used Messenger to chat when Nan was working on the computer at home. They would ask, "When will you be home?" or, "What are we having for dinner?" Sometimes, they would exchange messages about what one of them wanted to do to the other in bed that night. Lately, however, Jenny had discovered instant messaging so they had to stop that kind of talk. Jenny would get online and ask Ben if he'd play soccer with her when he got home. Ben loved the exchanges with Nan and Jenny. They were little breaks in his workday like sips of cool water on a long hike.

He clicked on the box and the familiar Messenger window opened. The message was from GoodGurl. *What's this? Did Nan change her username?* He opened the message. It read, "You never called or e-mailed me."

Ben typed a message back. "Who are you?"

"I'm a person who wants to meet you," was the reply on the screen. He decided it had to be Nan being coy.

"Oh, why?" Ben typed.

"Because, I want to. That's all."

"And then what?"

"Hmmm…"

"Okay, GoodGurl," Ben typed, "who are you really?"

"I'm Elizabeth."

"Elizabeth?" Ben typed.

"Kelly," was the reply. "Elizabeth Kelly from the bus."

Ben's heart skipped a beat. He hadn't thought about the raven-haired beauty from the bus since he'd seen her Wednesday morning. He'd tossed her card in the trash when he got to work and had forgotten about her—until now.

"I remember," he replied.

"I gave you my card and told you to call. You didn't. I feel rejected." At the end was a sad-face emoticon.

"I've been busy. I lost your card." Ben felt awkward.

"LOL. Now I really DO feel rejected." An even sadder emoticon appeared on the screen.

"Elizabeth," Ben typed, "how did you get my username?"

"Women have their ways."

"I see. What do you want from me? Do you know me?"

"I want to meet you," she replied.

"Why?"

"I want to… meet you."

Ben was beginning to understand. "Elizabeth, I'm married."

"That's okay," was the reply.

Ben wasn't comfortable with where the conversation was going. "I can't," he typed. "I won't."

Another sad-faced emoticon came up on the messenger box. Then, "BTW, I've put you on my friends list. Click on this link and you can access my personal information." A URL followed. "The number is my private cell phone. You can call me anytime."

Then another line came on Ben's screen. "Oh, and I hope you like my picture. LOL. Bye."

Ben stared at his computer screen. The URL was sitting in front of him waiting for him to click it. He knew he shouldn't open files from strangers. But this wasn't a file, it was a simple URL. It wouldn't cause a virus or crash his computer. Would it? Could Messenger carry a virus? Could this little instant messaging session threaten the files for the Katch pitch? Then, he remembered Nan's computer was hacked a few nights earlier.

He panicked. He quickly uploaded the Katch files from his computer onto the company server where they'd be safe behind a firewall and protected by the agency's anti-virus software. As soon as the last file finished uploading without a problem, he sat back, relieved.

He'd left open the messenger window with Elizabeth Kelly's URL. It beckoned. It wouldn't hurt to open it now. All of his files were safe. Maybe the information would tell him more about this mysterious woman so he could figure out why she contacted him. And she mentioned a picture...

Ben clicked on the URL and a browser window opened to a Facebook page with Elizabeth Kelly's information. On the top was a message that read, "You have just made GoodGurl your Facebook friend." The information about Elizabeth Kelly was simple and straightforward. The picture showed the beauty he had seen on the bus a few days before in a tasteful yet provocative pose. Her dress carefully accentuated her ample breasts. Her freckles showed and her green eyes beckoned.

She was indeed beautiful and Ben was flattered that she had contacted him. But he thought of his own beautiful wife and his precious child at home and he knew he shouldn't be interested in Elizabeth Kelly no matter how green her eyes were. Ben closed the browser window without reading the telephone number or e-mail address. He'd learned nothing about Elizabeth Kelly's intentions but when he thought about it, he didn't really care. If she sent him another message, he'd tell her not to bother him again.

Then, he opened a new e-mail and wrote a simple three-word message—*Here it is.* He attached the Katch creative brief with the essential truth he had pasted in, sent the e-mail to Andrew and John and it was done.

TWENTY-TWO

"DUDE, I NEED TO talk to you right away."

"Dirk?" Ben said rubbing his face. "You geek, you woke me up. What time is it anyway?"

"Ah... I don't know," Dirk answered. "After midnight I guess."

Ben checked the clock on his nightstand. "It's 1:45 in the morning!"

"Oh, yeah. Um, sorry. But I need to talk to you. Now."

"Now?"

"Now," Dirk insisted.

"Can't it wait until the morning?"

"No, I think you better see this. It's about Nan's computer."

Ben sighed. "All right. I'll be over in a few minutes." Ben hung up, and Nan rolled over in the bed next to him.

"Who was that?" she asked sleepily.

"Our friend the computer geek. He says he needs to talk to me."

"It's the middle of the night," Nan moaned. "Tomorrow is Sunday. You'll have all day to talk to him." She pulled on his arm to keep him in bed.

"He says it's about your computer."

"Oh." She let go of his arm. "Does he have my files?"

"Didn't say."

"Well, come back to me soon. I don't like being in bed alone."

He kissed her on the forehead. "I'll be back as soon as I can." His eyes were sticky with sleep as he pulled on his jeans and shirt in the dark. He stumbled down the stairs and grabbed the car keys off the kitchen table.

Five minutes later, he was knocking on Dirk's front door. The door opened and Dirk, wearing sweatpants and a Weezer T-shirt, let Ben in. "Hey, howya doing? Man, you should see your hair," Dirk laughed. "I can't tell if you look more like Lyle Lovett or Buckwheat."

Ben ran his hand through his hair. "Yeah, well what do you expect at two in the morning?"

"Sorry, but I thought you should see this right away. Follow me."

Ben followed Dirk into the house—a walkout rambler located on Minnehaha Creek that Dirk had bought with the money he made from Secure Digital. Dirk had turned the 1950's vintage house into a model of modernism. He'd taken out walls to open up the living area and replaced the half wall leading to the lower level with contemporary steel railings. The furniture was all B&B Italia with clean lines and a simple stature.

Dirk lead Ben through the living room, then into a bedroom converted into an office. Sitting on a desk running the entire length of the wall were three huge, flat-screen monitors. Behind them were dozens of wires and black boxes with blinking lights. Nan's laptop was on the desk with a wire leading to a computer underneath. Dirk motioned Ben toward a chair in front of the monitors. "You want some coffee?"

"What, and be up all night? Are you nuts? I plan to be back in my warm bed next to my beautiful wife as soon as I can. So, what do you have to show me?"

"Cool. Okay, remember the other night when I told you only a few people in the world had the talent to break through my firewall?"

"Yeah. You said something about 'seri-ass talent'."

"Exactly. Well, I found out who did it."

"Really? Who?"

Dirk rolled his mouse and a monitor blinked to life. A series of numbers came on the screen. After each number was what looked to Ben like computer code. "See here," Dirk explained, "all hackers leave a trace. There's no way around it. They use computer code to break through a firewall and into the computer. That code stays with the computer."

Dirk twitched in his chair like a kid playing a video game. His eyes were wide with excitement. "Well this guy was clever," he continued. "He crashed Nan's hard drive to erase the code, so I couldn't trace it. He did quite a number on it."

"You didn't get anything off the computer?" Ben asked. "But I thought you said you knew who did it?"

"I do, because he also had to leave a bit of code to get through the firewall. But he crashed that too. I couldn't find a thing."

"Oh, I get it," Ben said. "Since all the evidence was destroyed, you used your telepathic powers to find out who did it."

"Damn, I should've thought of that," Dirk exclaimed. "Would've saved a lot of time! No, wise guy. Now pay attention."

Dirk explained that the hackers didn't know what they were getting into until they were already in. They were probably surprised at the level of protection on Ben's home system. But once they started, they were committed. They'd already left code that identified them so they had to keep going. Once they cracked through, they were in and got what they wanted off Nan's computer. Then, they had to crash both the computer and the firewall to cover their tracks.

Ben was no longer sleepy. "Okay, Sherlock," he said. "So if the firewall got crashed too, how did you figure it out?"

"Elementary, my dear Watson," Dirk said. "Don't forget, I built this firewall. In all my systems I add a small, second processor to monitor what's going on in the main firewall. It's the same setup we had when we invited hackers to hack us at Secure Digital. We wanted to see what they were doing, so we put this little device in the firewall. There was no way for your hackers to know we were monitoring them. No reason for them to expect a home system would have this kind of firewall in the first place. Well, my little processor captured what I needed to catch them."

"That told you who it was?"

"Eventually it did." Dirk pointed to a monitor that showed lines and lines of what looked like random numbers. "See those? They're internet addresses. Every computer hooked up to the Internet has a unique address. Computers send instructions to each other in little packets of code and use the addresses to direct where the packets go. That's how they hacked into Nan's computer, with these little packets of code. Once I had the information from one of their packets, I just traced it back to its source."

"I see," Ben said. "Why are there so many numbers?"

"Because," Dirk replied, "it's never directly computer to computer. The packets are routed through a bunch of servers to get to their destination. I had to trace it back to its source through all these servers."

"And, pray tell, where did it lead to?" Ben asked.

"Right here. This computer," Dirk said pointing at the last set of numbers on the screen.

"So you've given me a set of ten numbers. Gosh, thanks, man. Well worth my trip here in the middle of the night."

Dirk folded his arms and turned solemn. "Ben, this address is for a computer located in the Wells Fargo Building in Minneapolis."

"The Wells Fargo Building? But who...?" Ben felt a shot of adrenalin. "Shit! Hanrahan Communications is in that building."

"Yes, sir, they are. But so are a hundred other companies."

"Dirk," Ben said, "there's something you should know. Katch is up for review. We're presenting next week and there's only one other agency pitching against us. Hanrahan. You don't suppose they did this to get information from me, do you? Can you tell whose computer it is?"

"Not without hacking into it," Dirk answered. "If I do, people this good would know." Dirk leaned toward Ben. "Look Ben, at first I just thought this was a random hacking, you know, someone who tripped over your firewall and wanted a challenge. But when I found out someone here in Minnesota did it… Well, it appears that it was done deliberately."

Dirk turned off the monitor. "I thought you'd find this worth getting out of bed for."

"Dirk," Ben said, "if Sheldon did this, I should go to the police."

"Yeah. In fact, you should probably go to the FBI. Didn't Nan say Theilen's campaign plan was on her computer?"

"Yeah, it was."

"That's seri-ass shit, dude," Dirk said. "However, there's a problem. I have a confidentiality agreement with Secure Digital. I'm bound by contract not to reveal any of my programming secrets for five years after I left. That was three years ago. What I've shown you is in violation of that contract. If this goes to the police, Secure Digital will sue me for everything I own. I didn't leave them on the best terms, if you know what I mean."

"So I can't go to the police."

"I'm not saying that," Dirk said. "I'm telling you this in case you need to. If you and Nan are in danger, then by all means, take it to the police. If Secure Digital sues me, I'll just move in with you."

"Oh, yeah. Nan would love that," Ben said. "Look Dirk, I'll just have to deal with this some other way."

Dirk raised a hand. "I dig, but you just might need to use this. But let me ask you something. What kind of security system do you have at J&M?"

"I don't know. It was installed by an outside vendor. It's managed by one of our Web designers."

"You're kidding? A fucking *Web designer* is in charge of your security?" Dirk shook his head. "Maybe I better check it out. If Hanrahan did this to Nan's computer, they might try to do something to your computers, too."

"Yeah, good idea." Ben said, remembering the Katch plans he'd saved on J&M's server. "You can come by first thing Monday and check it out."

"You sure?" Dirk asked. "We can go now. Or tomorrow—that's later today, I guess."

"No," Ben answered. "I gotta get back home. And I need to spend time with Nan and Jenny tomorrow—today."

Dirk got up and went into the kitchen. Ben followed him. "You sure you don't want any coffee? I just brewed some Cumbre Lavado from Cuba. Very hard to get. It's totally epic."

"No thanks. Although, I probably won't sleep much tonight," Ben said.

"Okay. You know the way out. See you later."

Ben started for the front door but stopped and followed Dirk into the kitchen. "Hey Dirk. I have a question. Is it easy to get someone's instant messaging username if you don't give it to them?"

"Veeery difficult. Why?" Dirk poured some dark coffee into a large black mug. The aroma was strong even from across the room.

"Someone sent me a message and knew who I was even though I didn't know them. Somehow, they got my username."

"They probably got it off your Messenger information."

"Can't be that. I have that info blocked from the public. Only Nan knows my username."

"You sure?"

"Positive."

"Well, that's strange," Dirk said, "because Messenger has a pretty seri-ass security system. No one's going to hack them to get just one username. Who is this person, anyway?"

"No one, really," Ben answered. "Someone I saw on the bus."

"Do they work for Hanrahan?"

"No. I'm sure it isn't connected to this thing with Nan's computer, if that's what you're thinking," Ben said. "She works at a law firm."

"A 'she', huh? Be careful with that shit, Benjamin."

"No, man, it's nothing like that. I blew her off anyway."

"Good. You better get back home to your wife."

"Dirk," Ben said. "Thanks."

"No problèma." Dirk lifted his coffee mug to his mouth. "Get some sleep."

"Yeah, right," Ben said.

*

As he drove home, for the first time Ben realized what he was up against. He and Nan were under attack by someone, most likely Sheldon Hanrahan. It was now Sunday morning and he wanted to stay away from the office so the creative department could work their magic with no one looking over their shoulders. He'd hoped to relax and recharge a little before Monday morning when he'd have to refocus on the Katch pitch and take up the challenge of leading J&M. In the morning, he'd go through the motions—he'd play tennis or basketball or soccer with Jenny and walk around the lake with Nan. But he doubted if he'd be able to relax.

And Monday would come sooner than he wanted it to.

TWENTY-THREE

"DO YOU LIKE my Zen garden?" Sheldon asked. "I've worked on it for over fifteen years. It will take another five until I have it precisely the way I want it."

"It's nice, I guess," his guest replied.

How could you not appreciate my garden? Sheldon thought. For Sheldon, his garden was a place of sublime serenity and he thought people should appreciate it—especially the person he was with who just looked at his feet as they walked. The garden covered six-thousand square feet in the middle of his back yard and just like the Parthenon, its dimensions precisely adhered to Pythagoras' Golden Ratio—1.618 times longer than its depth. An expanse of small white pebbles was raked into neat concentric circles around three islands of precisely placed boulders, meticulously sculpted green plants and closely trimmed moss. Along the back was a head-high stucco wall topped with curved gray-green tile. This was Sheldon's special place. It's where he came to think, to plan—and to remember.

The garden represented a turning point for Sheldon. At his lowest point, a year after the accident, he'd travelled to Kyoto, Japan and to the Zen garden of the Nanzen-ji Temple. The garden was stunning and perfectly elegant, and the contrast between its beauty and his own despair made him weep. He sat on the bench for hours gazing at it, and there he discovered what he had to live for. Beauty, order, elegance.

A few years later, after he'd made his fortune, he bought this house because it was on a massive lot. And then he went to work on his garden. The monks of Nanzen-ji had had eight-hundred years to shape their garden. Sheldon would achieve perfection in his garden in only twenty.

"What are your thoughts about what we discussed?" Sheldon asked. It was a gorgeous Sunday evening and the sun's low angle perfectly illuminated the garden's features.

"I don't know yet," the other one answered.

"You're still undecided?"

"It's a big move."

"Yes it is," Sheldon said. "But frankly, it's your only move." Through his dark glasses, Sheldon scanned the other person's face. "Don't do it if you aren't completely sure," he said. "I don't want you at Hanrahan Communications if you aren't committed.

"Of course," Sheldon continued, "this will be my only offer. If on Wednesday you make the presentation to Katch with J&M, I will not give you another offer to work for me. Is that clear?"

"Yeah, it's clear," the other one answered.

"Come," Sheldon said. "I want to show you something." Sheldon led his guest to one of the garden's islands and pointed to a five-foot-high evergreen. "Look at this tree," he said. "See how the branches spreading over the rocks resemble cumulus clouds rising over the mountains? The plant is a Japanese juniper and it's over two hundred years old. I imported it from Shikoku Island where five generations of Buddhist monks trained it to be in this precise form. I myself have been training the tree for the past thirteen years. It's strong and healthy and almost perfect. What do you think?"

"It's beautiful," the other one said. "I see what you mean about the clouds."

"Just like sculpting a tree," Sheldon said, "you must take control of your life. You must decide what you need, and cut out the rest."

"Yes, my life…"

"You won't be in control if you don't have a job."

"I know."

"If J&M loses Katch," Sheldon said, "it will go out of business. Then who would you work for? How would you pay your debts?"

"I don't know," the other one answered.

"On the other hand, if you come with us and HC doesn't win the account, we'll still be in business. You'd continue to work for me. You need the money."

There was no response.

"You must take control," Sheldon urged, "just like the monks did with the Juniper. I need your answer."

"We're putting together a solid presentation at J&M," his guest said. "Excellent work has been done."

"Will it win the account?" Sheldon asked.

"If we give them a good campaign, we might win."

"I'm surprised to hear you say that."

"Why?"

"Because your agency is weak without Tree," Sheldon said. "And we must destroy the weak so the strong can survive. It's the way of business. It's the way of nature."

"Isn't it for the board of directors to decide?" his guest asked.

"It's everyone's responsibility," replied Sheldon. "Everyone, especially the board members. The strong must survive."

"And the weak must be cut out," the other one said. "Just like Juniper's weak branches."

"Exactly," Sheldon nodded. "Good, you understand. So, what is your decision?"

Sheldon waited for an answer. Finally, the other one said, "I'll go with you."

"So you are committing to HC?"

"Yes."

"Are you sure?"

"Yes."

"Do you agree with the terms?"

"Yes."

"All of them?"

"Yes."

"Good," Sheldon said. They came to the end of the Zen garden and Sheldon motioned them to turn back. "Then, this is what you will do," Sheldon said. "Don't tell anyone about your decision. No one. Stay at J&M and do your job. Do it well. Don't contact me. Do you understand?"

"Yes, sir."

"Resign from J&M on Wednesday morning. Leave everything behind except your personal belongings. We don't need anything. Is that clear?"

"Yes, sir."

"Now, go home," Sheldon said, with a hand on the other's arm. "Relax. Enjoy the rest of the weekend. Leave everything to me."

Sheldon's new employee walked across the grass to the front of the house. There was the sound of a car starting and driving off.

Sheldon turned to his garden and thought about what he'd just done. He was pleased. This, along with his other plans would surely doom J&M and the Katch account would finally be his. And Theilen would struggle to restart her advertising campaign and Howard would win reelection in a landslide. Then, in two years, Howard would be president. Everything was coming together just as Sheldon had planned. It was perfect.

As he strolled along the Zen garden, something stopped him. He noticed a small crack in one of the Juniper's branches, probably caused by the storm from a few nights before. Sheldon took off his glasses to get a better look. He saw that he could not save the branch. The two-hundred-year-old tree would have to be destroyed.

He put on his glasses, focused beyond the garden and sighed.

TWENTY-FOUR

HE PLACED THE INTERNET CALL to the URL they made him memorize. He typed in the address, clicked on the "call" button and waited. A faint ringing sound came from his computer and then he heard a weak, "Yes?"

"We know who made the call to the police," he said. "It was your son David."

"David? Why? What does he want?"

"We've given him what he wants. He won't cause any more trouble. And the police have closed the case."

"David," the voice said, wheezing.

"I'm sorry."

"It's good you took care of it. We have to be careful."

"We are being careful. We'll be fine."

"Okay. Be sure to follow procedures. Delete this call record and do a clean sweep of your hard drive as you were taught to do."

"I will."

"John," the voice said sadly, "thank you."

"Of course," John Turner replied.

TWENTY-FIVE

WHEN BEN PUSHED the elevator button for the eighth floor early Monday morning, the doors closed immediately and took him to his floor. He had to get to work early because there were only two and a half days left to complete the presentation for Katch that would save his agency.

"Morning, Julie," Ben said as he stepped off the elevator into J&M's lobby.

"Good morning Ben," she replied with an unusually pleasant smile. "Tom Clarey is looking for you."

"He's here already?"

"Yes. He left a message. He wants to talk to you." She handed him a pink message slip and smiled again.

"And another week begins," Ben said.

As Ben walked to his office among the timber beams and the exposed yellow brick, J&M employees were turning on lights and starting their computers. As he went by they said, "Good morning, Ben." "Ben, have a good weekend?" "Mr. Smith, good morning!" *Mr. Smith?* They were showing him a level of respect he'd never had before. At first, it made him smile and lift his chin. But then he remembered he couldn't trust it.

He'd been here before. When his mother treated him like an adult after his father died and his Uncle Jim nodded at him approvingly when he helped clean up after Thanksgiving dinner. But it all ended when Ben's mother discovered pills in Ellen's purse. She told Ben he had to do something about his little sister. At seventeen years old, he wasn't sure what to do so he did nothing and Ellen's drug use got worse. He'd failed to help his sister then, and the same thing could happen now. J&M could lose the Katch pitch and no one would call him 'Mr. Smith' again. He remembered what Tree had said after every agency victory—a quote from Rudyard Kipling. *Meet with triumph and disaster and treat those two imposters the same.*

Triumph was indeed an imposter. He'd been here before.

Ben went into the account handling area and saw Jay. He was wearing a white shirt and khaki slacks. He was setting up in his cubicle. "Boss," Jay said, "good thing you're here already. You must have driven."

"No," Ben replied. "Early bus."

Jay followed Ben into his office. Ben removed a new ad layout from his chair placed there for his approval and sat at his desk. Someone had watered the philodendron on his bookshelf and it'd sprung to life in the sun.

"So, what's up?" Ben asked.

"Andrew wants to talk to you and Ginny about the creative direction for Katch. He has some questions."

"When?"

"Right away. He's already here and I just saw Ginny come in. And Jim Ross from Bug BeGone called. He approved the new plans. He actually said he's pleased."

Ben laughed and shook his head. "What a crazy business. By the way, Tom Clarey is looking for me. Do you know what it's about?"

"No," Jay said. "But, it's weird."

"Weird, how?"

"He isn't wearing a suit today. It's the first time I've ever seen him wear anything but one of his expensive suits."

Ben snickered. "I gotta see that. I should probably talk to him right away."

Ben said he'd have to take care of a few things before he met with Andrew and Ginny. He suggested a meeting at 9:30. Jay said he'd set it up and get the room ready. Ben told him to get him a few clean copies of the creative brief and the research report. Jay nodded and started to leave.

"Jay," Ben said stopping him at the door, "you're doing a great job. Thanks for all of your hard work."

"I'm not doing any more than you are," Jay said, waving over his shoulder as he left Ben's office.

Ben leaned one elbow on the arm of his chair. So Jim Ross accepted the replacement plan for Bug BeGone in Detroit. Miracles do happen. Just a week earlier, Jim was threatening to fire the agency because of the missed coupon insert and now, Jim was pleased with the plan to correct the mistake. That's the way it was in this crazy business. Clients were angry with you one day and loved you the next. It was true what Kipling had said—triumph and disaster were indeed both imposters.

Ben decided to go to Lucy Johnson's office instead of calling her with the good news that Jim had approved the Bug BeGone plan. When he got there Lucy was sitting at her worktable meeting with a media rep, a petite woman, who was showing Lucy charts and graphs on her iPad. "Oh, sorry, I didn't know you were in a meeting," Ben said.

"It's okay," Lucy said with a smile on her square face. "Do you know our Valassis rep, Lori Wyman?" Ben introduced himself. Lori, wearing a dark blue business suit, vigorously shook Ben's hand while handing him her business card.

He turned to Lucy. "Sorry to interrupt, but I wanted to tell you Jim Ross called and approved the replacement plan. He said he's pleased."

"That's great," Lucy said. "I'm glad it worked out. That's why I'm talking to Lori here. I had to pull a few favors from our friends at Valassis."

Indeed, she had. Last week, Ben had asked Lucy to do whatever was necessary to get the Bug BeGone campaign back on track. He'd said he would accept the responsibility for the mistake—even though it wasn't his—and told her he'd do everything he could to help. It was important to take care of the smaller clients, he had said, even though the agency's focus was on Katch. He challenged her to "pull off a Lucy Johnson miracle." His sincerity and the fact that he'd stayed late to work on his part of the Bug BeGone plan persuaded Lucy to make some calls and pull some strings. The result was Valassis and a few other media suppliers broke the rules so the campaign could get back on track.

"I saw the new media orders on my desk," Ben said. "I'll sign them and get them to you today."

"No need," Lucy said. "I can place the ads without your signature."

"No," Ben replied. "I'll sign them. It's my job."

Ben turned to Lori Wyman. "Thanks for your help, Lori. We appreciate it."

"You're welcome," Lori said with a quick smile. "I'll call you sometime for lunch to show you our latest readership numbers."

"Thanks. I have to get back to work."

Ben left Lucy's office and headed down the hall to talk to Tom. He didn't know what Tom wanted and he had to admit, he didn't much care. After last week, Tom wasn't his boss anymore so his position as senior vice president and head of account services had become nothing more than a sinecure.

On the way, Ben stopped at Tree's corner office and stuck his head inside. Until last week, this was where the leader of J&M sat, but now the office was dark and slightly musty from disuse. He remembered the employee's question at Tree's funeral—*Are you going to be the agency president now that Tree is gone?* He tried to picture himself sitting in the oversized chair behind the mahogany desk but the image didn't form.

"Hey, Ben," came a voice from a short distance up the hall. It was Joanne, the executive secretary, sitting at her desk outside Tom's office. She had her hair up in a youngish style, but it didn't make her look any younger. "Tom is looking for you. Can you meet with him now?"

"Sure." Ben glanced again into Tree's empty office, then went over to Joanne.

Joanne offered Ben water or coffee and he refused both. He went into Tom's office. Tom was at his walnut desk writing on some papers. He was, as Jay had said, not wearing a suit. Instead, he wore a blue Oxford shirt, black pleated slacks, and tasseled loafers. Papers and books filled Tom's desk and credenza. "You wanted to see me?" Ben asked.

"Hi, Ben," Tom replied. "Thanks for coming to see me."

"What's on your mind?"

Tom looked over the papers on his desk. "Well, over the weekend I was thinking about the part I should play on the Katch pitch. I have an idea."

"Tom, the creative brief and essential truth are done," Ben said. "We're going with mine."

"Yes, I know," Tom said with a nod. "That's not what I wanted to talk to you about."

"Oh?" Ben took a seat on Tom's couch. "Okay, shoot."

Tom picked up the papers from his desk and sat next to Ben on the couch. "Look at this. I worked on it over the weekend."

"Over the weekend?"

"Yes, over the weekend," Tom said with a glare. "Don't be so surprised."

"What is it?"

"Think about it. We'll be presenting to nine board members— eight of them we've never met. We not only have to sell our mutual funds campaign, we have to sell our agency, too. Katch needs an agency to go forward with, so the board will need general information about J&M and our approach to advertising."

"Yeah, you're right," Ben said as he skimmed through the papers. "I hadn't thought about that."

"I put together this presentation about our agency. It starts with a general overview and then goes into how we approach a marketing challenge like Katch has with mutual funds. It explains how we develop creative strategies and the essential truth. It's less than ten minutes long. I think it'd be a good introduction to our presentation. I should be the one who gives it."

Ben smiled. Tom was right; an overview of J&M's approach would be an important addition to the presentation. He looked at Tom sitting on the couch next to him and, for the first time since Ben knew him, Tom was completely sincere. "It makes sense," he said, handing the papers back to Tom. "You're right. We should include it in the presentation."

Tom took the papers and returned to his desk. "It needs some work, but I can have a first draft today."

"Good. Let me see it when you're done. I might have some thoughts. Okay?"

Tom didn't answer. "Tom," Ben said, "I'm coordinating the pitch. I need to see everything."

Tom hesitated and looked like he was getting ready to argue. Finally, he said, "Okay. I'll have it to you by three."

Ben headed for the door. "By the way, are you free at 9:30?"

"I can be. Why?"

"The pitch team is meeting in the Octagon. We have only two and a half days to put everything together. You should bring what you've done here and show it to the team."

"I'll be there," Tom nodded. "Thanks."

As Ben walked back to his office, he shook his head and smiled. Last week Tom was useless to the Katch pitch, yet he'd found a way to get back in. But Tom was back in only because he'd earned it.

And now, there was no question in anyone's mind, including

Tom's, that Ben was the person in charge.

TWENTY-SIX

WHEN BEN GOT BACK to his office, his phone was ringing. The caller ID was blocked. Probably Lori Wyman from Valassis—sales reps always blocked their IDs. Ben answered it anyway.

"Ben Smith," he said into the receiver.

"Ben, this is Joel Scheck at the *Times*. Did I catch you at a bad time?"

"Yeah, kind of. I'm busy." Ben picked up the new Bug BeGone media orders and signed them as he talked.

"I'll be quick," Joel said. "I'm calling about the Katch pitch. I'm working on a story for tomorrow's paper."

"I'm afraid I can't give you much, Joel." Joel had interviewed Ben years earlier and he knew he had to be careful with the reporter.

"What can you tell me?" Joel asked.

"We're going to give a great presentation and we expect to retain the account."

"Of course. Can I get a verbal peek at what you'll be presenting?"

"That wouldn't be appropriate."

"What will happen to the agency if you don't win the pitch?"

"I don't know," Ben answered. "Like I said, we're confident we'll keep the account."

"Who's running the agency now that Trevor Marin is gone?"

Ben paused. He remembered Tree's dark, empty office and what

John had told him at the coffee shop. He remembered the question from the employees at Tree's funeral reception. Then he said, "We're all working together. I wouldn't say anyone in particular is running the agency."

"You're pitching against Hanrahan," Joel said. "How do you feel about that?"

"HC is tough, but they don't know Katch like we do. We're the right agency for Katch, not HC."

"Can you comment on the effect winning or losing this pitch will have on the Theilen campaign? J&M is doing the advertising for Theilen. According to the polls, it's a close race."

It was a good question. Ben hadn't thought about the agency's work for Theilen's campaign for more than a week. Over the weekend, he'd seen clips of Senator Howard in London meeting with the British Prime Minister, and Nan had said the visibility would help him in the polls. She never asked Ben about J&M's commitment to Theilen, but Ben realized the Congresswoman's campaign needed J&M more than ever with Howard on the ten o'clock news every night. He felt a pang of guilt for not reassuring her about it. Then he said, "The election is still months away. Right now our focus is on the Katch pitch."

"And if you don't win it, will it hurt Theilen?"

"I don't know," Ben said. "Look, Joel, I gotta go."

"Okay. One more question. You said Sheldon Hanrahan is tough to pitch against. Can you comment on some information I have that his tactics are sometimes less than ethical?"

Ben thought about what Dirk had discovered about Nan's computer—someone in the Wells Fargo building broke through Dirk's firewall and HC occupied ten floors there. "I don't know anything about that," Ben answered.

"Well, part one of the story is out tomorrow. My deadline is six o'clock tonight. If you can think of anything to add, you have my number."

"Part one?"

"Yeah," Joel said. "There's too much here for just one story."

"Really. Well, I'll be sure to read it. Thanks for calling." Ben hung up. *Less than ethical tactics.* Sheldon Hanrahan might have had Nan's computer hacked. But as far as Ben knew, there wasn't anything happening to sabotage J&M's pitch for Katch.

As far as he knew...

Dirk. Dirk said he would come over and check J&M's security system. Ben dialed Dirk's number. "Yeah?" was the answer.

"Dirk, this is Ben. I'm thinking you should get over to check our security system as soon as you can. I'm getting a bad feeling."

"No problèma," Dirk said. "I need to make some coffee and I can be there in an hour."

"Perfect. Ask for me at the front desk. Thanks, man."

*

Ben turned to check his e-mail and saw the Messenger icon blinking on his monitor. He didn't want to open it—the message might be from Elizabeth Kelly. Then again, it could be from Nan. He clicked on the box and the message opened. The username was GoodGurl—Elizabeth Kelly.

The simple message read, "Call me," with a telephone number.

Ben typed back. "I can't. I won't. Please don't bother me anymore." He recalled the provocative photo on her Facebook profile. Her green eyes, freckles, full breasts...

A message came back. "It's important that you call me now." The telephone number was there again.

"Why?" Ben returned.

"I have information for you."

Information? Ben was perplexed. "What kind of information?" he typed.

"Important information. You must call me." The telephone

number was on the screen again.

"No," Ben replied. "Not unless I know what it's about."

"It's about Tree."

Ben was stunned. He stared at the screen for a full thirty seconds before he responded. "Trevor Marin?"

"Yes. Call me."

Ben wrote the number on a post-it note. He closed his door, and picked up the phone. He dialed the number. A woman's voice answered. "Hello, Ben."

"Who are you?" Ben asked angrily. "How do you know me? What do you want?"

"I told you, my name is Elizabeth Kelly." Her voice was smooth and controlled.

"What do you want?" Ben repeated.

"I don't want anything from you, but I have something you need."

"What is it?"

"Information."

"About Tree?"

"Yes."

"Okay, tell me."

"Not on the phone. I must meet you in person."

"In person? Why? You can't tell me over the phone?"

"No. It has to be in person. When can we meet?" Elizabeth Kelly asked. "It has to be soon."

"Look," Ben said. "I'm sorry. I really don't think I should meet you. Just tell me what this is about."

"I told you," she said. "It's about Trevor Marin. And I won't tell you over the phone. I must meet you in person. When can you do it?"

Ben ran his hand through his hair.

"It affects the Katch pitch," Elizabeth Kelly said. "It's important."

"It affects the Katch pitch?"

"Can you meet me soon?" she persisted.

"Okay. How about noon?"

"Noon is fine."

"Where?" Ben asked.

"The atrium courtyard in the old Midwest Savings building. On the skyway level. Do you know where it is?"

"The place with all the plants?" Ben's hands were clammy.

"Yes, in the far corner, away from the skyway entrance. It's a private place. We won't be bothered there. Meet me at noon. Don't be late. And Ben," she said, "it's very important you do not tell anyone about this meeting."

"Why?" Ben asked. The phone went dead.

"This is nuts," Ben said aloud.

TWENTY-SEVEN

DETECTIVE JACKSON HATED the morgue. When he was a teenager, his older brother Deon was murdered during a drug deal on Chicago's south side. To teach him a lesson, his father made Darren go to the Cook County morgue with him and his mother to identify the body. Darren never forgot the sorrow on their faces when they came out of the room. His mother was never the same and died of cancer three years later, pleading for Jesus to take her so she could see her dear Deon again. His father turned quiet and rarely talked to Darren. The Chicago police never did catch the person who killed his brother.

When Jackson walked through the morgue's swinging doors on Monday morning, it reminded him of that day he first stepped inside a morgue with his parents. The bright florescent lights reflecting off the tile floor and walls made his eyes hurt just as it did then. The morgue had the same smell. The chemicals used to cover the stench of partially decomposed remains didn't work well and the chemicals themselves had an acrid odor. To Jackson, the morgue smelled like death.

Jackson had come to talk to the medical examiner about a Latino gang member who someone had shot on Saturday. Over the weekend, the Shauna Tate incident had blown up into a full-scale gang war between a black gang called the Family Mob and a Latino gang called Vatos Locos. So far, the war had claimed three lives in addition to young Shauna. Jackson was now the lead detective on the case and he'd put in a month's worth of work during the past five days.

He went into the medical examiner's office off the main examining room. Dr. Emily Austin was about forty years old and her blue lab coat draped her obese body like a muumuu. "Mornin', Doc," Jackson said. "What do you have on the kid who was shot on Saturday night?"

"Hey Darren. He's over here. Name's Enrique Suarez." Dr. Austin pulled herself out of her chair and waddled over to a stainless-steel table with a blue sheet covering a body. She lifted the sheet and exposed the cold, naked body of a teenage Hispanic male. An exit wound as big as a golf ball exposed the young man's brain. Jackson wondered if his brother had looked this bad to his parents twenty years earlier in the Cook County morgue.

"As you can see," Dr. Austin said, "the cause of death was a shot in the back of the cranium with a nine-millimeter pistol. The slug came out here." The doctor pointed a fat finger at the hole in Enrique's forehead. "Those powder marks on the back of his skull mean he was shot up close, execution style."

"Lovely," Jackson said.

"When are you going to arrest some people and put an end to all this, Detective?"

"Soon. Maybe today."

"You think this boy is one of the people who killed Shauna Tate?" the doctor asked.

"I'm sure of it," Jackson answered. "What else can you tell me?"

"Well, before he was shot he was tortured," the doctor said. "Probably for several hours. Check out his feet." Jackson moved around to the end of the gurney. Enrique's feet were swollen to twice their normal size and were dark purple all the way up past the ankle.

Dr. Austin continued. "This bruising shows he was beaten on the bottom of the feet with a rod of some sort—like a switch or a golf club with the head cut off. Did you know there are more nerve endings on the bottom of the feet than just about anywhere else on the body?"

"Nope," Jackson said.

"They also cut out his tongue while he was still alive. Do you want to see?"

"I'll take your word on it," Jackson replied.

"I'd say young Mr. Suarez was thankful to get executed," Dr. Austin said. "Do you know who did it?"

"Got a pretty good idea," Jackson said with a nod. "Enrique here struck a deal with us and was helpin' us track down his fellow Vatos Locos shooters. It appears they found out what he was up to. That's why they cut out his tongue."

"I hope you get them, Detective," the doctor said shaking her head. "These are nasty people."

"We'll get 'em. Anythin' else unusual?"

"No. Everything will be in my report." Dr. Austin covered the body with the blue sheet.

"Thank you, ma'am. It's always a pleasure visitin' the morgue." Jackson turned to leave, but then turned back. "Hey, Doc, weren't you the one who did the exam on Trevor Marin last week? You know, the business guy who died in the car accident."

"Yeah, that was me," Dr. Austin said, returning to her desk. "Why? I thought the case was closed."

"Yeah, it is. I was just wonderin' if there was anythin' out of the ordinary."

"Now that you mention it, there was—or, rather, there is." Dr. Austin turned her chair, reached into a drawer, and pulled out a file. "When a body gets burned as badly as that one, we send for dental records just to be sure there isn't a mistaken identity. When we get them, we match them to the photos we took of the deceased's mouth. Well, we never got the records."

"His dentist didn't send 'em?" Jackson asked

"No, they sent them. They're right here." She handed Jackson the file. "But as you can see, there isn't anything useful. No dental chart, no x-rays, nothing. Just his general information, address, a record of his visits, stuff like that."

"I see. Did you call the dentist? Maybe they forgot to send the other stuff."

"Yes, we called them," the doctor said. "They said they gave us everything they had. They were as surprised as we were when we told them what was missing."

"Why didn't you let us know about this?"

"Sorry, Detective, but I thought the case was closed. And these other cases started to back us up," she said, pointing at Enrique Suarez.

Jackson nodded at the dental records. "What are you goin' to do with that file?"

"I was going to send it back."

"Do me a favor. Hang on to it for a while."

"I thought the case was closed?" Dr. Austin said.

"It is. Thanks," Jackson said with a wave.

*

Jackson left the morgue and walked the two blocks back to police headquarters. When he got to his desk, Lieutenant West was waiting for him. "You better see the captain right away," West said pointing a knuckly finger down the hall. "They got a tip on the location of the Suarez shooters and they want to collar them this morning. They want you there to make the arrests."

"You mean they want an African-American to make the arrest for the ten o'clock news," Jackson replied.

"You're getting smart, Jackson. You better get over there." West turned to go back into his office.

"Hey, Lieu," Jackson said. "I was just at the ME's office to talk to her about Suarez, and she mentioned somethin' funny on the Trevor Marin case."

West glared at Jackson. "I thought we agreed that case was closed?"

"Yeah, yeah, I know," Jackson said. "But listen to this. When they got the dental records from Marin's dentist, there were no records in the file. What I mean is, the file didn't have anythin' to match the pictures they took off of the body."

"No records?"

"You know the drawin' of your teeth the dentist marks up when you have a cavity?" Jackson said. "It wasn't in the file. There weren't any x-rays either."

"Yeah, so?"

"Well isn't it a coincidence that we don't have a body, we don't have the car and now we don't have the dental records either?"

"The case is closed," West said. "You gotta report to the captain."

"Yeah, I will. But I was thinkin', the one thing we do have is the fingerprints off the body. They're in the file."

"You mean the file of the case that's closed?"

"Yeah, I know it's closed, Lieu. But Marin was in the Air Force, right? So the department of defense has his prints on file. Let's just get 'em and see if they're a match."

West crossed his thick arms over his chest. "If I understand you right, Detective, you think it wasn't Marin in the Porsche? Right?"

"What I think is we don't know nothin' on this case."

"What case?" West said with his palms out. "The Marin case is closed."

Jackson rolled his eyes. "A'right, Lieutenant. Whatever you say. I'll forget about it. It just bothers me, that's all."

West nodded. He leaned against the door to his office. "Jackson, tell you what. If I have time—but only if I have time and it isn't likely because of all the extra shit I have to do to cover your ass while you're getting your face on TV—I'll pull a favor with the DOD and see if I can get a copy of Marin's prints just so you'll leave this damn thing alone. And you gotta promise to leave it alone. Okay?" He pointed his scarred chin at Jackson. "In the meantime, I don't want you digging around."

"Why should I do that?" Jackson asked with a smile. "The case is closed."

"Yeah, you're right Jackson!" West turned into his office. "Now get the hell over to see the captain."

TWENTY-EIGHT

"HE'S NOT AUTHORIZED to do this," Tony Mills said, tapping his foot at Ben inside J&M's cramped computer room.

"Tony," Ben said, "Dirk here is a friend and he knows what he's doing. I know you're in charge of our computer security, but it won't hurt to let him look at our system." Dirk was studying data on the system's monitor.

"No one's supposed to touch it except me." Tony's foot tapped faster.

Dirk gave Ben a quick look. "Ben, dude, your security system is crrrrrap."

"Bullshit," Tony said. "It's state-of-the-art. It's a level-two firewall. It's fine."

"Really?" Dirk turned away from the monitor and faced Tony. "Well Tony, Ben called me an hour ago to come over. Before I left, I did a little checking on your 'state-of-the-art' system. Took me less than fifteen minutes to hack it."

"Right," Tony scoffed. "Prove it."

"If you insist." Dirk reached inside his briefcase. "This is a printout of all the porn sites the security administrator—that would be you, right?—has visited from this computer over the past month. I pulled the report a half hour ago. It's quite a list! The number of lesbian spanking sites is especially impressive. Here, Ben, check it out." Dirk offered the printout to Ben.

Tony snatched it out of Dirk's hand before Ben could take it. "You can't prove it was me," he said without looking at the printout.

"Actually," Dirk said straight at Tony, "I can."

Tony turned red-faced and backed out of the room, clutching the printout. When he cleared the door, he scurried away.

Ben laughed out loud. "Man, you are cold. I guess we'll have to do something about Tony later."

"I'll give you what you need to fry his ass," Dirk said. He turned back to the computer monitor. "In the meantime, I'm going to fix this shitty security system for you. It will take me about an hour."

"It's all yours. I have to get to a meeting. Let me know if you need anything."

"Will do," Dirk said with a wave.

*

The meeting with Andrew on the Katch creative brief didn't start on time because Ben and everyone else was running behind. They agreed to meet in the Octagon when they could, which ended up being at 11:00a.m., an hour and a half after the meeting was scheduled. As Ben walked to the meeting through the J&M halls, he wondered what Elizabeth Kelly had to tell him at noon. She said she had information about Tree. And she'd told him not to tell anyone about the meeting. He thought about taking John with him anyway. Yeah, she said he should come alone, but he couldn't imagine why. It was all puzzling and a bit unnerving, but Ben had to let it go for the next hour. Right now, he had to concentrate on the Katch pitch.

When Ben walked into the Octagon, Ginny, John and Andrew were already there. Ginny and John were sitting at the huge conference room table, but Andrew was pacing as he usually did. He wore sandals and shorts and a green t-shirt with a picture of Che Guevara on the front. Ben couldn't tell if Andrew he was excited or upset. After ten years of working together, Ben knew there was little in-between with Andrew. If things were going poorly, he would stomp around yelling at people in the creative department as if they'd just committed a class 'A' felony. If things were going well—which meant the agency was busy and Andrew agreed with the direction of the work—he would pace up and down the creative department talking loudly, cracking jokes and telling his people they were all geniuses and deserved to be paid twice what J&M was paying them. His energy was infectious and people who didn't think he was completely nuts loved working for him.

Ben took a seat next to John and Ginny while Andrew continued to pace. Finally, Andrew said, "I really like where this is heading. Your creative direction, Ben—it really works. I especially like the essential truth. Simple, short and to the point. I already have a bunch of ideas. I just want to make sure I understand what you're thinking—to make sure we're on track since we don't have a lot of time."

"Sure thing," Ben said. "Let's discuss."

The Octagon conference room doors opened and Tom Clarey stepped in. "Sorry I'm late," he said. "I was working on my part of the presentation and lost track of time."

The others looked at Ben. "I asked Tom to join us," Ben said. "He has an idea for the Katch pitch I think we should consider. Tom, why don't you tell everyone about it?"

Tom sat and told the group what he and Ben had discussed earlier, how the presentation should start with an overview of J&M and its unique approach to advertising. He explained that the board of directors would need the information if they were to retain J&M long-term.

"I'm still working on it," Tom said, "but I'll have it done this afternoon."

"I think Tom should present it," Ben said. "It's a perfect role for him since he's in charge of new business." Everyone agreed.

"We were just starting to discuss the strategic platform," Ben said to Tom. "Andrew, you asked for an explanation of the essential truth.

Here it is."

Ben pushed himself forward. He started by explaining that Katch mutual funds have an image problem because their yearly performance is only average. Morningstar is the organization that monitors mutual funds and Katch is never at the top of their rankings, though Katch mutual funds performance was excellent over a ten-year period. The reason, Ben explained, is that Katch fund managers don't chase the latest trend or what they think will be the hottest new stock. Katch only invests in stocks that are consistent with the fund's strategies.

"That's called 'style purity'," Ben said. "And what do consumers want today? They want stability. Sure, they want the highest return they can get but not at the expense of losing it all the next year. Consumers today invest to make their financial plans work, to reach their goals.

"So, the essential truth?" Ben continued. "It's simple. It's 'Funds for your plans'."

"*Funds for your plans?*" Tom blurted. "That's it?"

"Fuckin-a, that's it," Andrew said still standing. "It's short and to the point. That's why it's called the *essential* truth. It's perfect, Ben."

"Ginny helped," Ben said with a nod to Ginny. "Do you want to add anything Ginny?"

"I think it works." Ginny removed her jacket as she spoke. It was rare for her to be less than formal. She looked excited about the plans.

She continued. "Investing is all about making your money work toward your objectives. If you don't have a plan, you really shouldn't be in the market or you'll chase every hot stock until you have nothing left. If you're investing wisely, you're investing according to your plan."

"Correct," Ben said. "And it's *your* plan. Not Katch's plan, not your stockbroker's plan, your plan. *Funds for your plans.*"

"And if you have a plan," John said, "you need stable funds." He was smiling at Ben. His hands were behind his head and his feet were on the chair next to him. "Makes sense to me. Katch Funds are funds you can plan on."

"Funds you can plan on!" Andrew said. "That's a great line. Write it down."

John laughed. "I had that line last week. I think I can remember it."

"So," Ben said, "the strategy is to take the thing that makes Katch Funds boring—style purity—and turn it into a benefit. Hell, Katch should brag about being boring."

"I love this." Andrew paced faster. He thrust his arms out as he talked. "It has a lot of creative potential. People will relate to the message. I wish I knew about this style purity shit for my own investing before the last stock market crash. I might not have lost so much."

"But the greatest thing about this strategy," Ben said, "is only Katch can own it. They're the only mutual fund company that didn't chase high returns during the last boom market. Back then, they got blasted for it. Today, they can point to it with pride and start rebuilding their reputation on it."

"Funds for your plans," John said. "It's a real essential truth."

Andrew grabbed his papers and stomped toward the door. "We gotta get some of these ideas down. I have a few more already. John, you comin'?"

"I guess our meeting is over and I have to get to work." John smiled as he followed Andrew out of the Octagon.

"Wow, that got Andrew jazzed up," Tom said. "Good work, Ben." Ben could tell he meant it.

"Ginny helped. She did a lot of work too and kept everything on track."

Ginny jumped in, "But it was Ben's thinking that pulled it all together."

Then Ben said with a smile, "Group hug?" All three burst into laughter. For the first time, the three of them were together on something. When the agency needed them to step forward, they all did. Tom found a way to help and Ben had to admit Tom's contribution would be important. He knew Tom would do an outstanding job starting off the presentation. Tom always presented a buttoned-up image. But this time, he'd found something important to present. And it was something Tom had thought of and worked on himself. Ben believed it would be the most convincing presentation Tom would make since joining J&M.

Ginny did her part too. Ben wasn't exaggerating when he said she kept everything organized and on schedule. Organization was her forte and it was critical for putting together a big presentation in a little over a week.

And in a few days, they'd have the creative ideas ready too. Andrew was motivated and he always produced inspired work when he was. John was into it too. Ben expected nothing less than the breakthrough campaign that Everet Katch was looking for.

It was all coming together. For the first time in over a week, Ben allowed himself to be optimistic. Perhaps J&M would keep the account after all. Perhaps they'd buck the odds and beat Sheldon Hanrahan in a pitch for the account that would keep J&M alive. Perhaps Ben would succeed in leading the agency through this trouble. Perhaps he was a leader after all.

Perhaps…

Elizabeth Kelly. He remembered the meeting with Elizabeth Kelly. *Don't tell anyone and don't be late,* she'd said. He checked his watch. It was 11:45. "I have to run," Ben said. "I… uh, have a lunch date." He bolted from the Octagon.

Ben worried he wouldn't make in on time as he ran for the elevators and punched the button for the first floor. The elevator took him to the lobby and he pushed through the front door and ran two blocks to where he could get on the skyway system. He went through a back entrance of the Industrial Arts building, up a set of escalators to the skyway level and headed toward the Midwest Savings building. The skyways were already crowded. People stood in lines at fast food counters or sat on benches reading newspapers. Several had on running shoes, power walking, talking loudly to companion walkers as they huffed through the hallways. Ben's wondered if Elizabeth Kelly would wait for him at the Midwest Savings Atrium if he was late.

He walked through a skyway over Nicollet Mall and saw the street level was as busy as the skyway. Everyone was spilling out of their offices for the lunch hour to refuel and recharge for the rest of the workday. Elizabeth Kelly said she had information about Tree. She used the name 'Tree,' not 'Trevor'. What did that mean? Perhaps she knew him. According to the business card she'd given him on the bus, she worked at a law firm. But if it was a legal matter, she'd have used Tree's formal name.

Ben came to the IDS Crystal Court, the hub of downtown Minneapolis. It was alive and jammed with people. Musicians played Bach to promote the Minnesota Orchestra Sommerfest. At the other end was a group promoting the United Way. He still had four blocks to go.

He crossed another skyway, then another. Ben tried to remember if he saw Elizabeth Kelly at Tree's funeral. No, she wasn't there. He would have noticed her.

Finally, he reached the skyway leading to the Midwest Savings building. It was where the skyway ended so there were only a few people here. Elizabeth Kelly had chosen her spot well for their secret meeting.

He checked his watch. He was only a few minutes late. Ben crossed the skyway to the atrium where Elizabeth had told him to meet her. The atrium was three stories high and like the Crystal Court, it was designed to take advantage of the skyway system. Granite benches, exotic plants and trees surrounded a shallow pond in the atrium's center. There were small private spaces with a single bench where people could read or eat lunch. It was quiet and smelled slightly musty like a greenhouse.

Where did Elizabeth Kelly say she wanted to meet? The far end of the atrium where they could be alone. Ben walked through the atrium to the side away from the skyway. Between the trees and plants, Ben saw a few people in the private areas quietly reading or eating a bag lunch.

And then he saw her. She was sitting in a secluded private area with her back to him. He recognized her black, silky hair and slender frame from when he'd seen her on the bus. He walked up a small granite stairway and approached her. She kept her back turned to him. She looked like she might be crying.

"Elizabeth?" Ben said.

She turned to him and when he saw her face, he took a full step back.

"Oh my God!" he gasped.

TWENTY-NINE

LIFE WASN'T FAIR, thought Sheldon Hanrahan. Especially for the weak. He felt sorry for them—he really did. But if humankind was to survive, they should not coddle the weak. Darwin was right. Survival of the fittest for survival of the species. After all, no one coddled him when he was struck down. He'd learned to survive. He'd learned to be strong. Life wasn't fair. He knew firsthand.

He sat at his glass desk in the Wells Fargo building and as usual, the lights were low, the vertical blinds pulled closed on the windows behind him. His dark glasses lay on his desk.

The intercom on the desk phone buzzed. A voice came from the speaker. "Mr. Hanrahan, I'm sorry to bother you sir, but I have a package for you. It's marked personal and confidential. Shall I bring it in?"

"Yes, Barbara." Sheldon put on his glasses, reached behind him and opened the blinds. A streak of sunlight angled into the steel and glass office.

A few seconds later, a petite woman with gray hair and a tailored suit stepped through the double doors carrying a plain, white envelope. "There's no return address," she said, approaching Sheldon, "and the delivery was made to the front desk. We don't know where it came from."

Sheldon took the envelope.

"Mr. Hanrahan, it's noon. Shall I have lunch brought in for you?"

"No," he answered, "I'll eat later."

"Very well." She left, closing the double doors behind her.

Sheldon opened the envelope. Inside was a note, several pages clipped together and Joel Scheck's business card. The handwritten note was on *Times* letterhead.

> *Mr. Hanrahan,*
>
> *Sorry for the personal reference on the envelope but I've been trying to get through to you for several days and haven't made it past your secretary. I want to talk to you about your business practices, especially with respect to account pitches. A small sample of information I've obtained is enclosed.*
>
> *I'm especially interested in talking to you in light of the Katch pitch. This is the largest pitch the Twin Cities has had in years and I'm sure it's one you'll do anything to win. I'm doing a story on it this week and I'd like to include your comments.*
>
> *I've enclosed my business card and telephone number. Please call me.*
>
> *Joel Scheck*
>
> *P.S. I'm also curious about the affect the Katch pitch will have on the senate race with HC doing the communications for Howard and J&M for Theilen. Hmmmm…*

Sheldon scanned the documents attached to the note. They chronicled the CompuSto pitch and the DUI car accident in San Francisco that caused Keith Ballard to lose the pitch. He noted that the information was correct. He read the handwritten letter again and could tell Joel was on a fishing expedition. If Sheldon talked to him, it would only raise Joel's suspicions further. He reached under his desk, pulled out a shredder, and shredded Joel's letter and the information on Keith Ballard and CompuSto.

He picked up his private phone and dialed a number. A man answered, "Dah?"

"Victor, this is Sheldon. The newspaper has information about our activities. It's not a coincidence they would get it now."

"How much is the detail?"

"Enough that we need to be concerned. What's the status of the activities on Ben Smith?"

"It is according to plan."

"I want to stop it," Sheldon said. "Now. Someone is on to us. Anyway, we have other plans."

"Cannot stop. Is too late. Is happening now," Victor said.

"There's nothing we can do?"

"No."

Sheldon paused to think. Then he said, "We might have to change our plans. I'll get back to you soon. Make sure I can get in touch with you at all times."

"Yes. I will do."

"I need to make some calls," Sheldon said. "In the meantime, stop everything we can."

"I said before, we can't stop. Is happening now, as we speak."

"Victor," Sheldon said, "listen to me. Do what you can."

THIRTY

WHEN BEN SAW Elizabeth Kelly's face, he wondered if he'd walked into a slasher movie. At first, he'd recoiled, but then he went to her. "What happened?" he asked.

Someone had assaulted Elizabeth Kelly and it'd happened just minutes before he arrived. Her lip was cut and blood trickled down her chin. A contusion above her left eye looked like it would soon swell horribly. Her hair was tangled and her blouse was ripped, exposing part of her breast.

He thought she'd be crying, but when he got close, he saw her green eyes were dry and focused. And she had her eyes focused on him. A pang of fear gripped him. This beautiful woman who someone had just beaten, glared at Ben as if she wanted to kill him.

Then, like a wounded animal, she sprang. Before he knew what was happening, she scratched his face with her fingernails. Ben's skin burned and he felt blood on his face. She tried to punch him, but he grabbed her wrist. She expertly twisted her arm to the side, broke his grip, and kneed him in the groin. Sharp pain shot into his stomach and down his legs. He slumped forward but kept his feet. She wiped her hand on her cut lip and carefully smeared her blood down Ben's shirt.

Then, she grabbed his cheeks with the thumb and fingers of her right hand and drove her free hand between his cheek and teeth. She pulled her hand out with a twisting motion covering it with Ben's saliva. She stepped back while he tried to regain his balance from the blow to his groin. Slowly, she wiped Ben's saliva on her face and the exposed part of her breast.

She glared at Ben with her green eyes blazing. And then she hissed, "You better run."

"Wh… what the hell are you doing?" Ben stammered.

"This," she replied. She lay on the atrium's granite floor, grinned at him wildly and screamed, "HELP! RAPE! RAAAAPE!" The sound of her voice echoed through the atrium.

Ben looked at the bruised and beaten woman on the floor in front of him and the atrium's musty smell became sharp, the green of the plants more vivid, and each sound was as clear as if it was amplified. Ben heard someone moving toward them. His heart pounded and his mind raced.

Run, he thought. *She's right, I have to run!*

He bolted for the skyway on the other side of the atrium. As he ran, a woman gawked at him with wide eyes. A man said, "Hey, buddy…" and moved to cut him off. Ben quickly sidestepped him and was in the skyway. He heard Elizabeth Kelly's sobs following him down the skyway. "HELP! HE TRIED TO RAPE ME! "

Ben ran as fast as he could. He had to get away from Elizabeth Kelly and her screams. He ran into the next building and saw an escalator leading to the street level. He took the escalator two steps at a time and pushed himself into the street. The warm air hit his face and made the scratch on his face burn. The bright sunlight made him squint and he didn't realize where he was. His thoughts were coming too fast. He shook his head trying to sort out what'd just happened, but his head wouldn't clear. The only thing that came was that he should run.

He saw the Mississippi River Parkway three blocks to his left. He started to run for it but realized that running would attract attention, so he took it at a fast walk. He felt blood dripping from the scratch and pain in his groin. It made him want to limp but he gritted his teeth and pulled himself straight.

Two blocks to go to the river. Ben tried to pick up his pace without being obvious. Then he stopped dead in his tracks. Why was he running away? he wondered. He didn't try to rape Elizabeth Kelly. "She attacked ME!" he said aloud. He had to go back to the atrium to tell everyone what'd really happened. He turned around, took three steps and stopped again. He pictured the petite Elizabeth Kelly with a battered face and torn blouse lying on the atrium floor. *No one will believe me*, he thought. So he turned around and ran as fast as he could all the way to the river.

When he reached the parkway, he stopped running and headed north. He was shaking and his head was spinning. He saw business people eating picnic lunches or taking a noontime stroll. He looked up at the sky and saw high cirrus clouds sliding in from the west. He realized he was walking too fast and slowed his pace. He noticed walkers staring at his face and that blood was dripping onto his shirt. He pulled out his handkerchief and wiped the blood away. There was still pain in his groin but it wasn't as sharp as before.

He started to think more clearly. He needed to do something. "She set me up!" he said. Maybe he should go to the police. But that wouldn't be any better than going back to the atrium. When he tried to tell his side of the story, they'd take one look at her and there was no way they'd believe him. Maybe he should talk to a lawyer. But Ben didn't know any criminal defense lawyers. He never thought he'd need one.

Nan. He should call Nan. My God, what would she think about this? She'd believe him of course. But she wouldn't know what to do either. She'd probably tell him to go to the police.

He came to a bridge over a deep ravine leading to the river. A jogger ran by and glanced at his face. The flow of blood had slowed, but it was still dripping on his shirt. He took out his handkerchief and pressed it hard against his cheek. The pressure on the wound stung but after a few minutes, it stopped bleeding.

He was still breathing hard and his pulse was too fast. He slowed down and tried to breathe normally. He thought about the people at J&M. And Nan. And Jenny. He was responsible for them. All of them. He had to think. Think!

He needed someone to tell him what to do. He felt for his phone. It was still in his pocket. He took it out, but couldn't think of who to call. Who would believe his side of the story?

John Turner.

Ben pushed the speed-dial for J&M. He put the phone over his scratch to hide it from the joggers. Julie from the front desk answered. "Jacob and Marin. How may I direct your call?"

"Julie, it's Ben. I need to talk to John Turner right away."

"Oh, hi Ben. I'll page him."

"Julie," Ben said firmly, "don't page him. Go find him and get him on the line. Now. This is important. Please."

"Oh, okay. Just a minute."

A few seconds later, John came on the line.

"Hey, Ben. Andrew and I are working through lunch on some ideas. I think we have…"

"John," Ben said, "I need to talk to you right now."

"Oh, sure, what's up?"

"Not on the phone," Ben said, turning away from another jogger. "In person. Something happened."

"Something happened?"

"Yeah, something bad."

There was a short pause. "I understand," John said. "Where are you?"

Ben told him.

"Don't leave," John said. "I'll be there as quickly as I can."

THIRTY-ONE

BEN'S FATHER WAS a carpenter and from all accounts, he was a good one. When Ben was ten, the country fell into a bad recession and his father found himself out of work for the first time in his life. His mother ran a neighborhood bakery whose clientele, hit hard by the recession, stopped buying her celebrated baked goods. The unemployment rate in Ben's south Minneapolis neighborhood was the highest it'd been since the Great Depression. People were desperate and the air was thick with worry.

But not in the Smith household. Ben's father filled his time helping neighbors and friends finish projects the recession had left undone. He and Ben built a sturdy workshop off the garage out of scrap lumber they had scrounged. Every day his mother and sister woke up before dawn to bake bread for charities. The family's mood was upbeat, and every night they went to bed tired and fulfilled.

"To be truly successful," Ben's father had said at dinner one day, "you have to overcome adversity. And the *way* you handle it defines your character—much more than how you handle success."

Ben thought of his father while he waited for John on a park bench overlooking the rolling Mississippi River. With a woman accusing him of rape, he wondered how it would be possible for his father to be proud of him. He thought of the people at J&M and what they'd think of him when they heard he'd been arrested for sexual assault. He'd tried to take charge of J&M, tried to stay positive and set a good example. And now this. It was not what would be expected from a leader.

Ben spotted John less than ten minutes after he'd called him. He was running up the bicycle path searching from side to side. He had taken off his vest and carried it as he ran. "Over here," Ben signaled.

John ran over. "Sweet Jesus!" he said out of breath. "What happened to you?" He sat next to Ben on the bench and wiped sweat from his forehead with a red handkerchief.

"I don't know, exactly," Ben replied. "I better start at the beginning."

Ben told John about seeing Elizabeth Kelly on the bus a week earlier, and that she'd somehow gotten his Messenger username. He told John about the telephone call that morning saying she had information about Tree. He said he'd agreed to meet her at the Midwest Bank atrium. And he told John about the attack. As he explained what happened, he could tell how bizarre it sounded and hoped John would believe him. He wasn't sure he believed it himself.

When Ben was done, John shook his head. "It's perfect," he said.

"Excuse me?" Ben exclaimed.

"No, no, forgive me," John said with a wave of his handkerchief. "I didn't mean it to sound like that. What I mean is you were set up perfectly."

"So you believe me?"

"Of course I do," John said. "I know you, Ben. You wouldn't do something like that."

Ben was silent for a while. His head was beginning to clear. "What's happening, John?" he asked "Why did she do it?"

"It's simple. She was paid to do it."

"Paid? That's crazy. Who would do that?"

"She was paid by Sheldon Hanrahan."

Suddenly, Ben's mind wasn't so clear. He'd heard what John said, but it didn't make sense. "What?" was all he could say.

"Yeah, Sheldon Hanrahan," John said. "Think about it. He set you up two days before the Katch pitch so you'd have a mess to deal with instead of preparing the presentation. And an arrest for sexual assault on the lead J&M account guy won't look good to the board members at Katch."

"That's absurd," Ben said. "Why would he go to this extreme to win a pitch he might win anyway?"

"Sheldon doesn't leave anything to chance, Ben. Anyway, you underestimate yourself. I believe we're putting together a winning presentation. I've been through a lot of pitches in my career. This is one of the best I've seen."

"But Katch can't be that important to Hanrahan Communications," Ben said. "Can it?"

"It is. It's that important to Sheldon." John wiped his head one more time and stuffed his red handkerchief back in his pocket. "Ben, my boy, you are going to have to turn yourself in to the police. But first, you have to listen to me for a while."

"Turn myself in?" Ben ran a hand through his hair.

"Yep, I'm afraid so. It's your only option. You can't run. You have to tell the police what happened."

"They'll never believe me, John. Never."

"No," John said. "Probably not. You'll need a good attorney."

"I'll need a *great* attorney," Ben said. "Problem is, I don't know any."

"Don't worry about it now," John said with a wave. "First, like I said, you need to know some things. And what I'm about to tell you will convince you I'm right about Sheldon."

As they sat on the park bench, two pleasure boats buzzed along the Mississippi. Behind them on the pathway, joggers huffed. Ben leaned back on the bench and tried to calm down. John looked out over the river.

Then, John began. He told Ben about two up-and-coming agency execs hired forty years earlier by Stein and Conklin during the Madman days. The two young men were Trevor Marin and Sheldon

Hanrahan. They shared an office, and it was obvious they'd both become stars in the advertising business. They became best friends, worked long hours, and partied hard after work.

After a few years at Stein and Conklin, Trevor and Sheldon formed an informal group called Lunch Hour Creative to work on small clients Stein and Conklin turned away. Lunch Hour Creative didn't charge for their work but they only took on clients who let them do great advertising. The members were Trevor and Sheldon, an art director named Louise Jacob, and a young copywriter right out of college.

"The copywriter was me," John said.

"You were part of Lunch Hour Creative?" Ben asked. "I didn't know."

"One of the original members," John said. "It was really something. There I was, a year out of college working elbow to elbow on campaigns with three people who'd soon be legends in the agency business. I don't know why they let me join them. They must have liked my writing. We became best friends. In fact, Sheldon and Louise Jacob were lovers."

John leaned back and put his hands behind his head. "It was an amazing time, Ben. I can't begin to tell you how exciting it was. We were doing work the industry had never seen before. One year, everything we submitted to the Clios in New York won an award. I mean every single submission. We even won Best of Show for the Basilica renovation campaign. It was unprecedented. We were like rock stars."

"Okay," Ben said. "This is all interesting, but what does it have to do with this?" He pointed to the scratch on his face.

"Be patient," John said patting Ben's knee. "Just try to relax and listen."

John told Ben about how Lunch Hour Creative became so famous that Stein and Conklin told them they couldn't do it anymore. But by then, Trevor and Sheldon had had a taste of success and decided to form their own agency.

Then, tragedy struck. One morning, the three partners were sailing on Lake Minnetonka discussing plans for their new agency. Sheldon was cooking bacon in the galley when the grease caught fire. He grabbed the pan, went above decks, and tossed it overboard. But he threw it into the wind and the flaming bacon grease blew back into his face badly burning his left eye. He spent the next month in the burn unit at Hennepin County Medical Center. The doctors were able to save his eye but he lost both the upper and lower lids. From then on, he was unable to close his eye.

"How awful," Ben said. "I always wondered why he wore those glasses."

"It's not just to protect his eye," John said. "I saw him after the accident, before he started wearing his oversized glasses. The burn disfigured him horribly."

"So, what happened to Lunch Hour Creative?" Ben asked.

John explained that the plans for the new agency went forward while Sheldon recovered. They had to move quickly—they were hot, and Stein and Conklin was pushing them out. But then, Louise and Sheldon broke up. Sheldon thought it was because of the way he looked and that might have been part of it. Louise was like that, John explained. Sheldon was furious and refused to go forward with the new agency. Tree stayed out of their personal conflict and started the new agency with Louise, and without Sheldon.

"What happened to you in all this?" Ben asked.

John leaned forward and clasped his hands in front of him. He sighed. "When Sheldon recovered from his accident, he took a sabbatical and came back a different man. He started his own agency and I went with him. You have to understand, Ben, I had this little problem with booze. Sheldon used my addiction to get me to join him. You see, Tree told me I had to get help with my problem or I couldn't join his agency. I told him to go to hell and when Sheldon came back from his sabbatical, I joined him instead. He made me believe I was fine. So I worked for Hanrahan Communications as their first creative director."

John continued. "At first everything was fine at HC. We took a few Lunch Hour Creative clients with us, and Tree and Louise took the rest. Both agencies grew and were successful. But my drinking got worse. I was in car accidents—one after they cancelled my insurance. My drinking ruined me financially. I lost my house and my wife took our son and headed back to Illinois. And then Sheldon fired me."

"Man," Ben said, "that's cold."

"Actually," John said, "Sheldon did the right thing. I was a liability. My work was terrible. I showed up to client meetings drunk. I deserved what I got and, frankly, I needed to hit bottom before I realized how bad my problem was. No, the firing was the best thing that could have happened. It forced me to get sober before I killed somebody and ended up in prison for the rest of my life."

Prison, Ben thought. Elizabeth Kelly. The attack in the atrium. "I gotta get to the police," he said.

"Yes you do," John said. "You need to tell them your side of the story. You need to tell them you were set up by Sheldon Hanrahan."

"John," Ben said, "sorry but your story doesn't connect to this. I don't care what Tree and Sheldon did thirty-five years ago. It doesn't prove he set me up."

"I'm not finished," John said. "You need to know one more thing. You need to know about Katch."

"Katch?" Ben asked, surprised.

"Yes, Katch," John answered. "Several years after Tree and Sheldon started their agencies, our old agency, Stein and Conklin, got in trouble because of a stupid racist thing Patrick Conklin did in a speech."

"Zulugate?" Ben asked.

"Yep. The photo of the Zulu boy kissing a cow's ass. Well, clients began to leave, and one of the biggest was Katch Financial. A pitch was set up and they invited both Jacob and Marin, and HC to present.

We all assumed HC would win the account because Sheldon had worked on Katch when he was with Stein and Conklin. But the account was given to J&M."

"Why?" Ben asked.

"Because after Louise broke up with Sheldon she had an affair with Everet Katch," John said. "She knew him from when she worked on Katch as an art director at Stein and Conklin."

"You've got to be kidding," Ben said.

"Nope. I'm not. Tree knew about the affair and didn't approve of it. But, to be honest, Tree let Louise influence Everet to get the account."

"*Tree* did that?"

John looked at Ben. "Mr. Trevor Marin was a great man, Ben. But he wasn't perfect. He wanted to beat Sheldon to prove he was the better ad man. I believe he regretted it later."

"What happened to Louise Jacob?"

"She was deeply in love with Everet," John answered, "but apparently, Everet didn't love her. He patched things up with his wife and dumped Louise. Of course, Louise couldn't continue to work at J&M with Katch Financial as their biggest client. So she sold out to Tree and left for California. I haven't seen her in over thirty years.

"But Ben," John said, "what's important for you to know is what it did to Sheldon. When he lost that pitch, he was furious. He'd been betrayed by Louise and cheated by Tree. Only a few years earlier, these were two people he'd loved. The entire affair—the accident, Louise leaving him, Tree betraying him—changed him. He resolved never to lose a pitch again. If he wanted a client, he got it, no matter what he had to do."

"Like frame me for sexual assault three days before a pitch," Ben said.

"Three days before the Katch pitch, Ben," John said. "The *Katch* pitch. Don't you see? It all fits. If Sheldon gets the account, he'll force Everet out at Katch. Then he'll have his revenge. Furthermore, if J&M

goes out of business, we can't help Theilen and Sheldon's boy Senator Howard wins the senate election in a landslide, and probably wins the presidency in two years. I guarantee he wants this account more than anything."

They stayed quiet for a while as Ben tried to sort through John's story. Eventually he said, "I don't think the police will believe it."

John laughed. "Yeah, you're probably right. But I have a feeling Sheldon's little stunt might backfire on him. Come on, I'll walk you to the police department."

Ben and John didn't talk as they went the four blocks to the police department. Ben felt better having spent time talking to John. It seemed outrageous that Sheldon would want to frame him. But John was right. He had to go to the police and tell his side of the story.

When they got to the police department, Ben turned to John. "Nan. What will I say to Nan?"

"I'll talk to her," John said. "Don't worry, she'll believe you. I'll give her the whole story. She needs to know. She's a good woman, Ben."

"What about the pitch?" Ben said. "And the employees? Damn." He shook his head. "I've blown it. I should've been more careful. I've let everyone down."

"No, you haven't. You haven't done anything wrong. You've done great work. Andrew and I have some exciting concepts. The media plans look good. The research supports our approach. Ginny is coordinating everything and Jay is working like a dog. Everyone has pulled together on it. We'll get it done, Ben. Don't worry."

"I guess there's nothing I can do," Ben said.

"It'll be okay," John said. "Turn yourself in, but don't say anything until you talk to an attorney."

"But I don't know an attorney," Ben said.

"Don't worry about that either. Just be patient."

"Thanks, John." Ben pointed a thumb to the police department building. "I guess I gotta deal with this. I'll take it from here."

Ben was scared as he walked through the building's front doors. He wondered if his father was ever scared when he was out of work. If he was, he never showed it. Neither did Tree when business was down. But he was about to be charged with a felony. This was a whole new level of adversity. And just like his father when he was laid off, Ben was going to have to do his best to overcome it.

THIRTY-TWO

"THERE ARE A LOT of allegations in this story, Joel," Charlie Case, the editor-in-chief for the *Twin Cities Times*, said over the top of his reading glasses. "Have you substantiated any of them?"

Charlie was reading Joel's story for the next day's *Times*. His thick gray mustache and bushy eyebrows twitched as he read. Edith DeGroot and Joel sat in soft chairs in front of his desk in his wood-paneled office. It was unusual for Charlie to review Joel's work, but he'd summoned Joel and Edith to his office to discuss Joel's story about the Katch pitch. Joel could tell from Charlie's twitching eyebrows that the meeting would not go well.

"I got the information from a confidential source," Joel replied. "I'm not able to reference it in the story. I've substantiated some of the facts, but I haven't been able to find anything directly incriminating Sheldon Hanrahan. However, the story does point to some rather large coincidences. I was very careful about that."

"You substantiated *some* facts?" Charlie pulled his safari shirt down over his paunch. "You haven't verified all of them?"

"No."

"That could be a problem." Charlie's mustache twitched at Joel. "Who's your source?"

Joel looked at Edith and back at Charlie. "Uh… you want me to reveal my source? That isn't right. Let me assure you, it's impeccable," Joel lied. He didn't know who the man smoking the pipe at the

Crowell construction site was, so he really didn't know if the source was credible or not. He'd tried to verify the information the man had given him, but he just ran into dead ends. He needed more, so in spite of his source's warning, he'd tried to contact Sheldon Hanrahan to see if he could trick him into saying something. That hadn't worked either and he'd had to go with the story based on unsubstantiated information.

"Joel, don't be dramatic," Charlie said. "This is just a story about an advertising account pitch. I want to know your source."

Edith spoke up. "Charlie, we never reveal sources. It shouldn't matter if it's a business story, a crime story or anything else. We need to maintain standards."

"I won't give it anyway." Joel said with a tinge of journalistic pride.

"Okay," Charlie said with an insincere smile. "Then, I'll need to edit your story. I can't let it run like this. You're making allegations against one of our top business leaders. I happen to know Sheldon Hanrahan personally. I don't believe he'd do the things you imply in your story. And, I might add, his agency places a lot of ads with our paper."

"Isn't it newspaper policy to keep business and editorial separate?" Edith protested. "If we don't, we'd never run anything controversial. Anyway, the story doesn't make direct accusations. I reviewed it. I believe it's well within our guidelines. It merely points out coincidences. We've run stories with a lot less support than this."

"We need to change it." Charlie's eyes were cold under his bushy brows.

Joel sat back in his chair and folded his arms. Charlie was railroading him and he didn't understand why the editor-in-chief, with a reputation for hard-nosed reporting and stirring up controversy, was being so cautious. If it was, as Charlie said, just a story about an advertising account pitch, why had he taken time to call Joel and Edith into his office to discuss it? Sure, the story raised questions about

Sheldon Hanrahan's business practices and asked why HC won all of their pitches. But the story didn't make any direct allegations. Joel didn't have the evidence he needed to go that far. It was, he thought, well balanced and professional—some of his best work in years. But it wouldn't run without the approval of the man sitting across the desk.

"Okay, what do you want me to change?" Joel asked.

"Nothing," Charlie said. "I'll make the changes myself."

"What?" Joel said. "It's my story. Just tell me what you want changed and I'll do it."

"No. *I'll* do it."

Edith pushed her glasses up her nose. "This is highly unusual," she said. "Why do you feel you need to do it yourself?"

"As I said," Charlie answered, "Sheldon Hanrahan is an important man. His agency places a lot of ads with us. We need to be careful. Although, I might be able to let it run as is if I know who your source is, Joel."

"I won't tell you."

"Okay, then I'm editing it."

"May I see it before it runs?" Joel asked.

"That won't be necessary."

"I have a reason for wanting to see it," Joel said. "This is only the first part of a series. There's a lot more to it than an advertising agency account pitch."

Charlie raised an eyebrow. "A series?"

"Yes, a three-part series," Joel answered. "Look, Sheldon Hanrahan will probably win this pitch. He always does. It might force J&M out of business. That's a story by itself. But there's more to it. J&M is doing the communications for Congresswoman Theilen's senatorial campaign and Hanrahan Communications represents Senator Howard. If J&M goes out of business, it'll hurt Theilen's campaign. I'm working with Michael Hanley on the political angle. These could be important stories."

"I see," Charlie said. "That's interesting, but I don't think you should pursue them, especially the political story."

"Why not?" Edith asked.

Charlie put his elbows on his desk and leaned forward, thrusting his mustache at Edith and Joel. "Because it's based on the premise that Sheldon Hanrahan is using unethical means to win accounts, a premise we don't have any evidence for and based on information from a questionable source. Furthermore, it implies he's doing so to defeat Theilen. Hell, Howard will probably beat Theilen no matter what happens to J&M. The two aren't connected. I won't support a story based on allegations and mysterious sources. Understand?"

Joel knew Charlie's tone meant he'd made his decision and the meeting was over. And he knew better than to go head-to-head with Charlie Case.

Joel stood and stomped to the door. Edith rose to leave too. As she did, Joel heard Charlie say, "Edith, stay a minute." Joel slammed the door as he left.

THIRTY-THREE

As HE SAT in the police interrogation room closed in by white walls and under bright florescent lights, Ben had to admit he looked guilty. Two cameras mounted in the corners near the ceiling recorded his every move, his every expression, his every word. He tried not to look guilty, but the harder he tried, the more he felt the cameras stare at him, and the guiltier he looked.

Ben had been sitting at a cheap eight-foot long table in a straight-backed chair for half an hour. He was thinking about how he should answer the police's questions when they finally came in the room. He didn't know about things involving the police—the procedures, if he should cooperate, or what they would do to him. John had told him not to say anything until he talked to an attorney. *But I'm not guilty!* he thought.

Finally, a muscular man in a tight-fitting dark golf shirt with a badge on his belt came in the room carrying a manila folder. "I'm Detective Peterson," he said. He sat across the table from Ben. He took out a pen and began writing on a form on the inside the folder. "You're Ben Smith?" he asked.

Ben answered that he was. The detective asked Ben his address, his age, where he worked and his birth date. Ben gave him the answer to each.

Then Detective Peterson said, "And you were involved in the incident at 12:10 this afternoon in the Midwest Savings building atrium?"

"Maybe I better talk to an attorney," Ben said.

"Why? You haven't been charged with anything."

"Is this being recorded?"

"Yes," Peterson answered.

"I better talk to an attorney."

"Mr. Smith," the detective said, "I think you better tell me what happened. Ms. Kelly said you wanted to meet her in the atrium at noon, that you met her on the bus last week and have been sending her instant messages ever since. She says you called her this morning because you wanted to meet her."

"That's not true!" Ben blurted. "None of it. She wanted to meet *me*! She said she had some information about Trevor Marin."

"Who's Trevor Marin?" Detective Peterson wrote the name on his pad.

"He is... was my boss at Jacob and Marin. He died last week in a car accident."

"So Ms. Kelly called you?"

"Yes... No. I guess I placed the call to her. She gave me her number. Oh, man... Maybe I better talk to an attorney."

Detective Peterson smiled condescendingly. "You haven't been charged with anything, Mr. Smith. Just tell me what happened in the atrium."

"I didn't do anything," Ben said.

Peterson put his pen down and stared at Ben. He told him that 'Ms. Kelly' as he called her, was in the hospital being treated for cuts and bruises from an assault. He pointed out that Ben had blood on his shirt that was probably hers and that he had a scratch on his face. He said that Ms. Kelly accused Ben of trying to kiss her on the face and breast and that the police would probably find Ben's DNA from the saliva he left behind. Witnesses saw a man fitting Ben's description running from the scene and several agreed to look at a line up. "I have a lot of evidence pointing to an aggravated sexual assault," Detective

Peterson said. "If something different happened, you better tell me right now."

Ben examined Detective Peterson and decided he should shut up. The detective wouldn't believe a word of his story. He'd probably seen hundreds of perverts in his career, and by the look on the Peterson's face, it was clear he thought Ben was just another one. The detective was working Ben as he was trained to do and Ben was allowing the detective to work him. "I'm sorry, Detective," Ben said, finally, "but I'm not saying anything until I talk to an attorney."

Detective Peterson glanced at the camera and a few seconds later a uniformed policeman came through the door. Peterson said, "Mr. Smith, will you please stand and put your hands behind your back." Ben did and the policeman went behind him and snapped on handcuffs.

"You're under arrest for aggravated sexual assault," Detective Peterson said. "You have the right to remain silent. Anything you say can and will…" Ben didn't hear the rest of the statement but at the end, he agreed he had. The uniformed officer grabbed Ben's arm and led him out of the room.

*

Ninety minutes later, Ben was back in the same interrogation room. They had photographed him and taken his fingerprints. They'd taken a swab of saliva from inside his cheek. They'd confiscated his shirt and had given him a cheap red nylon one from a box the police had on hand for just such situations. The uniformed policeman laughed when Ben put it on. They'd asked him what seemed like a thousand questions. Where was he born? When had he moved to Minnesota? What were his previous addresses and how long had he lived at each one? How long had Jacob & Marin employed him and where had he worked before?

And then they'd asked about his wife. As Ben sat in the

interrogation room, he wondered what Nan would think when she heard about the assault. John had said she would understand, and Ben believed she would. Still, she'd have to suffer the humiliation of being told her husband had been arrested for aggravated sexual assault of a beautiful woman ten years younger than her. He felt terrible for her and angry at the same time that someone—could it be Sheldon Hanrahan as John had said? —would put both of them through this.

The door opened to the interrogation room and Detective Peterson came in. Behind him was a tall, slender man in his late sixties sporting a thin gray mustache and dressed in a perfectly tailored pinstriped suit. Following him was a younger man who looked like he never lost at anything, and an attractive blonde woman in an expensive business dress and trendy glasses. They all carried briefcases.

"You wanted an attorney?" Peterson said. "You got three. Great ones at that."

"Thank you, Detective," the older man said. "I wish to be alone with my client." Peterson shot a look of disgust at Ben and left.

The older man extended his hand to Ben. "Hello, I am Leland Carmichael."

Leland Carmichael. Ben recognized him from when he'd seen his picture in the paper and on TV. Lee Carmichael was the best criminal defense lawyer in the state—and arguably one of the top five best in the country. He was the attorney for all the local high-profile criminal cases. He defended professional ball players when they got in trouble, wealthy business people, a rock star arrested for the statutory rape of a 15-year-old, a U.S. congressman who was accused of taking bribes, the Catholic archdiocese when one of its priests was accused of child molestation. And now he stood in front of Ben with his hand extended and was, apparently, Ben's attorney. Ben shook his hand, too surprised to say anything.

"These are my colleagues, Mr. Martin Mithun and Ms. Campbell Williams. We're here to represent you." They sat at the table with Ben.

The only thing Ben could think of saying was, "Mr. Carmichael, I can't afford you."

Leland Carmichael smiled. "You can call me Lee, and my fees are not any of your concern."

"But—"

"Don't ask, Ben. Just do as I tell you and you'll be fine. Okay?"

"Yes, sir." Ben said. Martin Mithun was watching Ben's every move, and Campbell Williams was writing everything he said down on a pad of paper.

"Good," the attorney said. "This is what you will do."

Leland Carmichael laid out the procedure Ben would go through in the next several hours and told Ben precisely what to do at each step. It was simple, really. Ben was only to respond to Leland Carmichael. He was only to answer questions Lee asked him and say absolutely nothing to anyone else. If Ben needed to go to the bathroom, he should ask Lee. If he needed a Kleenex after a sneeze, he should ask Lee for one. If his shoe came untied, he should ask Lee if he could tie it. From this point forward, Lee and Ben would be attached at the hip. Ben would be like a baby and Lee would be his overprotective mother.

Ben was more than glad to give himself over to Leland Carmichael. He hadn't known what to do from the moment he walked through the police department's front door, and now he didn't have to. He'd be in the care of the best criminal defense attorney money could buy.

But whose money? The three attorneys sitting in front of him had to cost well over two thousand dollars an hour. Who could afford that? Not Ben. But, when he thought about it, he decided he shouldn't care. Three hours earlier, there was a good chance he'd be convicted of aggravated sexual assault and would face the real possibility of going to prison. Now, his side of the story would at least be heard by the authorities and perhaps even believed. For the first time since he realized what the attack in the atrium would look like to the rest of the world, Ben felt hope.

"Do you want to hear my side of the story?" Ben asked.

"I have what I need at present." Leland's mustache barely moved when he talked. "We talked with your friend John," Lee said. "He told us what happened."

"And you believe it?" Ben asked.

"I do," Leland Carmichael replied with a nod. "We'll go over all of your details soon. We must know even the most insignificant fact. You'll get tired of Mr. Mithun's questions, I'm afraid. But right now, we need to concentrate on the arraignment."

Detective Peterson came through the interrogation room door. He looked angry. "Mr. Smith," he said, "all charges have been dropped. You're free to go."

"What?" Ben exclaimed. "Why did she…"

Leland Carmichael cut Ben off with a raised hand. He examined Detective Peterson for a moment, then said, "If that's the case, we'll be leaving at once." He grabbed Ben by the arm and led him out of the police department. Campbell Williams was on her cell phone as soon as they left the interrogation room and when they marched out to the street, a large, black Mercedes limousine was waiting for them. Leland put his hand on Ben's shoulder and directed him into the car. After they settled into the leather seats, Campbell Williams gave the driver Ben's home address.

As the limo headed south, Ben asked, "Why were the charges dropped?"

"I don't know," Leland Carmichael said. "We weren't expecting it. Apparently, Ms. Kelly didn't want to press charges. It seems she may have gone through a lot of trouble for nothing."

"Now what should I do?"

"Go home," Lee said. "Be with your wife, but don't talk to anyone else about the incident. If anyone contacts you about it, direct them to me." He nodded to Campbell Williams who gave Ben business cards for all three attorneys. "If anything unusual happens— and I mean anything—call me. If you can't get through to me, contact one of my colleagues. One of us will always be available, any hour of the day or night."

"Okay." Ben thought about the hacking of Nan's computer a week earlier and what Dirk had found out about it and wondered if he should tell his attorney. Then he remembered what Dirk had said about his non-compete agreement with Secure Digital and decided against it.

They were quiet as the limo entered Ben's neighborhood. From the moment they left the police department, Campbell Williams had been on her cell phone. Every once in a while, she would lean over and whisper something to Leland Carmichael. He would either nod or shake his head and she would convey the directions to the person on the phone.

As the big black Mercedes pulled onto his street, Ben said, "I didn't get my shirt back."

Leland Carmichael smiled. "They'll keep it in case Ms. Kelly changes her mind," he said.

Then, Ben turned to Leland Carmichael. "Can I know who is paying for you?"

The great attorney kept his eyes forward. "Ben, when you become an attorney you learn you should never ask a question for which you do not need the answer. You don't need to know, so please don't ask. Anyway, I'm not at liberty to tell you."

The limousine pulled up to Ben's house. The driver hustled out and opened the door for Ben. As Ben rose to get out of the car, Leland Carmichael put his hand on Ben's arm. "Remember what I told you. Don't say anything to anyone except your wife. We're investigating why they dropped the case. We'll talk to you soon."

Lee examined Ben's face. "You should put something on that scratch. I recommend an antiseptic cream with aloe vera. It makes the cut heal more quickly. And Ben," he said, "you'll be all right."

"Thank you," Ben said. He climbed out of the limo and went into his house.

THIRTY-FOUR

NAN WAS WAITING FOR him when Ben walked through the front door of his home. He didn't know what to expect from her. He also didn't know what he should say. But when he saw her standing at the front door, smiling at him sympathetically, he almost cried. They hugged for a long time.

Then, Nan said, "Nice shirt."

For the first time all day, Ben laughed. They kissed and he knew there was no doubt in her mind that he was innocent. He thought she'd understand. He'd hoped she would. Now that he knew for sure, he was relieved. Why had there been even a moment of doubt? He pushed away from the kiss and said, "I love you."

She waved her hand and said, "Of course you do. Let's get something on that scratch."

They went through the living room and headed to the bathroom. "The charges were dropped," Ben said. "They don't know why."

"I know why!" Nan said. "It's because you didn't do anything."

"I don't think it works that way. They don't drop charges just because the wife thinks the husband is innocent. You talked to John?"

"Yes, he called about three hours ago. I wanted to go to the police department, but he said I should wait until I heard from the attorney. An attorney from Leland Carmichael's office—I think her name was Campbell—called and told me to stay home. She said Mr. Carmichael was handling the case personally and I'd just get in the way. I wanted to go anyway, but she was firm. And, my goodness, it was Leland Carmichael's office! I didn't know you had such powerful friends. Hold still."

Nan gently washed Ben's scratch with a rag and warm, soapy water.

"I don't know who hired him," Ben said. "He wouldn't tell me. Strange things are going on, Nan. John thinks Sheldon Hanrahan set me up. That's crazy, but I don't have another explanation. Where's Jenny, by the way."

"My mother took her. I called and told her we had an emergency." Nan dabbed at the scratch with antiseptic cream.

"My God. You didn't tell her what happened, did you?"

"No, and she didn't ask, bless her heart. Jenny was happy to go. They're ordering pizza from Rocko's. Jenny loves Rocko's. Hold still! You're jumping around like a jack rabbit."

Now that Ben knew he was all right with Nan, he needed to know why Elizabeth Kelly had attacked him. She had assaulted him and he'd suffered the humiliation of being arrested for something he didn't do. He wanted to know why. He wanted the details. Who was Elizabeth Kelly? Who beat her up and how much was she paid? And, if Sheldon Hanrahan was behind it, did he really think Ben was that much of a threat? He wanted to make sense of the last five hours of his life so he could explain it all to Nan, her mother, and everyone at J&M. Most of all, he wanted Nan to know her faith in him was justified. But, as Nan applied an antiseptic cream to his scratch, he realized it didn't matter. She believed him and cared only that he was okay.

"I have to tell you something about your computer," Ben said. "Let's go for a walk around Lake Harriet. You're right. I'm jumping out of my skin. A walk will settle me down."

"Okay," Nan said. "You better change your shirt first."

*

Fifteen minutes later, Ben had put on one of his own shirts and he and Nan were strolling around Lake Harriet. It was a three-mile walk and they held hands the entire way. After-work joggers were pounding the path surrounding the lake, and a few sailboats lifted their colorful sails to catch the evening breeze.

They walked without talking for ten minutes. Ben kept picturing Sheldon Hanrahan talking to Elizabeth Kelly about the set up. He pictured her letting someone beat her up just before he met her in the atrium. He saw the meeting with Elizabeth Kelly as if he were watching it from above—the incredible scene of her wiping his saliva on her face and breast. He wondered if Sheldon Hanrahan told her what to do or if she thought of it herself.

Then Nan said, "You said you wanted to tell me something about my computer."

Ben snapped out of his reverie. "Yeah. I probably should've told you earlier, but I didn't want you to worry."

Then, Ben told Nan what Dirk had discovered about the hacking, that it'd been done by someone in the Wells Fargo building. He reminded Nan that Hanrahan Communications was in the Wells Fargo building, but they weren't certain someone at HC did it. Nan said they should go to the police but Ben told Nan it would be a problem because of Dirk's contract with Secure Digital.

"I don't know, Ben," Nan said. "This is pretty serious."

"Yeah," Ben said nodding his head. "Maybe I should tell Leland Carmichael."

Nan's cell phone rang. She didn't reach for it.

"Maybe you should check the caller ID," Ben said. "It might be important to this."

Nan got her phone and looked at the caller ID. "It's Theilen," she said. "I better take it." Nan pressed the screen to answer.

"Hi Janice… Oh, I see… Yes… Of course,… He's with me. We're walking around Lake Harriet… Fifteen minutes?… We'll see you then." Nan pressed the screen to end the call.

"What was that about?" Ben asked.

"Madame Congresswoman wants to talk to both of us. She's on her way from Saint Paul. She said her driver will drop her off at the band shell in fifteen minutes."

"She wants to meet with me, too?"

"That's what she said," Nan replied. "We better move it. We need to be on the other side of the lake in fifteen minutes."

*

When Ben and Nan got to the band shell, two dozen sailboats slid across the lake, getting ready to start a regatta. It would be a perfect evening for it. The wind was steady and strong from the west, puffy white clouds rolled across the sky. The band shell, with its three towering steeples, was being set up for a concert later that evening. Workers were busy tinkering with sound equipment. Ben and Nan sat on a bench and watched for the congresswoman.

A few minutes later, a white Lincoln Town Car pulled into the band shell parking lot and Janice Theilen got out of the back. She was no more than five foot-two and in her mid-fifties, was in better shape than most people thirty years younger. She wore a dark blue business suit, heels, and had pinned her brown hair in an up-do. In her suit, she looked out of place in the park.

Theilen spotted Nan and Ben and marched over to them. She held out a hand to Ben and he took it. He was surprised how strong her grip was.

"Ben," she said. "I heard you had some trouble today."

Ben was surprised. "You heard?"

"Nan, you need to keep your husband on a shorter leash," the congresswoman said in her quick, staccato style. "You can never tell what these good-looking types are up to." Coming from anyone else, the congresswoman's teasing would have been inappropriate, but from Janice Theilen, it had an amazing affect on Ben. He was glad she knew about his arrest.

"Let's walk," Theilen said pointing down the path. "I've been cramped up in meetings all day. Need to stretch my legs." She headed around the lake's east side. Ben and Nan followed, quickening their pace to keep up with her.

"Kids," Theilen said, "we have a few items to talk about. First, Ben, you need to know I heard about your little incident this afternoon from Lee Carmichael. He's a good friend and he's aware that Nan is heading my re-election campaign. Lee is incredibly thorough. Thinks of everything. That's why he's the best. He thought I should know what happened."

"I didn't attack her," Ben said. "She attacked me."

"Yes, and I know why." Across the lake, a cannon fired signaling the start of the regatta. A crowd gathered by the band shell began to cheer.

"You are smack in the middle of a big battle," Theilen said. "You need to know what's going on. This whole ordeal was orchestrated by Sheldon Hanrahan. Why? To win the Presidency of the United States for Bill Howard."

"So Ben's attack is related to Senator Howard?" Nan asked.

"Absolutely," Theilen replied. "Think about it. First of all, if J&M loses the Katch pitch, your agency, Ben, wouldn't be able to help with my campaign. No offense, but I could find someone to replace J&M fairly quickly. It'd cause some delays, but what's important is it wouldn't look good. My campaign would be associated with a company that failed. I'd look like I don't have it together. And as you both know, an election is all about image."

Theilen continued to march ahead with her eyes forward. "But that's only the half of it. Think how it would look if my campaign manager's husband was under indictment for aggravated sexual assault. The media would certainly pick it up. Combined with a J&M failure, it'd make me look like a fool. It would seriously hurt my bid for the senate."

"You said it was about the Presidency," Ben said.

"Ultimately it is." In the middle of the lake, the sailboats in the regatta had turned past the first buoy. The skippers shouted instructions to their crews. The crews trimmed their sails and the boats surged forward. A boat with red sails was in the lead six lengths ahead of a boat with blue sails. The rest were another six lengths behind the first two. They all heeled over in the brisk wind.

Theilen's heels clicked on the pavement as they walked. "Did you ever wonder why I chose to run against Howard? Nan? Ben? I was perfectly content being a five-term congresswoman. I'm on important committees in Congress. I have a lot of influence in Washington. Running against an incumbent like Howard is almost always political suicide. Ninety-five percent of all incumbents win their elections. Ninety-five percent! You really have to screw up not to get reelected. And Howard has managed himself perfectly over the last six years. Or, I should say, Sheldon Hanrahan has managed him perfectly. He'll be difficult to beat, and if I lose to him, it'll hurt me politically."

A walker recognized Theilen and held out a hand saying she supported the congresswoman. Theilen expertly shook the woman's hand, smiled and said 'thank you' without slowing her pace one step. "The reason I'm running," she continued, "is to expose Howard's platform. I want to force him into a dialogue for the record so the people know his agenda—or rather the agenda of Sheldon Hanrahan. If we do that, Howard might still win, but America will know what he's up to. And, when the presidential election comes up in two years, it'll be on the record for everyone to see."

Theilen examined Ben and Nan as they walked. "As I said before, elections are about image and I intend to expose Howard and Hanrahan for the monsters they really are. And that's where you two come in. You're the team to help me get the message out. So they staged the little incident this afternoon to take you both out of commission. I'm not surprised it happened."

"If Sheldon is trying to smear me to hurt your campaign," Ben said, "why would they drop the charges?"

"Apparently, he changed his mind."

"Shouldn't we go to the police or the FBI?" Nan asked. "Ben's a victim here."

"By now I bet the woman who attacked Ben is on her way to the Bahamas or Europe for a nice long vacation. I doubt if the police could find her if they tried. And, to be honest, we don't have any evidence against Sheldon. He's too good at covering his tracks."

"What should we do?" Ben asked.

"Well," Theilen replied, "I'm an attorney, but I'm not your attorney. You'll have to ask Lee Carmichael. I suggest you do exactly what he says.

"As for what you should do in your work, that's simple. Both of you need to put your heads down and work harder than ever. Do you want to get back at Sheldon Hanrahan for doing this to you, Ben? Then forget about this attack and concentrate on winning the Katch pitch. Do everything you can to get them to stay with J&M. I hear you have a good presentation for them. Make it great. Show your passion. You guys do outstanding work. If you demonstrate your passion for it, Katch will stay with J&M."

The Congresswoman turned to Nan. "Nan, you need to help me expose William Howard and his pack. I'll tell you more about their agenda soon. Once you know what it is, you'll understand why it's important for voters to know about it. Your future and the future of your daughter depend on keeping people like Howard and Sheldon out of power. I chose you as my campaign manager because I believed you can help me. Once you know what's at stake, I'm sure you'll be motivated."

The sailboats had made another turn and were racing past them. Waves splashed white against their hulls. Theilen stopped and watched them as they raced by. "Look. That one there," she said, pointing to the boat in second place. "The one with the blue sails. It'll win the race. Want to know how I can tell? The last leg will be into the wind. That boat's mast is set further forward so it will be able to catch the wind better on an upwind tack. It'll take the lead halfway through the last tack and win." She turned and smiled at Ben and Nan.

"I have to get back to Saint Paul. I have a banquet to attend." She waved her hand and the white Town Car appeared on the roadway. "Nan, we have a meeting tomorrow morning. We need to crank up the pressure on Howard. We'll talk.

"Ben," she said, "don't worry about the arrest. You're in good hands with Lee. He'll sort it out if they decide to press charges. Keep focused on the Katch pitch. Do well. After you win it, we'll get moving on my advertising. Thanks for your time, kids."

Congresswoman Theilen clicked over to the white Lincoln and climbed into the back seat. The car drove off.

*

Ben and Nan continued around the lake. They didn't say anything until they were nearly back at the band shell again.

Ben looked across the lake at the sailboats on the last leg of the race. Theilen was right. The boat with blue sails had passed the boat with the red sails. But as they approached the finish line, the boat with the red sails pulled even. The cannon fired to signal the race had a winner, but Ben couldn't see which boat won.

"Look at that," he said to Nan. "Theilen was right about the boat with the blue sails. It might have won the race."

"Let's go pick up Jenny," Nan said. "I want to spend as much time with her as I can."

"Good idea," Ben said. "We're going to be busy."

THIRTY-FIVE

"JACKSON, YOU LOOK like shit," Lieutenant West said as he lumbered past Jackson's desk. "When was the last time you had a full night's sleep?"

"Can't remember," Jackson groaned. "Probably since captain put me on this damn case. Feels like months."

"You need to get some rest before you keel over."

"Right," Jackson said. "I will when we get these guys locked up." He rubbed his eyes and tried to read through some telephone records.

A twist in the Shauna Tate case had caught the Minneapolis police department by surprise. Apparently, the head of the Family Mob, a man nicknamed Chill, hired some Vatos Locos Latino gang members to kill his own first lieutenant because he was screwing Chill's girlfriend. The Vatos Locos were more than happy to do it. When they shot up the wrong house, killing young Shauna, Chill claimed the Latinos were trying to kill him to gain turf in a drug war. Jackson had caught two Vatos Locos gang members who were now sitting in the county lockup under heavy surveillance. They were singing and they both sang the same tune—Chill had hired them.

When word got out about the murder-for-hire hit, it started a war inside the Family Mob gang, and the police were finding more dead bodies. Jackson thought the arrest of the two Vatos Locos gang members would end the case. Now he was sitting at his desk inspecting telephone records for where he might find Chill so he could arrest him before his own gang killed him.

"Darren," West said, "you should know you're doing a great job. This is a tough case. Too much politics going on."

"Thanks, Lieu," Jackson replied. He picked up the next sheet of telephone records.

"Hey Jackson," West said, stopping at his office door, "I got some good news for you."

"I need some. What is it?"

"My contact at the department of defense says he can get us Trevor Marin's fingerprint records. He's sending them."

"Really?" Jackson said. "That's great. But what're you doing workin' on it? I thought the case was closed."

"It is, wise guy," replied West. "And if you tell anyone I pulled a favor on a closed case, I'll get in trouble and then you'll get in trouble with me."

"Not if I find Chill I won't," Jackson said. "I'll be a damn hero around here. You won't be able to touch me."

"Don't count on it, Jackson," West said pointing a knuckle at his detective. "I didn't make lieutenant for nothing. Anyway, I thought you should know. We'll have the fingerprints in a day or two."

"Thanks, Lieu."

"Do you need help with those phone records?" West asked.

"Nah, I gotta get to the captain's office in a few minutes. He wants another briefin'."

"Okay." West disappeared behind his door, and Jackson turned his attention back to the telephone records.

THIRTY-SIX

"YOUR STORY in this morning wasn't what you said it would be," Michael Hanley said as he sat across from Joel at the Twin Cities Athletic Club eating his eggs Benedict. "What happened?" Hanley's coat hung on the chair next to him and he'd tucked his club tie into his starched white shirt. As usual, his perfect white hair didn't move as he ate.

Joel had ordered waffles instead of scrambled eggs, thinking it was impossible for the TCAC to ruin waffles. He was wrong. They tasted stale and the syrup was watery. He pushed the waffles around his plate and planned to grab a bagel after the meeting.

"I'm pissed about it," Joel said. "It isn't what I wrote. Charlie Case got hold of it and took out most of the punch. Why'd he do that? He usually likes hard-hitting stories. This series could be great, just like Stein and Conklin."

"Did he give you a reason?"

Joel shrugged. "He said I didn't have enough substantiation for making accusations against an important businessman like Sheldon Hanrahan. I wasn't making accusations! I was just pointing out some coincidences, that's all. We've run a lot more controversial stories with far less, so I don't know what Charlie's problem is."

Hanley examined Joel over the top of his coffee cup as he took a sip. He held his gaze as he set the cup down. "Joel, you ignored the first rule of journalism—you write for your editor first, then your readers. The reason Charlie changed your story is because he's friends with Sheldon Hanrahan."

"Oh," Joel said. "I didn't know that."

"Those are the sorts of things you should know to be a successful journalist. How did you last this long? By the way, who did you interview for the article?"

"I talked to a few people at J&M, some ex-Hanrahan employees. No one knew anything. I tried to get through to Sheldon himself, but he never called me back."

"You tried to interview Sheldon without having substantiation first?" Hanley asked, pointing his knife at Joel. "Don't you know better? That's the *second* rule of journalism. You wait until you have irrefutable evidence before you ask your subject about it. That way they can't stop you. You jumped the gun, Joel."

"I know, I know," Joel said shaking his head. "But I didn't have anything concrete and the agencies are making their presentations tomorrow. I didn't know what else to do." Joel continued to push his waffles around his plate with his fork.

"You should have waited," Hanley said, returning to his breakfast. "What about the political angle? Did Charlie talk to you about it?"

"He discounted it. He told me not to pursue anything beyond what ran this morning. He said there was no connection between the Katch pitch and the senate race. I don't know. He might be right."

"He's wrong," Hanley said. "There is a connection, and if we can make it, Charlie will have to run the story in spite of his friendship with Sheldon Hanrahan. He didn't get to be editor-in-chief by kowtowing to everyone he knows. I think it's time for me to get involved. But make no mistake, Charlie's right. We can't sling mud at someone like Sheldon Hanrahan unless we have the evidence to justify it. You didn't dig deep enough for your story, Joel. You didn't have anything to incriminate Sheldon. Until you do, your story will be about nothing more than two advertising agencies pitching for an account, which is exactly what ran this morning."

"But what about the information I got about Sheldon's business dealings?" Joel asked.

"What about it?" Hanley replied. "First of all, it doesn't add up to a hill of beans if it isn't substantiated. Second, all of it is in the past and doesn't mean much to the current situation if you can't make a clear connection."

"So what should I do?"

Hanley finished his eggs and signaled for the waiter. A waiter as old and musty as the Twin Cities Athletic Club itself shuffled over and handed Hanley his bill. "Like I said, I'm getting involved. I'll talk to my sources in the Howard and the Theilen camps. I'll ask them about the implications of the Katch pitch on their campaigns. In the meantime, you work the other end. I want you to keep your eye on the pitch. This information about Sheldon is only relevant if something suspicious happens. What we really need is a smoking gun."

"A smoking gun? Like what?"

"Irrefutable evidence that Sheldon is using questionable means to help Howard win in November," Michael Hanley said.

"You mean to win the Katch pitch," Joel said.

"It's the same thing."

"All right," Joel said staring at his waffle. "I'll dig more. One question. If I uncover something, whose story is this, yours or mine?"

Hanley signed the bill, then took his tie out of his shirt. "You said Charlie told you not to pursue it, so I'm pursuing it instead. You don't have another story. I'm not sure I do either. We need much more than we have now. But I'll tell you what, if I get a story out of this and you provide something that helps, you can have a byline."

"A byline?" Joel took his napkin from his lap and tossed it on the table. "Just a minute. I've done all the work so far. I got the information about Hanrahan. This should be *my* story. I should be a co-author at least."

"From what I can see," Hanley replied, "your story ran this morning. You pulled the trigger before you had what you needed for anything bigger. Furthermore, I have the connections and the resources for the political story, not you. Now, do you want the byline or not?"

Staring at the senior writer for the *Times*, Joel realized the possibility of a three-part series like the one he'd done for Stein and Conklin was gone. Charlie had told him not to pursue the series, and now, if there was something more to the story, Michael Hanley would write it. Sure, Hanley had the connections and influence to tackle the political side. But the story hinged on the Katch pitch and the advertising industry was Joel's expertise. He deserved more than a byline.

"If I uncover a smoking gun," Joel said, "I want to co-author it. If not, I'll accept a byline."

Hanley stood from the table and put on his coat. His white hair was perfectly smooth. "It will have to be a hell of a smoking gun, Joel. But okay, you have a deal. Let me know what you find out." Hanley turned and walked out of the restaurant.

Joel pushed his plate of uneaten waffles aside. Hanley was right, he needed a smoking gun. But what would he find to connect Sheldon Hanrahan to foul play? He'd been working for days to substantiate the information the pipe-smoking man at the Crowell construction site gave him, and he'd found nothing.

And now he needed a smoking gun just to get a co-authored story with Hanley—a smoking gun from Sheldon Hanrahan who obviously very good at covering his tracks.

THIRTY-SEVEN

WHEN BEN CAME into the office on Tuesday morning, nobody asked him about the scratch on his face or why he never came back from lunch the day before. People avoided eye contact and avoided talking to him, too. Only the day before, everyone had greeted him as if he was someone special, the person responsible for the Katch pitch that would save their jobs. Now, they were scared again.

Ben was determined to show everyone he was no different than before the attack. He was innocent and had nothing to be ashamed of. So he kept his chin up, his eyes forward, and went about his business, just like Janice Theilen had told him to do. If someone asked him about the incident, he'd tell them a crazy woman attacked him in the Midwest Savings atrium which, in his opinion, was what happened. Elizabeth Kelly—or whatever her name was—had to be nuts to let someone beat her so badly simply to frame him.

However, he would not tell anyone that John and Theilen had thought Sheldon Hanrahan was behind the attack. Even though there was evidence, even though, as John said, it all added up, the accusation would look desperate and wouldn't be what the employees would want to hear from their leader. So he kept the theory about Sheldon Hanrahan to himself.

Anyway, if Sheldon was trying to set him up, why did he drop the charges? As he saw it, Elizabeth Kelly—or Sheldon Hanrahan—had him cold. The police would never believe Ben's account of the attack.

They would prosecute him for sexual assault and he'd have to place his future in the hands of Leland Carmichael. And who was paying for him? John, at a copywriter's salary? Doubtful. Congresswoman Theilen? She had influence, but she didn't have that kind of money. Or maybe Leland Carmichael was volunteering his services. That wasn't likely, either.

Elizabeth Kelly, Sheldon Hanrahan, Leland Carmichael, Janice Theilen, Senator Howard and the presidency of the United States—it all made Ben's head spin. But he had to let it go. He had a presentation to finish and he'd be damned if Sheldon Hanrahan or anyone else would prevent him from doing his very best. What had John told him about being a leader? *A leader is someone who has the courage to fight.* Damn right he'd fight. If Sheldon Hanrahan had set him up with Elizabeth Kelly, his best revenge would be to win the Katch pitch.

When Ben got to his office and checked his calendar, he saw Andrew had scheduled a meeting at nine in the Octagon to review the Katch creative concepts. The meeting would be attended by everyone who would be at the pitch—Ben, Andrew, Tom, Ginny, and John. Ben answered a few e-mails, reviewed the Katch creative brief, and headed to the Octagon.

He arrived at the meeting early. He was eager to see the ideas Andrew, John, and the rest of the creative department had developed.

Ben knew how hard it was to develop a great campaign. Most people—even most clients—didn't have a clue. Under a deadline, the pressure to be creative was incredibly stressful. It took long days and late nights of exhausting work, tossing ideas around and seeing how they measured up against the strategy. They filled walls with headlines, taglines, sketches, storyboards and copy. Then, they'd rip all but the best ones down and start over. They consumed gallons of Mountain Dew and Red Bull, ordered Chinese after everyone else in the agency had gone home. Then they'd order pizza at midnight. Their currency was great ideas. Their layouts were akin to fine art and their copy was like poetry. But if the strategy was off, the ideas came out wrong and all their work was for nothing. And ultimately the quality of their work was entirely subjective and anyone in authority could destroy even a great campaign by saying, "I dunno. I just don't like it."

So Ben knew that deep down creative people—even the best ones—felt their highly-honed skills were unappreciated. It was hard to keep them motivated. But Ben had given them the correct strategy and written a strong essential truth. It was his best work ever, just what the creative team needed to do its job. He was sure that their ideas would be great.

After a few minutes, Ginny and Tom came in and sat next to Ben. To his relief, they didn't ask about his scratch. Then, Andrew and John came in. Andrew was carrying a large stack of presentation boards. He was in an especially good mood. He thrust his chin forward and wore a goofy grin. He had pulled out his shirt from his jeans. He took a seat at the head of the table and sorted through the boards as if they were cards in a sure-bet poker hand.

"Let's get going," Ben said. "How about if I set this up for you, Andrew?"

"Go ahead," Andrew replied, still sorting.

Ben reminded everyone that the main strategy for the campaign is to take Katch's commitment to style purity—the fact that each Katch mutual fund remains true to its investment strategy—and turn it into a positive. The task, he said, was to take the target audience's perception that Katch funds are boring and turn it on its head by positioning Katch funds as the smart investment choice for people with long-term plans. That's how they arrived at the essential truth— 'Funds for Your Plans.'

As he spoke, Ben began to forget all the awful things that had happened to him. He was in the moment—the rush of getting a presentation together—and he was thoroughly enjoying it.

He wrapped up his part of the meeting and said, "Andrew, take it away."

All eyes shifted to Andrew and he was in his element. He stood, paused dramatically, and met the eyes of everyone in the room. He still wore a goofy grin. Just when it appeared that he was about to begin, he raised a finger and said, "One minute." He grabbed the remote that controlled the lights and took several minutes adjusting them until they were just right. Then he reshuffled the stack of presentation boards and scanned his audience again. He was grinning more broadly now, and the excitement in the room was electric.

Ben smiled to himself. Andrew had been a fine amateur actor before he got into advertising, and he used all his acting skills in his creative presentations. He'd worked on major accounts for some of the best agencies in New York and Chicago before moving back to his hometown of Minneapolis. He had a reputation as one of the best presenters in the business. He could keep an audience enthralled for over an hour, even if what he was presenting wasn't all that good. This time, apparently, Andrew was presenting outstanding work. It would be a wonderful show.

Andrew began. "We have two campaign ideas to show you this morning," he said as if he were on a Broadway stage. "The first is called…" He paused and met the eyes of each person in the room again. Then he said, "Fairy Tales." He slowly turned the boards over one by one, presenting them as if they were the crown jewels. The pages on the boards were mock ups with rough artwork but they represented the ideas clearly. The ads for Fairy Tales were like pages from a children's book, dense with copy and whimsical artwork. They focused on two well-known fairy tales—the Tortoise and the Hare, and Billy Goats Gruff. The message of the Tortoise and the Hare was, 'slow and steady wins the race,' and the message of Billy Goats Gruff was, 'the grass is not always greener on the other side of the bridge.' Both ads, the accompanying e-mail campaign, and the brochures delivered the message of style purity perfectly. Andrew showed the ads pasted in *Fortune* magazine and pointed out how they contrasted with the boring sameness of the competitors' ads.

"It's brilliant," Ginny said.

"Why, thank you for those kind words, Ms. Rubenstein," Andrew replied gaily. His dark eyes sparkled. "But it isn't our top choice. Would you like to see our top choice, Ms. Rubenstein?"

Ginny laughed. "Why yes I would!" she replied. "Thank you Mr. Birk."

"Will you two children please stop playing around so Andrew can present the next campaign?" Ben said with a smile. For the first time in over a week, the pitch team members were enjoying themselves. They'd put together something special—just what Everet Katch had asked for—and they were feeling good about their chances.

The second campaign was named 'Letters', and, as Andrew said, it was the one they recommended. Andrew called it "buzzy," meaning when it ran, the press would write about it multiplying the impact of the campaign. He turned over the first board to show an ad in the form of an open letter to the president of Morningstar, the company that tracked the performance of mutual funds. The letter, from Everet Katch and written on Katch letterhead, issued a challenge to Morningstar to report not only the mutual fund's returns, but also the fund's performance on style purity. It implied that Morningstar was doing a disservice to investors by only reporting returns and gave as evidence the wild fluctuations during the latest boom and bust years. The letter concluded with a statement saying that Katch was fiercely dedicated to the stated investment strategy for each of their mutual funds and was therefore, "Funds you could plan on."

Other ads in the campaign were letters from Katch's individual fund managers addressed to the managers of competing mutual funds. They challenged them to join Katch in helping investors understand the importance of style purity. They were tastefully, yet forcefully worded—obviously, John had written them. The creative team had designed the accompanying brochures, e-mail campaign and web site to educate investors on style purity—especially if investors were using funds to meet their long-term financial goals.

Andrew stomped around the room, gleefully thrusting a fist into the air. His childlike enthusiasm was infectious. "Buzz! BUZZ!" he shouted. "This campaign will get press. It'll stir up controversy and, hopefully, piss off a few people. It'll light up social media! And that's what Katch needs to do—a buzzy campaign. In fact, this campaign is more than buzz, it's *buzz that brands*. Any idiot agency can do a stunt and get some press for its client. This campaign will get buzz, *and* it brands Katch as the most responsible mutual funds company in the business. It's fuckin' buzz that fuckin' brands."

Everyone nodded in agreement. The campaign would indeed get press and pressure Morningstar and the entire industry to pay attention to style purity. In the process, it would completely turn the tables on Katch's competitors and their erratic, short-term returns. The campaign was indeed brilliant, and Ben could tell it was just what Katch needed to turn its mutual funds business around.

In short, the campaign was perfect.

When Andrew was done, Tom spoke first. "I like the fairy tale campaign best. It really stands out. The open letter campaign—I don't know, it might be a bit bold."

"The fairy tale campaign is great but bold is what Katch needs," Ben replied. "It'll be controversial, but I think we should push them to do it."

"Yeah, you should," Andrew said. John and Ginny nodded.

"That's settled then," Ben said. "We show both, but push for the letter campaign. Great work, guys."

"Thanks," John said.

"Of course it's great work," Andrew said, suddenly less animated.

"Okay. What do we need to do before tomorrow?" Ben asked.

Ginny pulled out a list. She said she was getting the PowerPoint presentation proofed and needed to tweak the media plans with Lucy based on the buzzy creative ideas. She had the printing costs for the mailers and brochures and would put them into the plan. "I still need Tom's presentation," she said.

"Tom, when will you have your part done?" Ben asked.

"This afternoon," Tom answered. "I have a few more changes to make."

"Okay," Ben said. "Andrew and John, you'll need to clean up these boards. Our presentation is tomorrow at two. We'll print everything in the morning and do a rehearsal at 11:30. Okay?" Everyone agreed.

"One more thing," Ben said. "Our people are scared again. I suppose they wonder what happened to me yesterday. Well, what happened to me isn't important. Right now, our job is to be confident and to instill confidence in our people. We can't appear to be scared and we have no reason to be. We're absolutely the right agency for Katch and we have the best presentation I've ever seen. I can't wait to make it. It's marvelous work and everyone should be proud of it whether we win the pitch or not."

"Yes, we should," John replied. Ginny and Tom nodded. Andrew gathered up the boards with his back to the others and didn't respond.

The meeting was over and they started to leave. Ben caught John by the arm. "John, do you have a minute?"

"Of course," John said.

When the others had left, Ben said, "I want to thank you for yesterday. I didn't know who to turn to."

"You're welcome," John said. "I hear the charges were dropped."

"Yeah. I don't know why. Did you contact Lee Carmichael?"

"No."

"Who did then?" Ben asked. "Who did you call after you left me?"

"A few friends. One of them must have called Lee."

"Yes, but who? And who's paying him?"

John slid closer to Ben. "Ben, the charges have been dropped. If you have any legal problems, you have one of the best criminal defense attorneys in the world working for you. Frankly, you don't need to know who called Lee Carmichael."

Ben shook his head. "I also talked with Theilen yesterday," he said. "She supports your theory that the whole thing was set up by Sheldon Hanrahan. I mean, that's crazy."

"Ben, listen to me. Don't worry about what happened yesterday. You have to focus on the presentation. There's still a lot to do."

"Yeah, yeah. Of course, you're right," Ben said. "If Sheldon set me up, I want to beat him at this pitch."

"Yeah, me too," John said. "We have some creative ideas that just might do it, don't you think?"

"They're terrific," Ben said with a smile. "Some of the best ever."

"All based on your work, my boy. *Your work*. You deserve a lot of credit. If we win this pitch—and I think we will—you'll be the one everyone points to as the one who pulled it out."

"Yeah, I suppose."

As he rose to leave, John smiled and patted Ben's shoulder. "I think you'll do just fine as the next president of Jacob and Marin."

"What?" Ben exclaimed.

John chuckled as he walked out of the Octagon conference room.

THIRTY-EIGHT

"VICTOR, WHERE IS she now?" Sheldon asked through the Aston Martin's hands-free phone system. He dropped the visor to shield his eyes from the setting sun. Traffic heading west out of downtown was heavy for this time of night.

"She is in Saint Maarten," Victor responded in his thick Russian accent. "No one finds her. She will be on island for all of winter. She is happy to go. Hates winter. Will go back to Florida next year. She have a young man there."

"What will the police do?"

"Nothing. They drop case. They have other things they worry about."

"Someone might want to investigate," Sheldon said.

"They will find nothing. Good we stopped when we did."

It'd been a precautionary move—whisking the girl away before the police could get any information on her. They wouldn't find her and Victor was right, they wouldn't even try. The letter from Joel Scheck with details about Sheldon's business practices was reason enough to kill the plan. No need to give Joel anything to ask questions about. Anyway, Sheldon had other plans that would escape the attention of a snoopy reporter.

"Victor, I still want the Katch account." The sun had dropped below the Aston Martin's visor and cast rays directly into Sheldon's face. He turned his head to protect his bad eye. "An important person

234

at J&M has agreed to work for me. This person has a significant role in J&M's presentation to Katch. The move will happen tomorrow morning."

"Okay."

"This alone may not be enough, Victor," Sheldon said.

"Has to be," the Russian said. "We should not do more."

"I want the Katch account."

"Someone is watching," Victor replied. "Is dangerous."

"You said everything is secure with the girl?" Sheldon asked.

"Yes."

"Then it will be no different than what we'd planned before."

"You want I should go ahead with other plans?"

"Yes."

"Okay," Victor said. "You are boss."

"And Victor, make sure it works. I don't want Jacob & Marin to make their presentation tomorrow. Understand?"

"Yes."

Sheldon hung up without saying goodbye. He raised his head a little and saw a rusted-out Camry had stopped in front of him. He slammed on the brakes and the tires screeched as the Aston Martin came to within inches of plowing into the Toyota.

That was close, Sheldon thought. The traffic rolled again and Sheldon continued driving. The Katch account. He was going to have it. And whoever had fed Joel the information about Sheldon—a disgruntled employee, a competitor, someone at J&M, or possibly a political rival—would not outmaneuver him.

THIRTY-NINE

"YOU ONLY GET one defining moment in a career, Ben," Tree had said when Ben was new at J&M. "And more often than not, it's in a presentation."

Over the years, Ben realized that Tree was right. Of course, the hard work that went into a presentation—the strategy, the detailed plans, the creative work—were critical. But if it wasn't presented well, if the thoughts and ideas didn't come out with energy and passion, the work didn't matter.

Ben knew that the Katch pitch would be his one defining moment. So he barely slept the night before. He kept running the presentation through his mind until he had every word memorized. He got up twice in the middle of the night to make notes and, when he sat up in bed a third time, the glowing red numbers on the alarm clock read 2:52. Nan grabbed his arm and said, "Leave it alone. Get some sleep." He lay down, threw an arm around her waist and fell back to sleep.

He was awake before the alarm went off. When he got up, Nan rolled over and mumbled something about 'five more minutes'. Ben shoved his feet into his slippers and went downstairs to start the coffee. As the coffee brewed, he went over his notes again. He liked what he read. Everything was there—solid research with insightful analysis, sound strategies, a clear creative direction, and an essential truth even Tree would have been proud of. And the creative work was brilliant. Everet Katch and his board of directors needed proof that Ben and J&M could turn the mutual funds business around, and they had produced the work to assure them. Now they just needed to make a great presentation.

As he sat at the kitchen table reading through the presentation, he heard something dripping. Coffee was spreading over the counter and spilling over the edge. "Damn!" he said, jumping up to the coffee maker.

"What is it?" Nan was standing in the kitchen doorway in her pink bathrobe and slippers rubbing a hand through her tangled blonde hair.

"It's the coffee maker. It's leaking."

"I'll get it," Nan said. She shuffled over to the sink to get a dishrag.

"Thanks." Ben returned to his chair.

"Today's the big day," Nan said, wiping up the coffee.

"I'm feeling good about our work."

Nan smiled. "I knew you could do it. I'm proud of you."

"We still need to present it," Ben said, "but I have to say, I'm confident, knock on wood." Ben rapped his knuckles on the table.

"That's not wood," Nan said. "It's Formica."

Ben laughed. "Come, give me a kiss good morning."

Nan came over and sat in Ben's lap. She kissed him tenderly and ran a hand through his hair. "You'll do great. What time's the presentation?"

"Two. I'm taking my car today. We still have to put everything together. It all needs to be proofed, printed, and assembled. We need to mount the ads on boards. Then we're rehearsing at 11:30. There's still a lot of work to do."

Nan gave Ben a peck on the cheek and slipped off his lap. "I better get you some coffee."

Ben smiled. He had a feeling this was going to be a good day, but he'd be glad when it was over.

Ben went back upstairs, showered, and put on the Armani suit he'd set out the night before. He felt uncomfortable in such an expensive suit, but as he checked himself in the mirror, he saw it gave him stature. Maybe Tom Clarey had a point about dressing up for work. Ben ran a comb through his hair. The scratch on his face was healing quickly and wasn't very noticeable. He went back downstairs, wolfed down a bagel with cream cheese and guzzled some coffee. Nan gave him a once-over and told him he looked great. He asked Nan to give Jenny a hug for him when she woke up and tell her he'd play basketball with her later that night. He kissed Nan goodbye and jumped in the car. He was at J&M by 7:15.

The agency was dark when he arrived. He snapped on the lights and walked past the timber columns and yellow brick to his office. He began making final changes to his presentation. At 7:50, Jay poked his head into Ben's office. "Hey, boss, how can I help this morning?"

"Morning, Jay," Ben replied. He was happy to see Jay. The kid would be a star someday. He had good instincts for the agency business, and with a little experience, he'd soon be handling accounts on his own.

"Do we have Andrew and Tom's presentations yet?" Ben asked.

"No." Jay slid into a chair in front of Ben's desk. "Neither one got 'em to us. I asked Andrew about it late yesterday. He waved me off and said he needed to finish the boards. Said he'd have it to us this morning. I haven't gotten anything from Tom either, but he was working on it. We should have everything this morning."

"I hope so. We need to put it together and load it onto my laptop."

Jay raised a palm. "Want me to handle it?"

"That'd help a lot. If you get any push-back from Andrew or Tom, let me know."

"Will do," Jay said. "That means I'll need to get yours right away, too. *You're* not going to give me any push-back are you?"

Ben laughed. "Okay, chief. I just need a few minutes to make some changes."

"Five minutes," Jay said pointing a finger at Ben. "Then save it to the server. Anything else I should do?"

"No. We rehearse at eleven-thirty. Everything has to be ready to go. I don't want any last-minute rushes. We do that too much around here. I want us to be cool and confident. We can't if we rush."

"Gottcha." Jay left Ben's office.

Ben turned back to his computer screen. He went to the beginning of the presentation to go over it once more. Then he realized he didn't need to. Yet another edit would not improve it. It was time to let it go and send it off to the server. He took in a deep breath and was filled with satisfaction. His work was done.

He clicked 'save' and selected the folder on J&M's server that held the Katch presentation files. The hourglass icon came on the screen indicating the computer was saving the file.

As the file saved, Ben gazed out the window. He'd done it. He'd found the courage to stand up to Tom to do things right, the courage to overcome the attack by Elizabeth Kelly, the courage to overcome his own self-doubt. He'd done the hard work and now, all he had to do was make a great presentation.

He looked back at his screen. The save to the server was taking longer than usual. Ben rolled the mouse but the cursor didn't respond. He felt a tinge of panic as he thought his computer might be crashing. He couldn't remember if he'd saved his presentation this morning. "Jay!" he yelled out the door.

"Yeah?" came Jay's voice from outside.

"Why are these files taking so long to save to the server?"

"Give it a minute," Jay shouted. "People log onto the server in the morning and it slows it down."

Ben waited and watched the hourglass icon. It didn't move. Finally, the icon went away and the cursor on Ben's computer responded to the mouse. *That took way longer than it should have,* Ben thought.

He left his office and headed down the hall to check in with

Ginny. People were beginning to arrive and he felt their respect once again. This was the day of the big presentation and, in spite of the incident with Elizabeth Kelly, Ben had led the agency in putting it together. Everyone had heard the presentation was great and from their faces, Ben could tell they were optimistic. He was too.

When he turned into Ginny's office, she was sifting through the contents of a box on her desk. "Are you moving out?" Ben asked.

"Not yet," she said. Ginny was dressed in a perfectly tailored dark blue suit and matching designer shoes. Ben had to admit, she looked more comfortable in her high-end designer clothes than he felt in his. She looked good and would present well.

"How are the hard copies and the research deck coming?" Ben asked. "Will they be ready for the rehearsal?"

"That's what's in this box," Ginny answered. "I went over them again last night and caught a few typos. I'll have one of my people make the changes. Then we'll save them to the server and start printing them out. We'll need ten copies."

Ben leaned against her doorway. "How do you feel about the presentation?"

"Honestly, I think it came together beautifully," she said. "But..."

"But?"

"I hope it's enough."

Ben saw the worry in her face. "All we can do is the best we can, Ginny," he said. "Be confident."

Ginny forced a smile and nodded. "I'll get these changes made. They'll be ready."

"Ginny," Ben met her eyes with his, "thanks for everything. You've been terrific."

She smiled again only this time it wasn't forced. "I'll see you at eleven thirty." She returned to the box's contents.

Ben went back to Jay's office and saw him staring into his computer screen. "Did you get to Andrew and Tom about their parts of the presentation?"

Jay didn't look up from the computer screen. "Andrew's in, but Tom isn't here yet. Damn, the server really is slow this morning."

Ben looked over Jay's shoulder and saw the hourglass icon on Jay's computer screen wasn't moving. "Yeah, that's what happened to me earlier."

"Maybe the creative staff is doing something on it," Jay said. "Their files are huge. Could be slowing it down."

Jay's computer screen blinked to black, then back on. The hourglass icon was gone but everything else on the monitor was the same as before. "What was that?" Jay exclaimed.

Ben and Jay looked at each other. "Check the server to see if our files are there," Ben said.

Jay clicked on the server icon, and the hourglass returned but didn't move. After a few seconds, the computer monitor blinked off again and this time it stayed black. "What the…?" Jay said.

"Let me try my computer," Ben said. Jay followed as Ben rushed into his office. He sat at his computer and opened the link to the server. The connection opened without a problem and they saw the files for the presentation were where they should be.

"That's weird," Jay said. "It must be something with my computer."

"No, it was slow for me this morning too, remember?"

"What should we do?"

Ben remembered that Dirk had fixed J&M's security system just two days earlier. And Dirk was among the best security guy in the world. But Nan's computer—with Dirk's security system—had been hacked a week before. Ben began to panic. "Let's get this presentation together as quickly as possible," he said. "I'll get Andrew's presentation. You watch for Tom. Where is he, anyway? He agreed to get here early today. As soon as he comes in, get his files. Keep things off the server as much as possible."

"Good idea."

"I'm gonna find Andrew," Ben said.

Ben hurried to the creative department and when he got there, he saw John Turner and three others from the creative staff in front of Andrew's door.

"What's going on?" Ben pushed his way through.

John looked at Ben, shook his head. "You better talk to him." John moved away from the door and corralled the others to leave with him.

Ben stepped into Andrew's office. "What's this about?" he asked. Andrew was standing alongside his desk putting a few pictures he'd taken from his wall into a box. "What are you doing?"

"This is hard." Andrew's voice was strained, his face was pale. He wasn't wearing a suit.

"What's hard? And how come you aren't dressed for the presentation?"

"I'm sorry Ben," Andrew said into the box. "I can't do the presentation with you."

"What? Why?"

"Because, I'm quitting," Andrew said. "I've been offered another job."

"Another job? Where?"

"At Hanrahan," Andrew said, softly.

Ben folded his arms across his chest. "You, working for Sheldon Hanrahan?"

"It's a guarantee," Andrew said looking up from the box. "I'm guaranteed to have a job after the Katch pitch whether they win or lose. Can you say the same?"

Ben thought about it for a moment. He closed Andrew's door and took a seat on the couch. He crossed his legs. "No. To be honest Andrew, we can't guarantee we'll even be in business next week. But if we are, you'll be the creative director, and you won't have to work for Sheldon Hanrahan."

"I can't take that risk," Andrew said. "You don't understand. I need a job." He paused, then said, "You see, I'm not too good with money, Ben. I spend too much. I invest poorly. I lost all my savings in the stock market. I ended up owing on margin calls. I still owe—a lot—and if I lose my job here… My house, my wife …"

"Maybe we can help," Ben said evenly.

Andrew sneered. "How can you help if we lose Katch?"

"I don't know, but we'd do what we could."

"You have one hundred and forty people here who'd need help if we go out of business. You can't help them all, Ben. You can't." Andrew bowed his head. "I'd like nothing more than to stay. You have a great campaign to present. If you win the pitch, I'll kick myself. But I just can't take the risk. I'm sorry."

Ben stayed seated on the couch with his legs crossed and studied Andrew. He tapped a finger on the couch's arm. "Are you sure?"

Andrew shook his head. "I have no choice."

Ben took a deep breath. Then he stood from the couch and faced Andrew. "Okay, your resignation is accepted. You must leave immediately. I'll walk you out."

Andrew was startled. "What are you doing?"

"You just quit and I'm escorting you out." Ben pointed at the box on Andrew's desk. "Do you have all your stuff?"

"Yeah, I have everything."

"And, I assume you're not taking anything belonging to J&M, including any of our work?"

"No, I'm not," Andrew said. "Listen, Ben…"

"Let's go." Ben opened the door. Andrew hesitated, then picked up the box and walked out of the office as Ben followed. The entire creative department stared at them as they walked. When they got to the elevators, Andrew turned toward Ben. "I'm sorry, Ben."

"I am too, Andrew," Ben said without emotion. "We'll see you around."

Andrew stepped into the elevator, pushed the button for the ground floor, and stared blankly as the doors closed.

FORTY

BEN FELT STRANGELY quiet as he went back to the creative department and into John's office. He closed the door behind him and leaned his back against it.

"Andrew is gone," Ben said. "He's going to work for HC."

John folded his arms across his chest. "I thought that's what was happening."

"You'll have to do the presentation in his place," Ben said.

"I guessed that would happen too," John said with a nod. "Fine, I'll be ready. I'll meet you in the Octagon at 11:30."

Ben set his jaw. "That bastard Sheldon played Andrew. First, he tried to frame me with Elizabeth Kelly, and when that didn't work, he took advantage of Andrew. I want to win this pitch, John. I want to win it more than I've ever wanted to win anything."

"Yeah, me too," John said.

Ben felt his nostrils flair and he stared at John. "That son of a bitch." John nodded.

When Ben opened the door to leave, Jean Ash approached. Her face was set in a frown. "We might have trouble getting the mockups done for the presentation," she said. "We can't get the printers to work. The computers lock up. Nothing's working."

Ben looked at John. "I had the same problem earlier. You don't suppose…"

John turned to his computer. "Let me try." He opened a file and sent it off to the printer. The images on his monitor froze. John rolled the mouse and punched keys on his keyboard but the computer didn't respond. "This didn't happen earlier," he said.

Ben's stomach knotted and his heart raced. "Shut everything down," he ordered. "Right away. We could lose our files."

Ben pushed his way past Jean and sprinted toward Ginny's office. He charged through the door. "Are you having computer problems?" he asked.

"Yes." She stared at her computer screen. "It keeps locking up on me and now I can't reboot."

"Unplug it and disconnect it from the network. Then don't touch it."

"Okay, but what . . ."

Ben bolted from Ginny's office. He ran to Tom's office and burst in. Joanne and Tom were hunched over Tom's computer. "Turn off your computer," Ben said. "Right now."

"What?" Tom looked up, startled. "What's going on? I just got in and my computer isn't working"

"We might lose everything if we don't shut it down," Ben said. "Joanne, get on the paging system and tell everyone to shut off their computers and unplug them from the network. Do it now." Joanne scurried out of Tom's office and in a few seconds, she was relaying Ben's instructions to the agency.

"What the heck?" Tom asked. "I have to get my presentation to Jay. He told me you wanted them early."

"We have a bigger problem than that," Ben said. "None of the computers are working—not even the Macs in the creative department. I think we've been hacked."

"How are we going to do the presentation?" Tom asked.

Ben stood in the middle of Tom's office without moving. Anger boiled from his stomach to his chest. He felt his fist clench. His jaw jut out. He took a deep breath and pushed the anger back down. This was not a time to lose it. He had to decide what to do next.

"Okay," he said. "First, you should know Andrew just quit. He's going to work for HC. John is going to step in for him."

"You're kidding?" Tom said.

Ben slowly shook his head. "No, I'm not."

"Damn, we're screwed." Tom slumped in his chair.

"No we aren't," Ben said. "We're not giving up, Tom. We're going to make this presentation. Gather what you've printed out. Find Ginny and John and meet me in the Octagon in five minutes. I need to make some phone calls." Ben turned on his heel and headed out of Tom's door.

Ben returned to his office, closed his door and picked up the phone. He dialed Katch headquarters and asked to speak to Everet Katch. The receptionist forwarded his call to Everet's secretary.

"Hi, Ben. Sorry, but Everet is with the board of directors. Hanrahan Communications is making their presentation now."

"Lora," Ben said firmly, "it's very important. Please."

"Okay," she said. "I'll see if he'll take the call."

A few minutes later, Everet Katch came on the line. "Ben, this isn't appropriate." He was clearly irritated.

"Everet, I'm sorry, but we have a problem." Ben explained the situation with their computers and that he thought they'd been hacked. He told Everet they were doing everything they could to get the presentation together but they wouldn't be ready at two.

To Ben's surprise, Everet's irritation disappeared. "I can push your presentation back an hour—maybe an hour and a half—but no more. Some of the board members have flights tonight."

"Okay," Ben said. "Thanks."

"Ben," Everet said, "do everything you can to get here before 3:30—no later. I'll cover for you."

"Yes sir," Ben replied.

Ben hung up and dialed Dirk's number. The phone rang and rang without an answer. "Come on, come on," Ben said into the receiver. Finally, Dirk answered on the twelfth ring.

"When I don't answer, it means I'm working," Dirk said, angrily. "Who the hell is this?"

"Dirk," Ben said, "I need your help."

FORTY-ONE

"GIVE ME TWENTY MINUTES," Dirk said after Ben had explained the problem.

Ben headed to the Octagon to talk to Tom, Ginny, and John. As he walked through the halls, the agency was in a panic. Everyone knew that with the computers down, the presentation they had all worked so hard on wouldn't be done in time. And the news that Andrew defected to HC had spread throughout the agency like wildfire. Ben had to take action, fast.

When he got to the Octagon, Tom, Ginny and John were already sitting at the table waiting for him. Their worried faces greeted him. "I called Everet Katch," Ben said as he took a seat at the table. "He's given us until 3:30 at the very latest."

"Wow," Ginny said. "He never accepts anything late."

John said. "Maybe he knows something."

"Well, whatever it is, we need to fix the computers first," Ben said. "I have someone coming. He'll be here soon."

"I hope he's good," Tom said. "The network is really screwed up."

Ben nodded. "If anyone can, he can, but it'll take some time. In the meantime, we have to talk to our employees. They're starting to panic."

"I heard Andrew quit," Ginny said.

"Sorry, Ginny, I didn't have time to tell you. Yeah, he's going to

HC. He said he couldn't afford to be without a job."

"None of us can," Tom scoffed.

"That's true," Ben replied. "Andrew wanted to stay but he's in too much debt. I believe him. Now, we have to talk to our people about Andrew, about the computers and about the presentation. They need to be reassured. Once our computers are back up, we'll need all hands to finish putting the presentation together."

"And you're the one who needs to talk to them, Ben," John said.

"Yeah," Ben replied, "I know."

*

Ben stayed in the Octagon while the others went to gather the employees. He closed his eyes and his mind drifted back thirty years. "Talk to your sister," his mother had cried back then. Ellen was in her room, packing a small suitcase. At age sixteen, she was leaving home. "California," she said, where she'd be far away from all the "bullshit".

"Sorry, Benji," Ellen said when she finally noticed him standing at her door. "I just don't know why I should stay."

Ben looked at his sister. She was a mess. She was pale and anorexic thin. A week before, she'd cut her black hair short and spiky. She was always cold and was sick nearly every week. Ben had tried to talk to her about her drug use and the scary friends she hung out with. He wanted to talk to her, tell her why she should stay. But the words didn't come so he stood there in her bedroom doorway, looking at his feet and said nothing.

An hour later, Ellen was gone and Ben's mother no longer talked to him like he was a man. He was supposed to have been the family's leader, and he had failed. He couldn't save his sister and he couldn't even find the right words to comfort his mother. He felt like a loser and swore he'd never let himself be in that position again.

Ben opened his eyes when the first people began to file into the conference room. As they came in, they all looked at him as Ellen had done thirty years before. His stomach roiled and his pulse quickened. They sat at the table, leaned against the brick walls, sat on the floor. Ben stood at the head of the conference room table. They were all there—John, Jay, Ginny, Lucy, Tom—all one hundred and forty employees of Jacob & Marin Advertising. When they had all gathered, he returned their stares. They were clearly afraid and needed him to reassure them. Ben stepped forward and tried to think of the words to say, but the words didn't come. There was a long, uncomfortable silence.

Then he met Jay's eyes and thought about his pregnant wife and the house they wanted to buy before the baby came. He remembered Janice Esteban talking excitedly about plans for a once-in-a-lifetime Mediterranean cruise over the winter holidays. He saw Rob Hansen, who was scraping by to pay for night school to get his MBA. He scanned the room and saw the people he was responsible for, worried about their jobs, their mortgages, their car loans, their dream vacations, their retirement savings, and college tuition for their kids. Then, his thinking came to a halt and he realized the words needed to come from his heart, not his head.

"I... uh," he began. He leaned forward, put his hands on the cool marble table and something rose from deep inside him. A calmness, like meditation, washed over him. Then he heard himself say, "I want to tell you all how proud I am of each and every one of you."

And then the words gushed from him without effort or thought. He talked about Tree and the great agency he had built and how each of them had contributed to its greatness in their own special way. He recalled successful campaigns the agency had created over the years and how delighted their clients were when the campaigns worked so well. He talked about Andrew and said no one should be angry with him because just like them, Andrew did what he thought was right. And he talked about Ginny and Jay and John and Tom and Lucy and how everyone had worked so hard to put together a great pitch for Katch.

He talked for a half hour and when he was done, several people had tears in their eyes. No one said anything for a long time. Then someone asked, "Do you think we'll keep the Katch account?"

Ben didn't answer right away. "Will we keep the account?" he repeated finally. He shrugged and smiled. "I don't know. I really don't. I only know one thing. This is the best campaign we've done since I've been here. Everything about it… it's terrific. We should all be proud of it. I know being proud of our work may not make our mortgage payments or save for our retirement, but doing great work gives us something we can carry with us forever. So, if we win the pitch or not, I'm confident each of us will be just fine."

People nodded in silent agreement and Ben knew he'd broken the panic. He'd given the employees of Jacob & Marin what they needed—no lies, no platitudes—just honest, straightforward talk.

As he stood in front of his friends and colleagues, he remembered what John had said a lifetime ago. *A leader has the courage to fight.* Ben had fought to save the agency and the employees had followed his lead and put together a great presentation.

Perhaps he'd found his essential truth.

"Yo, is anyone here?" came a voice from outside the conference room. The conference room door swung open and there stood Dirk wearing a gray sweatshirt, ripped blue jeans, flip-flops and carrying a large computer bag. "Oh, sorry man," he said when he saw the crowd inside, "I didn't know you guys were meeting."

"It's okay," Ben said. "Employees of Jacob and Marin, this is Dirk Anderson, the smartest computer guy I know. He's going to fix our computers so we can make our presentation."

"Epic." Dirk said as he raised his hand to the assembly. "You guys got any coffee?" Everyone laughed at Dirk's perfect caricature of a computer geek.

"I'll get you some," Janice Esteban said, heading for the door. "I assume you like it strong and black."

"You got it," Dirk replied with a smile.

"I need to get Dirk working on our computers," Ben said. "In the meantime, let's do everything we can for the presentation. Once we can get to our files, we can finish putting it together. Ginny, you take charge of coordinating everything. John is responsible for the creative." As Ben left with Dirk, the employees started to talk about what they needed to do for the presentation and Ben knew he'd done his job. If Dirk could get the computers fixed, they'd still be able to make the presentation before three-thirty.

*

Ten minutes later, Dirk was standing in the doorway of Ben's office. "Dude, you've got a problem." He stepped into Ben's office and shut the door behind him.

"What is it? When can we get the computer back up? We don't have much time."

"I can get the computers back up right away but . . ." Dirk shook his head, "all your files are gone."

"Excuse me?" Ben said.

"Ben, dude, you've lost everything."

Ben's breathing stopped. He felt like he was drowning. "I can't believe it. Everything is on our computers. Everything! It will be like we are starting from scratch. We have to present this afternoon!"

"Ben," Dirk said, "there's something else. When I upgraded your security system, I remembered how they hacked into Nan's computer. So, I used a new system I've been working on. And they got through it. There are fewer than five people in the world who know about this approach. Me, a guy in Silicon Valley, and a few guys in Russia. And they crashed your hard drive to cover it up, just like they did with Nan's computer. But I got 'em. This time, I had your computer hack them back while they were hacking you. They never knew, but now I know who it is. It's a computer belonging to Hanrahan Communications."

Ben jumped to his feet. "Sheldon Hanrahan. Sheldon Hanrahan has my presentation. He stole *my* presentation! That bastard!"

Dirk showed Ben a thumb drive. Here's the information you need. Make a copy and take it to the police," Dirk said. "Nail that son-of-a-bitch."

"I can't," Ben said, pacing. "If I do, he'll destroy my presentation, and I won't have time to rewrite it. I've got to get it back. I've got to make my presentation this afternoon. I've got to win the pitch!"

"Listen, Ben. You have to go to the police. Don't worry about my contract with Secure Digital. I think it's time I make up with those guys. I'll tell them about my new system and make a deal. You should go to the police."

Ben clenched his fists. "But Sheldon Hanrahan has my presentation. *My* presentation! If I go to the police, he'll destroy it! I'm not going to let him. I have to make the presentation this afternoon." Ben ran his hand through his hair. He saw the presentation in his mind—each word, each chart and graph, the strategies, the media plan, his essential truth. He was certain it was a winning presentation, only he didn't have it for the board of directors this afternoon.

"I don't know," Dirk said. "You're dealing with some pretty seri-ass dudes."

"I can't lose my presentation, Dirk. Don't you understand? I have to make that presentation! I can't fail this time. *I can't!*"

"Ben, chill out," Dirk said. "Don't go psycho, man."

Ben rubbed his temples. Then he dropped his hands. "Give me that thumb drive," he said. "I need to make a call."

Dirk handed the drive to Ben.

"You said you can get our computers back up?" Ben asked.

"Your computer should be working now. It just won't connect to the network yet. I can get the network back up in fifteen minutes."

"Anything you need—anything—just let me know. I have to make this call now."

Dirk opened the door to leave. "Ben, you sure you're okay?"

"Close the door behind you," Ben said.

Dirk left and Ben plugged the thumb drive into his computer.

Then, he picked up his phone and dialed the number for Hanrahan Communications.

FORTY-TWO

"MR. HANRAHAN, how did the presentation go at Katch?" asked Barbara as Sheldon stepped through the glass doors of Hanrahan Communications.

"Very well," Sheldon said from behind his dark glasses. "I'm sure we made a good impression on the board." Barbara followed as Sheldon went into his office.

"That's wonderful," the gray-haired woman said. "I'm sorry to intercept you like this, sir, but someone has been calling for the past forty minutes insisting he talk with you. In fact, he's holding on the line right now. I told him you were out but he said you would want to talk to him as soon as you got back. He said you have something of his and he has something you will want."

"Who is it?" Sheldon asked as he walked through the double doors into his steel and glass office.

"A Mr. Ben Smith."

Sheldon took off his suit coat, loosened his tie. Ben Smith. He thought this might happen.

"Sir?" Barbara inquired. "What shall I tell him? As I said, he's holding on the line."

"Tell him I don't want to talk to him and that he should not call back. We have no reason to talk."

"Yes, Mr. Hanrahan. Although, he said I should give you some numbers if you refused."

"Numbers? What numbers?" Sheldon settled in behind his desk.

"Well, sir, I wrote them down." Barbara lifted her reading glasses to her eyes and read off a piece of paper. "They are 2422323441. That's it, sir, ten numbers." She let her glasses drop and waited for Sheldon's response. "Shall I repeat them, sir?"

"No," Sheldon said. "I'll take the call. Close the door on your way out."

Barbara went back to her desk and put the call through. Sheldon answered on his speakerphone. "This is Sheldon Hanrahan."

"And this is Ben Smith," came Ben's voice over the speakerphone. "You have my presentation."

"Your presentation?"

"Yes, my presentation for Katch." Ben's tone was even. "You have it and I want it back."

"I see." Sheldon rose from his chair and strolled around his desk. He took a stack of documents off his desk and thumbed through them as he spoke to the speakerphone. "What makes you think I have your presentation?"

"You took my call," Ben said. "That's how I know."

"Oh?"

"You wouldn't take a call from me unless you had a reason to. The reason you took my call is because your secretary told you the numbers I gave her."

Sheldon smiled. He had to admit, not just anyone could outwit Sheldon Hanrahan.

"The numbers," Ben's voice continued from the speakerphone, "24, dot 223 dot 234 dot 41, is the Internet address of the computer that hacked into J&M's server this morning. Obviously, you recognized the numbers or you wouldn't have taken my call. I know it's your computer, Mr. Hanrahan. You also set me up with Elizabeth Kelly in the Midwest Bank atrium. I know it was you. That didn't work, and this won't work either."

"Really, why would I go to such extremes?"

"Because you cheat, Sheldon. You think you're above the law so you cheat, no matter who gets hurt, including, by the way, Andrew Birk."

"You think I cheat?" Sheldon replied. "Maybe I'm just destined to win."

"I don't want to talk about it," Ben said. "I want my presentation back. I intend to make it this afternoon. I intend to beat you fare and square."

"I'm sorry to hear you lost your presentation, Ben." Sheldon laid the papers back on his desk. "Assuming I have it, you said you have something I might want in exchange. What is it?"

"I'll give you the information that proves you hacked into our computers. It will ruin you. I have it on a thumb drive."

"You do?" asked Sheldon.

"Yes I do," Ben said. "You give me my files, I give you this drive and I won't go to the police. I make my presentation and we compete on equal footing. Best man wins."

"I see." Sheldon sat at his desk and crossed his arms across his chest. "Best man wins? I'll tell you what, Ben. I'm curious to hear your point of view about who should win and who should lose. Let's meet. Perhaps this afternoon? In the meantime, I'll see if we have your presentation. If we do, I'll be sure to bring it. When shall we meet?"

"Right away. It's 12:15 and I need time to print everything out."

"I'm afraid I can't meet just now, Ben," Sheldon said evenly. "How about if we meet in an hour?"

"You bastard. You know I need to present to Katch this afternoon."

"One-thirty, Ben. Or not at all," Sheldon glared at the speakerphone.

The line was silent. Finally, Ben said, "Okay. Let's meet somewhere with people around. I don't trust you. How about Sadie's?"

"I have a better idea," Sheldon said. "Let's meet at the baseball game. The Twins have a noon game. Section 129 is a good place. Meet me there."

"You want to meet at Target Field?"

"Yes. Section 129. The Home Run Porch. It's a perfect place to discuss winners and losers."

"Fine," Ben said. "Bring my files—all of them—or I'll give this thumb drive to the police. And don't be late."

"I'll see you at one-thirty, Mr. Smith." Sheldon pressed the speakerphone button to hang up. He picked up his private phone and dialed a number. A voice answered.

"Victor," Sheldon said, "We have a problem."

FORTY-THREE

"JACKSON," WEST SAID from inside his office. Jackson wasn't listening. He was obsessing about the Trevor Marin case again because the Shauna Tate case was finally over. Jackson had found Chill, the leader of the Family Mob, in an abandoned warehouse in Saint Paul and had thrown him in the high security section of Hennepin County lockup. The police had him cold on murder-for-hire. He was facing a life sentence without parole and the news media and even Reverend Terrance White were praising the police for quickly settling a very difficult case. Now all he had to do was the paperwork.

Jackson worked slowly, carefully typing the reports into his computer one finger at a time. But his mind kept drifting to the Marin case. The unanswered questions still needled him. There were too many loose ends and Jackson needed answers before he'd let it go.

"Jackson!" West repeated.

"Yeah?" Jackson answered without looking up from his keyboard.

West's large head leaned out of his office door. "Jackson, dammit, get in here. I have something for you."

"Gimme a minute."

"Okay, fine. I'll just send Trevor Marin's prints back to the Department of Defense." West's head disappeared behind the door.

Jackson pushed away from his desk. "You got 'em already? You got Marin's fingerprints?" he asked as he went into West's office. West was sitting at his desk wearing a toothy grin.

"Yeah, I told you I know some people over there." West handed Jackson a CD. It had a navy-blue DOD emblem on the jewel case.

"Happy?" West asked.

Jackson examined the CD. "Yeah, thanks, man. I gotta get these to the lab right away."

"Whoa, whoa, whoa," West said, raising a beefy hand. "You gotta learn to be more discreet. Trevor Marin's case has been closed for a week. Don't let people know you're on one of your damn crusades or they'll wonder what it's about. And Jackson," West said with a stare, "if these prints don't match what we took off the corpse, you come to me before you do anything. Clear?"

"Gottcha, Lieu. Randy in the lab owes me one so I'll just ask him for a favor. Anyway, I got some juice around here now, if you haven't noticed."

"Yeah, well, juice dries up fast, wise guy." West said. "Once you get the paperwork done on the Shauna Tate case, you'll be mine again and you'll be just another detective on my squad."

Jackson laughed. "Man, you don't let a brother have even one day of glory."

West smiled. "No, that's not true. You can have today. Just don't screw up the paperwork."

"Gosh, thanks." Jackson turned to go back to his desk.

"Hey Darren," West said, serious again, "we're all proud of you for what you did on the Shauna Tate case. It was top-notch detective work."

"Thanks, Lieu," Darren said with a nod. "And thanks for these prints. I'll let you know what I find out."

*

Before heading off to lunch, Jackson dropped off the prints with Randy in the forensics lab and asked him to compare them with Trevor Marin's fingerprints from the case file. Randy asked for a case number but Jackson told him the case was closed and asked if Randy would do it for him as a favor. Randy said he had some other work to finish first, but if Jackson came back in an hour and a half, he'd have the comparison done. Jackson agreed and went to the Red Wagon for lunch.

Jackson ordered his steak rare and smothered with fried onions. It was delicious. He'd been grabbing fast food since they'd assigned him to the Shauna Tate case, so he savored his meal while he read the entire *Times*. The front-page story was about Shauna Tate again and the story noted Jackson as one of the important figures in solving the case.

Jackson ate the last bite of his steak and wiped his chin with a napkin. He paid his bill on the way out. At the police station, he took the stairs to the third floor forensics lab. Randy was at his desk surrounded by two large computer monitors. A giant of a man at six feet eleven inches tall, Randy had a short ponytail, thick glasses and a loose green shirt and jeans. He was inspecting a computer screen as Jackson approached.

"Hey Randy," Jackson said. "Did you run the prints?"

Randy turned to face Jackson. "Yep. They're here on the monitor."

"And?"

"See for yourself." Randy pointed a long finger at a monitor. Two sets of prints were side-by-side on one of Randy's screens. Randy rolled the mouse and the prints moved together. They matched perfectly. "As you can see," Randy said, "the prints from the DOD match the prints off the corpse."

"They match? Are you sure?"

"Yep. A perfect ten-point match."

"Yeah, I guess they do." Jackson felt a tinge of disappointment. "Thanks. I owe you one."

"One thing," Randy said as he took the CD out of the computer and examined it. "Where'd you get these prints?"

"From the DOD. Why?"

"I know you got them from the DOD,. Says it right here on the case. What I mean is who'd you get them from at the DOD?"

"I dunno. West got 'em from someone he knows there. Why?"

"Nothing, I guess." Randy unfolded his long legs and stretched them in front of him. "It's just that the computer program the DOD uses isn't the same as what's on this CD. I usually have to convert their files to our system. I didn't have to this time."

"I see," Jackson said. "Does that happen often?"

"First time it's ever happened. It's no big deal. I was just curious. Anyway, the answer to your question is the prints match." Randy slid the CD into its case and handed it to Jackson.

"Thanks, Randy," Jackson said.

*

Jackson took the stairs back down to homicide. West wasn't in his office so he laid the CD on his chair. He wondered if he should tell West about what Randy had said about the file type. But as he sat at his desk to finish filling out the paperwork on the Shauna Tate case, he decided not to. He knew his obsessions were annoying, and West had already bent over backward. He'd even broken the rules to help him.

Maybe it was time to let the Trevor Marin case go.

FORTY-FOUR

"Where are you going?" John asked as Ben marched past him toward the elevators.

"I'm going to get my presentation back," Ben replied without changing his focus.

John hurried to follow Ben. "Where? How?"

"I'm going to get it back from that son-of-a-bitch Sheldon Hanrahan." Ben arrived at the elevator and punched the down button.

"Wait, Ben," John said. "Don't do it."

"I'm not going to let him ruin everything. We're going to make that presentation this afternoon." A ding announced the elevator's arrival and the doors opened. Ben stepped in. He was barely aware that John stood in front of him.

"Ben, don't," John implored.

Ben punched the elevator button for the first floor. "I'm not going to fail. Not this time. We're going to win the pitch."

The elevator doors closed and took him to the first floor without stopping. He hurried through the building lobby, into the street, and headed to Target Field.

*

When Ben arrived at the Twins stadium, he bought a ticket and pushed through the turnstile. He'd taken off his tie at the office and looked like just another businessman playing hooky to catch the last half of the game. Inside his suit coat pocket, he carried the thumb drive Dirk had given him.

Ben walked through the concourse to section 129 in left field. Sometimes, when work was slow, he'd meet a friend at an afternoon game and sit in the porch's first few rows. It was a great place to watch a game because sluggers often dropped home runs right there. Today, however, the crowd was large for an afternoon game and there were no seats in the first five rows which were filled with fans dressed in Twins jerseys and hats.

Ben decided he should be far enough away from the crowd so he'd have some privacy with Sheldon but near enough to people in case he tried anything. Just what Sheldon would try, Ben didn't know. As he slipped into an empty area in row ten, he wondered what he'd expected when he agreed to meet Sheldon here. He knew Sheldon had stolen his presentation—the evidence was inside his coat pocket. But as he sat waiting, he wondered if Sheldon would bring his files.

Perhaps, Ben thought, he was making a mistake and should go to the police like Dirk had told him to. Sheldon was a large man—Ben had heard he was a tight end for Harvard. And there was no guarantee Sheldon would come alone. But if Ben went to the police, Sheldon would surely destroy his presentation and it would take days to redo.

As Ben waited, the game was already in the eighth inning with no score. It was a pitcher's duel. The White Sox had been in first place since opening day. However, for the past month, the Twins had started to rally and the Sox faded. On the radio driving to work, Ben had heard that the Twins, who had won the series' first two games, would take the division lead from the Sox with a win today.

Normally, this would be a series Ben would have watched closely. But for the past ten days, the Katch pitch had consumed him and he didn't care about the Twins. He only cared about getting his files back from Sheldon. So, as the crowd cheered, Ben sat and waited. The crowd gasped. In the stadium's bright, vast openness, Ben watched the Twins centerfielder make a leaping catch to steal a double from a

White Sox slugger ending the top half of the eighth inning. The crowd roared and clapped their hands as the organ egged them on. Ben stayed seated.

He looked around. No Sheldon. Maybe the instructions weren't clear. Maybe Sheldon was waiting for Ben in a different section. Ben was sure Sheldon had said section 129. He scanned the sections around him to see if Sheldon was waiting. He didn't see him.

The first Twins batter in the bottom half of the eighth inning dug in at home plate and the fans settled into their seats. Ben checked his watch. It was 2:10. He had less than ninety minutes to get the files back from Sheldon, run back to the agency and print everything out to present to the Katch board. It'd be barely enough time.

The crowd moaned. The first Twin's batter struck out, then the next one did too. The last batter hit a weak fly ball to the center fielder and the White Sox players trotted off the field. The organ played again while the Twins players warmed up in the field and the first Sox batter came to the plate to start the ninth inning. On the first pitch, the batter hit the ball to the gap in right field and ended up safe on second base. Ben watched half-heartedly as the Twins quickly gave up two runs before the Sox half of the inning was over with the Sox leading 2–0.

Ben checked his watch again. It was 2:25. He looked around again but didn't see Sheldon. What if he didn't show up at all? What if he was using this time to cover his tracks by dumping the incriminating computer and destroying the J&M files while Ben was wasting time at Target Field? But what choice did he have? If he didn't get the files back, he couldn't make the presentation and J&M would lose the Katch account.

The first Twins batter in the bottom half of the ninth inning dug in at home plate, took ball one. On the next pitch, he swung weakly at the Sox' closer's fastball and hit a dribbler to first base. One out. The crowd moaned and went quiet. A few people started to leave.

"Too bad," came a voice came from behind Ben, "The Twins

need this game."

Ben jerked around to see Sheldon sitting one row above him off of his right shoulder. He wore the same dark-tinted glasses as when Ben saw him at Tree's funeral.

"I want my presentation back," Ben demanded. "Do you have it?"

"Don't be in such a hurry, Ben," Sheldon said, looking out at the field. "Let's enjoy the game. Baseball is the most elegant sport. The symmetry is breathtaking. Anyway, I thought we were going to talk first. Over the phone, you were saying something about winners and losers." Sheldon crossed his legs and folded his arms across his chest.

"I don't have time to talk. I want my files back."

"Well *I* want to talk," Sheldon said. "By the way, meet my friend Victor. He's the man who just took the seat to your left."

Ben swung around and next to him was a huge, muscular man wearing a black leather jacket. He had short blonde hair, bushy eyebrows and his steel-blue eyes were as cold as Siberia in January. Ben stiffened and pressed his arm against the coat pocket that held the thumb drive.

"So, you think I'm a cheat," Sheldon said over Ben's right shoulder.

"I don't want any trouble," Ben said, still looking at Victor. "I just want my files back."

"You already said that. Don't worry about Victor. Tell me what you meant when you called me a cheat."

"You win because you don't play by the rules." Ben turned back over his right shoulder to address Sheldon. "As a matter of fact, you broke the law when you hacked into our computers and stole my presentation. And when you set me up for aggravated sexual assault with Elizabeth Kelly, too."

Sheldon didn't seem to hear Ben. He pointed out at the field. "Do you realize that in one hundred and thirty years of baseball, the velocity infielders throw the ball and the speed of base runners increased at precisely the same rate? It's the same with pitching and hitting. Pitchers throw much harder today, but hitters swing faster, too. Batting averages and home run rates have been relatively constant over the decades." Sheldon shook his head. "It's remarkable," he said.

The crowd moaned again. Apparently, a Twins batter had made the second out. A few more people began to leave the stadium.

Sheldon looked down at Ben. "Oh, I'm sorry. We were talking about rules. You accused me of cheating. So Mr. Smith, do you believe rules and laws are absolute?"

"I can't talk, Mr. Hanrahan. I don't have time."

"Answer my question," Sheldon said. "Do the rules apply equally to everybody?"

"Yes, of course they do," Ben answered. Apparently, he wasn't going to get his files back until he talked with Sheldon.

"So a rich, intelligent criminal is just as likely to be convicted of a crime as a poor, stupid one?"

"No, probably not, but they should be."

"But I didn't ask you if the laws *should be* absolute," Sheldon said. "I asked you if they *were* and you just agreed they are not. Rules are subjective and applied inconsistently. Even baseball has no firm rules. The all-star hitter gets a smaller strike zone and more pitches to hit than a rookie. The rules aren't the same for everyone in anything, Ben, not even baseball."

Ben looked out at the field. The crowd cheered and he saw a Twins batter slide safe into second base.

"Okay," Ben said, annoyed. He barely had enough time to make the presentation, even if Sheldon gave him his files right now. "I stand corrected. Whatever you say. Now can I have my files?"

"Did you ever wonder why the rich, intelligent criminal gets off and the famous hitter gets more balls to hit?" Sheldon asked. "Do you know why the rules are applied differently, Ben?"

"I suppose you'll tell me."

Sheldon leaned forward with his elbows on his knees. He was inches from Ben's ear. "It's because there's a higher principle in

267

force," he said. "You think we're a society based on laws, but we aren't. At the core of our being, we know the strong must survive. We must allow the successful businessman or the big homerun hitter to survive and even thrive in spite of the rules. We don't enforce the rules for them, for the survival and advancement of our entire species."

Ben didn't answer. The crowd was getting more animated and loud. They stood, stomped their feet and cheered with each pitch. People were no longer leaving. Two Twins runners were now on base. Normally, he'd be excited too but, now, all he wanted was to get his presentation and get away from the large man next to him.

"If I break your rules, Ben," Sheldon said, "it's because I learned a lesson a long time ago that rules designed to make life fair, are meaningless. The only important thing is that the strong survive. I understand this principle and that's why I win. You believe in rules and that's why you lose."

"I think I understand your theory," Ben replied, turning back to face Sheldon. "The strong and intelligent must survive. And the good-looking, too, right?"

Sheldon leaned back. "Appearance means nothing," he said speaking over the crowd noise.

"Really?" Ben said. "Looks mean nothing? So if that's true, why do you wear those glasses? Did you make the presentation to Katch this morning with them on or off?"

Sheldon glowered at Ben through his glasses. "Too bad, Ben. I thought you'd understand. But you and Tree and Everet and Louise—you're all wrong. Fine. Wallow in your delusion of fairness. In the meantime, I'll continue to play my game and win. So, do you have the thumb drive?"

"Yes," Ben answered.

"I assume it's the only copy?"

Ben froze. It *was* the only copy. He'd forgotten to make a copy of the files on the thumb drive as Dirk had said. The large man on his left could take the only leverage he had and Ben would not get his presentation files back. Ben had let his emotions get the best of him. Maybe Sheldon was right. Maybe the strong were the only ones who should survive. The fans stamped their feet and cheered.

Sheldon continued, shouting now over the crowd. "I can tell by your hesitation you have the only copy. Give it to me now."

"Give me my files first," Ben said.

"Sorry, Ben," Sheldon said. "I don't have your files. But, I want your thumb drive. Don't make me ask Victor to take it from you."

The large man wrapped a vice-like hand around Ben's arm. Suddenly, the crowd let out a huge roar. Victor tightened his grip on Ben's arm as both men looked out at the field. The Sox left fielder was racing back to the warning track and Ben saw a baseball spinning toward them. Victor must have seen it too, because he let go of Ben's arm. For a split second, Ben thought the baseball would fly over their heads, but as it cleared the outfield wall, it headed right for Victor. At the last second, Victor dove to his left and the baseball crashed into his seat. The ball ricocheted off the seat and over Ben's right shoulder.

Ben heard Sheldon grunt. He turned and saw that the ball had knocked Sheldon's glasses off. Ben looked directly into Sheldon's uncovered eyes. His left eye was bugged out and there were no upper or lower lids. Wrinkly, white scar tissue surrounded his eye like something from a bad horror movie. Sheldon's ghastly eye glowered hatefully at Ben.

"I'm sorry for you, Sheldon," Ben said, "but you can go to hell." And then he ran.

Behind him, he heard Sheldon shout, "Victor, don't let him get away."

FORTY-FIVE

BEN SPRINTED ACROSS the row but fans scrambling to fetch the winning homerun ball kept getting in his way. He dodged them as best as he could and soon was climbing the stairs leading to the concourse and the stadium exits. The stairs were filling with fans cheering and exchanging high-fives for the now first-place Twins. Ben glanced back and saw Victor had pushed past the fans and was climbing the stairs after him. He moved quicker than Ben had thought possible for such a big man.

Ben took the stairs two at a time, moving from side to side to avoid running into people. He pushed past a couple with a young child, almost knocking the woman down. The man shouted, "Hey, buddy, watch it!" He was more than halfway to the concourse now with only a few more people in his way.

He glanced back again. The big man was only a few strides below him and Ben saw he'd be caught before he reached the concourse. He took three more strides and felt a hand at his leg. He pulled his leg free, turned right and sprinted across an empty row of seats in section 128. The maneuver bought him some distance from Victor and, on the flat row, he was faster than the big man. He reached the next set of steps and pumped his legs, taking the steps three at a time now. He was only a few strides from the concourse but Victor was behind him again and gaining on him again.

Ben's heart was pounding. The stadium's bright lights were a blur;

the noise of the crowd was cacophonous. He got to the top of the stairs with Victor right behind him. He burst into the concourse jammed with fans chanting, "We're number one! We're number one!" Ben faked to his right, and then shot to his left back toward the exit. Apparently, Victor went for his fake because he heard a woman scream and a jostling of people as Victor crashed into them. He heard people shouting and a ruckus begin. He turned and saw that a scrum of half-drunk fans surrounded Victor and was yelling at him for knocking down the woman. Victor kept his eyes focused on Ben, but the angry fans were giving Ben the time he needed to get away.

Ben pushed through the crowd but saw there was a logjam at the exit. He went up another set of stairs to the level with box suites. Here, the crowd was thin. He glanced over his shoulder and didn't see Victor.

He turned to run down the concourse but stopped in his tracks. Standing in front of him was Sheldon wearing his glasses again. Before Ben could react, Sheldon grabbed his arm and pushed him through an open door of a private suite. Ben stumbled in and almost fell to the floor.

The suite was unoccupied and smelled like stale beer. In front of a large window were ten seats facing the field and in the back, where Ben stood gathering himself, was a small, messy kitchen area with two bar tables and stools. The door where Sheldon stood was the only escape.

Sheldon leaned out the door. "Victor, in here," he shouted.

A few seconds later, Victor followed Sheldon into the suite. Both men stood three feet in front of Ben. "The thumb drive," Sheldon said, his hand out, "give it to me."

Ben clenched his jaw. "I already told you," he said, "go to hell."

"Don't be a fool, Ben. You don't want Victor to take it from you."

"Victor," Ben said eyeing the big man. "A Russian. Lotta computer hackers in Russia."

Sheldon slowly shook his head. "Okay, Mr. Smith, I'm done talking. We'll do it your way. Victor?"

Victor took a step toward Ben. Ben's heart raced and his muscles tightened. He knew it'd be suicide to fight this brute, but he'd fought so hard during the past few weeks to save the Katch account and everything that went with it. And by fighting, he had brought himself to the edge of victory. Now, even though he wouldn't get his files back and wouldn't make the presentation to Katch, he'd continue to fight. What was it that John had said? *A leader is someone with the courage to fight*

Instinctively, he brought his fists to his chin and turned his shoulder toward Victor like a boxer. Victor stopped his advance, smiled, then laughed. "Okay!" he said. "We fight." The large man positioned himself to attack.

"Ben, don't be a fool," Sheldon said.

Ben's mind raced with what Victor would do first and how he, Ben, should react. But he wasn't a fighter and had no clue what to do. He couldn't breathe and his arms felt heavy. His eyes weren't focusing. Still, he held his position.

"I suggest you leave him alone, Sheldon," came a voice from the door of the suite. Ben glanced at the doorway and saw a mustached man standing there. He quickly looked back at Victor who stayed ready to attack.

Ben looked at the man in the doorway again. He was dressed in an expensive gray suit and two other men flanked him. Slowly, he realized it was Leland Carmichael. On his right was Martin Mithun and on his left was a man even larger than Victor wearing a tight fitting polo shirt.

Leland Carmichael stepped forward and the other two men followed. "Sheldon, there are witnesses." Carmichael's thin, gray mustache stiffened.

Sheldon turned and addressed the attorney. "Ah, Lee Carmichael. Perhaps you should think about what you're doing. You've stayed neutral all these years like a good attorney should. Do you really want to take sides now?"

"Indeed, Sheldon," Lee said. "I've thought about that question a lot. Right now, I'm here for my client, Mr. Smith. Call off your muscle."

The large man next to Leland Carmichael advanced toward Victor. Victor turned toward him and both men sized each other up for several seconds. Then Victor looked at Sheldon.

Sheldon thrust his chin out and held it a moment. "Lee, Lee, Lee," he said. "I'm disappointed in you. Okay, you have this one. Victor and I will leave. But it isn't over." Victor glared at the big man in the polo shirt and grinned maliciously as he walked to the door with Sheldon following.

As Sheldon walked past Lee Carmichael, he said under his breath, "Be careful, Lee." Sheldon and Victor pushed through the suite door and disappeared into the concourse.

Leland Carmichael turned to Ben. "You can drop your fists now," he said. "They're gone."

Ben stood for a moment, trying to comprehend what'd just happened. He realized he still held his fists by his chin. He dropped his hands and stared blankly at each person in the room.

"You'll be fine," Lee Carmichael said. "Apparently, we got here just in time."

Ben began to gather himself. "How'd you know I was here?"

The attorney unbuttoned his suit coat and pulled up a bar stool. The large man in the polo shirt went to the door and locked it. Martin Mithun stood next to Leland Carmichael and watched Ben closely. "John Turner called me when you left the agency. He told us you were meeting Sheldon Hanrahan, so we followed Mr. Hanrahan from his office to here. We saw everything. We thought we'd lost you for a moment, but we found you in here, ready to fight a man twice your size." Leland Carmichael let out a small chuckle. "I do believe you would have given him a tussle! By the way, what was Sheldon after?"

Ben reached into his pocket and retrieved the thumb drive. "This," he said. "It's data that proves he hacked into our computers and probably into my wife's computer at home. A friend of mine got it for me."

"Dirk Anderson," Martin Mithun said without taking his eyes off of Ben. "I'm sure the information is reliable."

"I better take it," Leland said.

Ben handed him the thumb drive. "I probably should have turned it over to the police."

"Or to me," Leland Carmichael said, firmly. Then he flipped the thumb drive over in his hand and handed it to Martin Mithun. "I won't turn it over to the police right away, though. I believe Mr. Scheck at the newspaper will be able to do more with it. This could help expose Mr. Hanrahan. Then again, he's very good at slipping through the cracks."

"What was Sheldon saying about you taking sides?" Ben asked.

"It's a long story Ben," Lee said. "You don't have time for it. You need to get to Katch."

Ben checked his watch. It was 3:05. "It's too late. We have to be at Katch by 3:30, and I don't have a presentation. Sheldon stole all our files. That's what I was trying to do—get them back."

"I guarantee he destroyed everything as soon as you tipped him off. He'd never have given you anything."

Ben shrugged. "Yeah, you're probably right. But I had to try. Now I don't know how we'll keep the Katch account."

"I know how," said Leland Carmichael. Lee held a hand out to Martin Mithun. Martin pulled a cell phone from his pocket, punched in some numbers, and handed it to Leland Carmichael. The attorney pressed the phone to his ear and after a few seconds said, "Hello, it's Lee. I have him right here. We're at Target Field... Yes, he's just fine... You said you wanted to talk to him as soon as we got him... Okay. Here he is."

Lee handed the phone to Ben. "Hello?" he said.

"Ben? Are you all right?" a voice said at the other end of the line.

"John?"

"Yeah," John Turner replied. "I'm glad Lee found you. You have to get to Katch as soon as possible. We're ready to do the presentation. I'll meet you there with everything."

Ben pulled himself over to a barstool and sat heavily. He pressed the phone into his ear. "You got the files back?"

"No, we didn't," John said.

"Then how can we make the presentation? You said you have everything."

"We do!" John said. "You see, Ben, after you talked to the employees, the entire agency pulled together and redid the presentation. All one hundred-and-forty people. Everyone chipped in—Ginny, Jay, Lucy, Tom, all the secretaries, the media people, the entire creative staff. Hell, even Jeff Novak and the accounting department helped. Everyone. I've never seen anything like it."

Ben ran a hand through his hair. "How is it possible?"

"It was you, Ben!" John answered. "Don't you understand? It was what you said in the Octagon. It was because everyone has been watching you work your butt off for the past week and a half. It was your leadership, Ben, plain and simple. You inspired all of us, so for the past two hours while you've been running around trying to get the files back, we've been rewriting the presentation. And I mean every single page of it. I gotta tell ya, it's just as good as it was before, maybe even better."

Ben was dumbstruck. "I can't believe it."

"Well it's true," John said. "You have to get to Katch. I'll bring your tie. We're heading out now. See you soon."

Ben handed the phone to Leland Carmichael and the attorney handed the phone to Martin Mithun. He placed a hand on Ben's shoulder. "I guess you'll be able to make your presentation after all, Ben. I can give you a ride to Katch. Are you ready?"

Ben slowly nodded, then smiled. "Yeah. I'm ready," he said.

"Let's go."

FORTY-SIX

BEN SMITH STOOD in the lobby waiting for the elevator to take him to the Jacob & Marin advertising agency. He pushed the 'up' button a second time, but the elevator didn't come. He smiled and shook his head. Today it didn't bother him when the elevator didn't come right away. It would arrive when it was programmed to, and he'd be just fine with it.

Ben had wanted to get to work early because over the weekend, Ken Swanson, the new director of marketing for Katch, informed him they needed an IRA campaign fast. The request from Ken came through an e-mail sent the day before—Sunday of all days—that Ben had read when he checked his e-mail from home.

IRA sales dropped 12 percent over the third quarter, the e-mail had said. *We can't allow this to continue. We need a new campaign that will reverse the fall ASAP. We're confident J&M can get us the campaign we need.*

They're confident we can get them the campaign they need? Of course, we can thought Ben.

Finally, the elevator came and took Ben to the eighth floor. When he stepped into J&M's lobby, he was thankful he had a job he loved so much. A few months earlier, he wasn't sure he'd have a job. And, he didn't realize then how much he truly loved what he did. He was good at it—he knew that now. It was what he was meant to do. He couldn't imagine doing anything else.

"Morning, Julie," Ben said as he walked into the lobby.

"Good morning, Mr. Smith," Julie replied from behind the reception desk.

"I'll never get used to you calling me Mr. Smith," Ben said. "Are you sure you can't call me Ben like you used to?"

"Oh, no. It just wouldn't be right," Julie said with a pleasant smile. "By the way, John Turner is looking for you. He wants to talk to you first thing." She handed him a pink message slip. "Oh and I made lunch reservations at Manny's for you and Mrs. Smith as you requested."

"Thanks, Julie. You're the best." Julie beamed as she turned her attention to her computer screen.

As Ben walked among the timber beams and the exposed yellow brick to his office, the Jacob & Marin Advertising Agency was beginning its day. Employees talked on phones or typed on keyboards as they stared into computer screens. Some packed briefcases for client meetings. Others leaned against cubicle walls talking casually over the dividers. They had all been able to keep their jobs, thanks to Ben.

After the ordeal in Target Field, Ben had given the most inspired presentation of his career to the Katch board of directors. Of course, the strategies and plans were bulletproof and the campaigns were brilliant. But it was Ben who'd made the presentation magical. He was pumped with adrenalin and the confidence that came from knowing he'd inspired the entire agency to do this great work. He had filled the Katch boardroom with that confidence and the board was infected by it.

At the end, Everet Katch gave Ben a nod and Ben knew he'd met his challenge. "You need to give us something that impresses nine board members," Everet had said. And Ben had done just that.

After the presentation, Everet had called to inform Ben that the vote by the board of directors was seven to two and J&M had won the pitch. When Ben announced the win in an agency-wide meeting the next morning, everyone cheered. They hugged, gave each other high-fives and more than a few people openly wept.

They had done it and the fruit of their effort was now the thriving advertising agency he was walking through. Ben swelled with pride looking at these people, his friends and colleagues who were running a great agency.

Before Ben got to his office, Jay Stone intercepted him. "Boss, good thing you're here. You must have driven."

"Nope," Ben said. "I still take the bus, Jay. Every day. It was just on time for once."

"Yeah, well, we got a call from Jim Ross at Bug BeGone. He says we messed up the URL on the cockroach ad for *Better Homes and Gardens*."

"What?" Ben moved toward his office.

"That's what he said. He checked November's advanced copy and the URL was wrong. He's really pissed off. The ad was supposed to drive people to the Web where they could print off a coupon. If the URL is wrong, they won't be able to."

Ben stopped in front of his office and turned to face Jay. He put his hand on Jay's shoulder. "That's a big problem, Jay. It's a problem I'm confident you can handle."

"But . . ."

"Jay, Bug BeGone is your account now. You need to talk to Lucy to see if we can get the magazine to change the URL before they're printed. If not, you'll have to work out a plan to correct the mistake. You'll need to make Jim Ross happy again. You can do it."

"Yeah, I know," Jay said. "Sorry. I'm still not used to being in charge."

"If you need my help, let me know."

"Nah, I can do it," Jay said with a wave of his hand.

"So," Ben said before Jay left, "when do you close on the new house?"

Jay smiled. "Wednesday afternoon. I can't wait. The baby is due in a month."

"Congratulations. I'm happy for you."

"Thanks, Ben," Jay said, sincerely. "Thanks for everything."

"You're welcome," Ben said. "Just get the Bug BeGone mess cleaned up."

"Yeah, I will. Gotta see Lucy." Jay said as he scurried away.

Ben turned into his office and snapped on the lights. He took one step in and stopped. He still wasn't used to it. The corner office. The president's office. It had been Tree's office but now, it was his. He took off his overcoat and hung it on the coat rack behind the door. He went to the mahogany desk and sat in the oversized chair. He gazed out the windows at the Minneapolis skyline. Two months earlier, he would've laughed if someone had told him he would sit at this desk. Back then, he didn't believe he was qualified. He wasn't even sure he wanted the position. But here he was, president of the Jacob & Marin Advertising Agency.

There was a knock on the door and John Turner stepped in. He was wearing his gray tweed sports jacket. "Good morning!" John said.

"John!" Ben said. "How's J&M's creative director this morning?"

"I'm great, thanks. You?"

Ben looked around his office and said, "I just can't get used to being in this office."

John grinned. He settled into a black chair in front of Ben's desk. "Well, Mr. President, I read the e-mail you forwarded from Katch. Apparently, we have some work to do on IRAs."

"Yeah, we do," Ben replied, "and I'm out for the next few days, remember."

"That's right. France with Everet Katch."

"I still don't know why Everet wants me to go to France with him," Ben said.

"I thought it was so you could help with the plans for the expansion into Europe?" John asked crossing his legs.

"That's what he said," Ben answered. "But we don't do international advertising. I don't think I'll be much help."

"You'll have an interesting trip, I'm sure. When do you leave?"

"Tonight at eight. We're taking the Katch private jet. We land in Paris tomorrow morning. I'll be back Wednesday night."

"Ginny and I can get started on the IRA campaign while you're gone," John said. "Do you want Tom involved?"

Ben thought for a moment. "I think it's best if we keep him on new business. He's done well lately. Two new accounts in two months. Not bad."

"He took it hard when you put Ginny in charge of account handling."

"I know," Ben said with a nod. "But he'll do fine at new business as long as we keep him focused."

John smiled and there was a glimmer in his eye. "Ben, what did I tell you? You're doing great as the president of the Jacob & Marin advertising agency."

"Thanks to you," Ben said.

John waved a hand. "Nah. You did the work. And anyway, it was already in you." John stood to leave. "I gotta start on the IRA campaign. Have a good trip. We'll see you when you get back."

It was already in me, Ben thought. *Yeah, I guess it was.* He wasn't ready for it when his father died. Who would be at age fourteen? And then when Ellen left home, he thought he'd failed. This time, however, it had turned out differently.

He ran his hand over the smooth mahogany desk and stared out the window again. In two weeks of hard work and strife, who he thought he was had changed. He was ready now—leading people was what he was born to do. President of J&M? Leader of one hundred and forty smart and talented people?

He humbly and graciously accepted it.

FORTY-SEVEN

BEN SIPPED A Diet Coke at a table in a quiet corner at Manny's Steakhouse while waiting for Nan. She was almost always on time, but the senate campaign was in its last months, and she was busy.

Ben gladly waited for her. She had supported him his entire career. Now it was her turn to shine and he'd do anything for her. She deserved it.

Finally, Ben saw her at the maitre d' station. She wore a brown leather overcoat and matching calf-high boots. She had a matching leather and fur-lined hat and her silky blonde hair fell gracefully to her neck. Ben couldn't take his eyes off her while the maitre d' escorted her to his table.

"My God, you're beautiful," Ben said as she took off her hat and shook out her hair.

"I clean up well, don't I?" she said, a little embarrassed. She sat across from him. "We had a press conference this morning about the poll that just came out. The numbers don't look good so I had to." She took a sip of water.

"Theilen is still leading, isn't she?"

Nan frowned. "Howard has recovered nearly everything he lost after the *Times* series about Sheldon Hanrahan. The U.S. Attorney's decision last week to drop the investigation gave Howard a big boost. It's a close race again."

"I can't believe they dropped the investigation," Ben said, shaking his head. "Sheldon must have powerful friends."

Nan rolled her eyes. "He's a snake. Get this. The poll numbers show Howard stronger on crime. Stronger on crime? His campaign manager broke the law! It was Watergate all over again! I'll say this, Sheldon is good at spin. Just this morning, a direct mail campaign came out hinting that Theilen might be a lesbian. A lesbian! She has two kids and has been married twenty-five years. But the press will pick up the story and we'll be on the defensive. I tell you, Ben, this election is turning nasty."

"I'm sorry, Nan," Ben said. "I do have some good news for you, though. That's why I wanted to meet you for lunch. I wanted to tell you about it before I left for France."

A waiter in a stiff white apron came to the table. Ben ordered a small steak and Nan ordered a salad.

"France." Nan gave Ben a look. "Next time, go when you can take your wife. I'll miss you while you're gone. Jenny will too. Thanks again, by the way, for caring for her while I've been crazy busy."

"Of course," Ben said. "I'm finally beginning to learn the difference between those skating jumps."

"You said you had good news?" Nan's blue eyes widened. "I know. You bought an airplane ticket for me to France? As if I had the time…"

"I wish you could go," Ben said, "but no. It's about your ad campaign. I've seen our concepts for the last big push. Nan, it's some of our best work. We're all excited about them. They might help Theilen win."

"Wow, that's almost as good as a ticket to France. Can you give me a verbal peek?"

Ben shook his head. "It's agency policy to never show a client their ads until they're ready. I'm only telling you this much because you get special privileges."

"Yeah," she said with a flirtatious smile. "I know the agency president." She leaned into him. "I have wild sex with him to get those special privileges."

"You must be good."

"I'm very, very good," she said with a wink.

Ben laughed. The food came and while they ate, they talked about how Jenny was doing at school and a possible holiday vacation somewhere warm. When they were finished, the waiter in the white apron brought the bill.

Nan checked her watch. "I gotta run. I'm meeting the strategy team to talk about the lesbian thing. I'll be late. I'll try to get home before you leave."

As they rose from the table, Ben took her hand and squeezed it. "I love you," he said.

"I love you too," she replied. "If I don't see you, have a great trip."

FORTY-EIGHT

DETECTIVE JACKSON WAS nervous standing at the head of the Minneapolis Police Headquarters briefing room. He looked out to a bevy of TV cameras and lights pointed at him. Chief Daniels was on his right and Lieutenant West was on his left. A few people from Jackson's precinct sat in chairs in the back.

As Jackson shuffled his feet and wondered where he should put his hands, Reverend Terrance White strolled in. The Reverend's white three-piece suit contrasted perfectly with his coal-black skin and complimented his flawless white teeth. He pumped the hands of several reporters before he settled his wide frame into a chair.

Chief Daniels, fit, trim and dressed in a gray business suit stepped to the lectern. "Let's begin," he said. The lights on the TV cameras blinked to life, the reporters clicked on their tape recorders and held them out toward the lectern.

"We're here this afternoon to recognize one of our detectives for his outstanding work on the Shauna Tate case," Daniels began. "Detective Darren Jackson has been selected to receive the Meritorious Service Award." Daniels went on to describe the case's challenges and explain how Jackson had worked tirelessly until he'd brought the young girl's shooters to justice. He concluded by saying that Jackson was an outstanding example of the hard working, dedicated people on the Minneapolis police force.

Jackson stepped forward and Daniels handed him a shiny silver medal in a mahogany box. Jackson held the medal to the cameras while Chief Daniels shook his hand and the cameras clicked and flashed.

Finally, Daniels said, "Detective, would you like to say a few words?"

Jackson took the lectern, stared at the cameras, lights and reporters with their tape recorders pointed at him and he couldn't remember what he'd planned to say. After a few awkward seconds, "Thank you," was all he said and stepped back from the lectern. The audience applauded politely and the ceremony was over eight minutes after it began.

Several photographers came to the front and asked for a photograph of Jackson. As they set up, Reverend White pushed his way to the front with his hand held out. His ivory smile was broad and Jackson wondered how so many teeth could fit into one mouth.

"Congratulations, Detective." White grabbed Jackson's hand and held on. His teeth clicked as he talked. "We need more recognition of the African-American community's contribution to our city."

Still holding Jackson's hand, White turned to the reporters. "How about a picture with me and the detective?" Reverend White turned Jackson to the cameras and more flashes went off.

When the cameras stopped clicking, White let go of Jackson's hand and waddled off after a reporter and Jackson realized he hadn't said a single word to the Reverend.

As the room cleared, Lieutenant West approached Jackson and extended a knuckly hand. "Nice speech," he said.

Jackson shook the Lieutenant's hand. "Yeah, well . . ."

West laughed. "Seriously, congratulations, Darren. We're all proud of you."

"Thanks, Lieu," Jackson said. "I really don't like these things, you know."

"Well, you better get used to it," West said with a slap on Jackson's back. "You're a great detective. I think there'll be more of them in your future. See you at the precinct later." West turned and left the briefing room with the others.

The room was almost empty when Chief Daniels came up to Jackson and shook his hand one more time. "Sorry about the speech, Chief," Jackson said.

"Don't worry about it." Daniels turned them both toward the exit. "Making speeches is my job. You did just fine."

As they reached the door, Jackson remembered the Trevor Marin case. He hadn't thought about it for months. But with Chief Daniels by his side, the unanswered questions came rushing back—especially Chief Daniels himself releasing Marin's body so quickly. Jackson's obsession—the one that now made him a decorated detective—was back.

As they walked through the door, Daniels smiled cordially. "Darren," he said, "let me know if there's anything I can do for you."

As Daniels headed back to his office, Jackson said, "There is one thing, Chief."

Daniels turned back. "Oh?"

"Ya know, I was workin' on the Trevor Marin case before I got put on the Tate case and, well, I was just wonderin'—it was you who released Marin's body that mornin.' The policy is to hold bodies for 24 hours. Why'd you release it so soon?"

Daniels' face stayed genial but his hazel eyes turned icy. "Detective Jackson, you have a bright future with the Minneapolis Police Department. Keep up the good work."

The chief of police turned and walked away.

FORTY-NINE

"GET AS MUCH SLEEP as you can, Ben," Everet said shortly after Katch's corporate Bombardier 5000 jet took off for Charles De Gaulle airport. After downing a double scotch on the rocks, Everet reclined in one of the big leather chairs and began snoring impressively. Ben tried to sleep too, but he wasn't tired. He tried to read but he couldn't concentrate. He looked out the window and his mind drifted and he remembered.

They'd gotten the call from the Los Angeles Police Department as Ben was getting ready for his freshman year at Minnesota. They hadn't heard from Ellen in over a year. The call came in just as Ben and his mother were sitting down for dinner. It was a Tuesday.

Ben's mother answered the phone and listened for a few minutes. Then she closed her eyes and bowed her head. She handed the phone to Ben. She turned off the stove and went to her bedroom.

It was a heroin overdose, the police officer had said. Someone found Ellen's body in a motel room in Compton. She'd been turning tricks to pay for her drugs and had been in trouble several times before. Ellen's body was in the Los Angeles County morgue and the police wanted to know what they should do with it. Ben didn't know what to do, so he hung up the phone and called his Uncle Jim. "I'll take care of it," Uncle Jim had said. Ben knew then and there he'd let everyone down. His mother, Uncle Jim, his father, Ellen. He hadn't been able to be the head of the family and his failure had killed his sister. His mother never really connected with him after Ellen died and Uncle Jim regarded him as a loser. And, for years, he believed he was.

Finally, as the jet glided over the Atlantic into the Tuesday dawn, Ben drifted off into a shallow sleep. Hours later, he woke to the sound of jet engines reversing thrust and Ben realized they'd touched down. He blinked his eyes open and saw Everet Katch smiling at him through his salt and pepper beard. "Ah, France," Everet said. "There's no better place than France in October." Ben nodded, though he'd never even been to France before.

The jet taxied to a private tarmac, stopped and turned off its engines. After a few minutes, the pilot dropped the jet's stairs and two uniformed French customs officers boarded. They checked Everet's and Ben's passports, inspected their luggage, asked a few questions. Whatever Everet answered in French seemed to satisfy the officers and they stamped the passports and disembarked. Ben followed Everet off the plane and into the back of a black Peugeot. A uniformed driver helped the pilot shove their bags into the trunk. Then he climbed behind the wheel and pointed the car south toward the Loire Valley.

The drive took three hours. The sky was sapphire blue and the fall air, cool and dry. They were harvesting grapes in the vineyards, and wood-sided trucks filled with the harvest rumbled over dusty dirt roads toward the quaint wineries. Everet and Ben exchanged idle chat, Everet trying to educate Ben about the particulars of French wines.

After a long silence Everet said, "You know, Ben, I'd have never let Hanrahan Communications take over my advertising. Never."

It took a few seconds for what Everet said to sink in. "Then why the review?" Ben asked finally.

"I told you the week before your presentation. I had to get some of my shareholders off my back."

"I see," said Ben. "What would've happened if we hadn't been able to give the presentation? Or what if our presentation stunk?"

Everet turned his gaze at the vineyards. "First of all, I believed you'd do a great presentation. I had confidence in you. You have the magic, Ben, just like Tree."

"Thanks," replied Ben. "It was good work, wasn't it?"

Everet turned and grinned at Ben. "Some of the best. And the results prove it. Mutual fund sales are coming back. And the buzz from the open letter campaign is way beyond what we expected. It's working wonderfully."

"We almost didn't get to present it," Ben said.

"Well, if you hadn't, I'd have found a way to hold off the decision until you did," Everet said. "And if the board still voted for HC, I would have threatened to resign and the board would have gone with my decision anyway."

"So the pitch was just to get a few shareholders off your back?"

Everet nodded. "That and more."

"More?" asked Ben. Everet didn't answer.

*

The Peugeot turned off the road onto a gravel drive. The gravel crunched under the tires and dust billowed up behind the car. The drive wound through a small vineyard and lead to a two-story château with a steep-pitched slate roof and faded green shutters. Sculpted junipers lined the stucco walls. To the left was a one-story barn with the same green shutters.

The car stopped at the front of the château and the driver opened the door for Everet and Ben. Ben asked, "Is this where our meeting is?"

"Yep." Everet stretched his legs. "Château Ballard."

The chateau's front door opened and a slim man in his fifties stepped through. He was wearing a black turtleneck and black pleated slacks. Ben thought he recognized him. "Everet! How wonderful to see you again." The man had an English accent.

"Keith," Everet replied as a greeting. The two men shook hands like old friends.

Everet pointed to Ben. "Keith Ballard, meet Ben Smith."

"Keith Ballard of Ballard Advertising in San Francisco?" Ben asked as he shook the man's hand. Keith had a smoking pipe in his other hand.

"One and the same," Keith Ballard replied. "Pleasure to meet you, Ben. I've heard a lot about you. I have been looking forward to this meeting for quite some time now. Welcome to my family's château in the lovely Loire Valley. Come in! Come in!"

Ben followed Keith and Everet into the house. A center hall with parquet flooring opened to a large living area with twelve-foot ceilings and furnished with what looked like vintage French furniture. The ceilings were coved and *fleur-de-lis* adorned the tops of each doorway. Streaks of sunlight angled through large windows facing vineyards that ran all the way to the Loire River.

"You're just in time for tea," Keith said. "We're having it in the garden." He pointed to the back of the house with the stem of his pipe. "It's a lovely day for it, don't you agree?"

Keith Ballard led Ben and Everet out to a patio. Beyond the patio, a lawn sloped down to the vineyard above the valley. A table and chairs were set up on the lawn and a middle-aged woman and elderly man were sitting at it gazing out over the valley. Ben followed Keith and Everet across the patio onto the lawn. As he got closer, he wondered if he was dreaming. He thought he recognized Sarah Marin.

As he approached, Ben realized it was really her. She smiled. "I'm glad you could come, Ben," she said.

"Sarah?" Ben exclaimed. "What are you doing here?

Her answer was a look from Ben to the elderly man sitting at the patio table.

"Hello, Ben," the man said wheezing. His hair had gone completely gray. His skin was pasty like Ellen's was when she'd left home. And he was rail thin. He wore a thick wool sweater and a red blanket was draped across his legs.

"Tree?" Ben gasped. "I attended your funeral."

Everet pulled out a chair and Ben slumped into it facing the sickly man in front of him. Trevor Marin had always been a picture of vigor, and now he was frail and vulnerable. Ben was shocked at the site of him.

Finally, Tree spoke. His voice was weak. "I guess I have to explain a few things, Ben." Then he said to Keith Ballard, "Keith, my friend, we should probably hold off tea for a while. I think Ben here needs some time."

"But of course," Keith said. "Not a problem at all. Perhaps the rest of us should let these two talk."

"Good idea," Everet said. "I want to check out this year's grapes. I hear it'll be a classic vintage." Everet and Keith went back to the house. Sarah kissed Tree on the top of the head and smiled sadly at Ben. She then followed the other two into the house.

Ben studied Tree for a long time and then said, "I'm so glad to see you again. I never thought I would. I don't understand. Why did you do this?"

"I'm dying, Ben," Tree said without emotion. "Multiple myeloma—a particularly virulent strain, I'm told. I probably won't see the end of the year. Keith has graciously allowed me to die here, at his family's château. I can't think of a better place."

Ben looked out over the valley. "My God, Tree," he said.

Tree pushed the blanket off his legs. "Help me up," he said. "I want to walk while I still can. Sarah doesn't like it when I do. She wants me to conserve my strength but I'd rather use what's left to feel as human as I can. Keith has lovely grounds here."

Ben helped Tree to his feet and the frail man held Ben's arm as they slowly strolled across the green grass.

"I faked my death for a number of reasons, Ben," Tree began. "When I learned I was going to die, I decided I wanted to die on my own terms. I want people to remember me as I was when I was healthy. I didn't want their last images of me as a weak, sick old man. I guess I have too much of an ego," he said with a wry smile.

"And there were other reasons too," Tree said.

They walked around the side of the house along a vineyard thick with grapes. The sweet, musty smell of grapes was heavy in the fall air. "When a man's facing death," Tree continued, "he takes stock of his life and there were things I wanted to do before I died. One was to correct a mistake I made years ago. Another was to see that J&M survived. So I hatched a plan."

"A plan?" Ben asked.

"Yes. The mistake I made years ago was with Sheldon Hanrahan. He and I used to be great friends, Ben. We loved each other like brothers. But I took advantage of him after his accident and I've regretted it ever since." Tree leaned a little harder on Ben.

"John told me the story about Sheldon and Louise Jacob and how you got Katch as a client," Ben said.

"I was wrong. And I'm sorry to say it changed Sheldon. It corrupted him. He hurt a lot of people including Keith Ballard here to win the CompuSto account. I tried to talk to Sheldon about it a number of times, but he wouldn't listen. He told me he was just practicing the lesson I taught him about survival.

"And the more success he had, the more corrupt he became. Someone had to stop him before he puts Bill Howard in the White House. His views are... dangerous. Many of us believe if he gets in power, he'll destroy our good country."

Tree coughed and wheezed. Ben stopped walking but Tree motioned them to continue. "So, I thought of a way. I set a trap and the bait was the Katch account. I knew with me gone, he'd use his dirty tricks to go after Katch. I thought we'd expose him. We almost did when that woman attacked you. But Sheldon was too quick. Then, when we learned your friend Dirk had traced the computer hackings to him, we thought we had him there, too."

"We?" asked Ben. "Who else was in on it?"

"A lot of people are concerned about Mr. Hanrahan," Tree said.

"Everet and Keith were involved. Keith wanted to settle an old score—the CompuSto pitch. And Chief Daniels has been trying to catch Sheldon for years. My plan almost worked. There was only one hitch."

"A hitch?" Ben asked. They turn the corner around the barn and headed back.

Tree's eyes turned sad. "I was a successful businessman, Ben, and a good husband. But I wasn't always a good father. We had to tell my oldest son David about the plan. I couldn't deceive my children about my death. David and I have been estranged for years. He threatened to go to the police—he even made a call to them—unless we gave him some money. We did and he backed off."

"So your plan didn't work?"

"Well, we slowed Sheldon down at least. He might think twice about what he does from now on.

"But Ben," Tree said, halting them both with a pull of Ben's arm, "stopping Sheldon was only part of the plan. The other part was to save J&M. The other part was for you."

"Me?" Ben asked.

Tree motioned for them to return to the patio table. "You know, Ben," Tree said, "the two great loves of my life are Sarah and J&M. I'm sad that I'm leaving them. Sarah will be alright. She's strong. But the agency..."

They'd returned to the patio table. Ben helped Tree into his chair and sat next to him. After a few labored breaths, Tree continued. "I always thought you'd be the person to take over J&M after me. You were reluctant for some reason. I even brought in Tom Clarey because I thought it'd piss you off and make you step up. But something always held you back."

"Yeah, I suppose you're right," Ben said.

Tree nodded and smiled weakly at Ben. "I set up the pitch with Everet to force you to take charge of the agency. Ben my boy, it's hard being a leader. It's far easier to follow. But I knew you'd rise to the challenge. It's in you, Ben. You just needed a push. I'm sorry we had to do it this way. Please understand, I didn't have much time."

As Ben sat with his dying friend gazing out over the Loire Valley, he finally realized how his father's and Ellen's death had affected him all these years. It had held him back, made him reluctant to fulfill his true potential. But the work he'd done on Katch and the way he was forced to take charge of the agency had changed him. Tree was right, he'd needed a push. And with the push, Ben had found the courage to be a leader. It was, after all, his essential truth.

FIFTY

SHELDON HANRAHAN RESTED his feet on the glass of his desktop. As usual, his office was dark even though it was the middle of the day. He studied the latest poll results for the senate election. The numbers showed that his man Howard was probably going to win.

He'd had to move quickly to stay out of trouble after the *Times* ran the story on his business practices. He had powerful associates in high places, the best legal advice money could buy, and had been able to avoid prosecution. And then he had to pull off a miracle to get Howard's election back on track. He'd pulled out nearly every trick in his bag and now, he was on the brink of success. And in two years, there was the presidential election.

The telephone rang. It was his private line. He answered, "This is Sheldon."

"This Victor." The Russian's voice was low and gravely. "You right. He is alive. In France, at Keith Ballard château in Loire Valley. He is dying."

Sheldon did not respond.

"What do you want to do?" Victor asked.

"How much time does he have?"

"Not long. Few months, maybe."

Sheldon took off his dark glasses and rubbed the bridge of his nose. After several seconds he answered, "We will do nothing.

Nothing against Tree and nothing against Keith Ballard. Understand?"

"Yes. Is clear."

"And Victor, keep me apprised of Mr. Marin's condition. I want to know when he dies."

"I will do."

Sheldon hung up. Trevor Marin. When Sheldon was first told of his old friend's death, he thought back to the days when he was with Tree and Louise. Tree was the only man he'd ever loved and Sheldon wept remembering what they'd had so many years earlier. But then when he discovered someone had given the *Times* information on his business practices, he knew his old friend was still alive and had set a trap for him. Now, Tree would be dead soon and Sheldon wondered if he would ever know love again.

First things first. He had to be sure to win Howard's senate race. He reached back and cracked opened the vertical blinds just enough to throw a thin ray of light across his desk where a single file folder rested. He opened it. Inside were several photos, bank statements, tax returns, a floor plan of a house, and pages and pages of information on… Nan Smith.

He pulled out a photograph and examined it. Nan had intelligent, blue eyes, silky blonde hair and an athlete's body. She was beautiful.

Sheldon set the photo down. He reached back to close the blinds and the room was dark again.

Louise Jacob. Tree Marin. Nan Smith.

Yes, he would win the senate race for William Howard. Then, someday, he would have love again.

Someday.

***

ABOUT THE AUTHOR

Photo by Greg Thoen

FOR OVER THIRTY years, Bill Andrews was a marketing/brand executive/copywriter with several Twin Cities ad agencies and *Fortune* 500 companies. At night and on weekends (and sometimes during the workday!) Bill wrote fiction.

Bill's novel, DAUGHTERS OF THE DRAGON—A Comfort Woman's Story, (Lake Union Publishing 2017) won an IPPY for historical fiction and has made several bestseller lists.

Today, Bill is retired and focused on his writing.

OTHER BOOKS BY WILLIAM ANDREWS:

An Exercise in Sacrifice

Daughters of the Dragon – A Comfort Woman's Story

The Dragon Queen

See Following Pages for Summaries

DAUGHTERS OF THE DRAGON
A Comfort Woman's Story

A Novel by William Andrews

DURING WORLD WAR II, the Japanese forced 200,000 young Korean women to be sex slaves or "comfort women" for their soldiers. This is one woman's riveting story of strength, courage and promises kept.

The Japanese take Jae-hee, a 14-year-old Korean girl to be a sex slave, or "comfort woman" for the Imperial Army. Ja-hee suffers terribly at the hands of the Japanese. Now with Japanese gone, she must carry on an important family legacy.

Her terrible ordeal shapes the rest of her life as she finds and loses true love in the surreal communism of North Korea. After escaping to the south, she's forced to run a *kijichon* (brothel) for the American military in South Korea. Finally, she finds success in the cold capitalism of South Korea's economic boom until her coworkers discover that she was a comfort woman. But through courage and strength, she's able to fulfill her duty to her family.

Set within the tumultuous backdrop of 20th century Korea, Amazon #1 bestseller for Historical Fiction, *Daughters of the Dragon* will make you cry and cheer for Ja-hee. And in the end, you'll have a better understanding of the Land of the Morning Calm.

Daughters of the Dragon is inspired by *The Kite Runner*, by Khaled Hosseini, *Memiors of a Geisha* by Arthur Golden, the books of Amy Tan and Lisa See.

Praise for DAUGHTERS OF THE DRAGON

William Andrews has created a masterpiece of fiction.
- Midwest Book Reviews

This book is an easy 5/5 stars, with its passion swept across the pages. This book spoke to my very soul. EVERYONE should read this story and pass it on.
- Brittany McCann – Author and Reviewer

I finished reading "Daughters of the Dragon" and remained still in my chair with the book in my lap. I was enveloped in the characters and their stories. The author's descriptive passages made me sense the beauty of the country, the desperation of war, and the humanity, good and evil, of each character.
- AMiB: Amazon Power Reviewer

Very emotional story that is hard to put down. Well-developed characters and vivid descriptions bring the experience to life. Sad that it is based on historical truths, but definitely a story that needs to be told. Reading this book provides a poignant look into the Korean culture and a true sense of the strength it takes to be a survivor.
-KE Burke" Barnes and Noble reviewer

I have to admit, I was not sure about this book. A white man telling this story.... I just didn't know if he could pull it off. But he did. It was powerful, unsentimental, and not gratuitous. I am beyond impressed. The reality of this story is still VERY raw across Asia, and it is important that it be told in order to understand the current relations between Japan and its neighbors.
-Rosanne: GoodReads Reviewer

Have you ever read a book that you don't want to end because it is that good? That is how I felt about Daughters of the Dragon: A Comfort Woman's Story. The author handles this difficult subject with great care; the story is captivating and well-paced. I will look forward to reading the next book by William Andrews.

-Minty Mom: Amazon reviewer

This was an awesome book, about something that you never hear of. The devastation is impossible for anyone to comprehend, and yet the courage and strength that these women had is fantastic. I HIGHLY recommend this book. I read often, and many, and this book easily rates in my top 15. I can't wait to read more by this author.

-Ryan Ober: Amazon reviewer

This book is both a tragic and triumphant telling of the atrocities that over 200,000 Korean women had to endure at the hands of the Japanese soldiers during WWII. It is an unforgettable story that for too long has not been told. The author provides historical information that is easily read and powerful. I highly recommend this book to everyone who loves to read and shares a thirst for knowledge. I am looking forward to more from this author!

-Karen Rogers: Amazon reviewer

AVERAGE AMAZON REVIEW: 4.8 stars out of 5 from thousands of reviews.

THE DRAGON QUEEN
A Novel by William Andrews

From the bestselling author of *Daughters of the Dragon* comes the story of one of the most extraordinary queens in history.

AS TENSIONS RISE on the Korean peninsula, US diplomat Nate Simon is sent to Seoul to gauge the political situation and advise the president. He also needs to find out why someone sent the president an ancient, intricately carved comb with an ivory inlay of a two-headed dragon. Though familiar with Korea's language and culture, Nate knows little of its troubled history. Beautiful and mysterious embassy aide Anna Carlson believes it's time he learns, starting with the extraordinary story of Korea's last queen.

Seoul, 1866. The beautiful orphan Ja-young is chosen to be the child bride of Gojong, Korea's boy king. Highly intelligent but shy, Ja-young faces a choice: she can be a stone queen—silent and submissive—or she can be a dragon queen and oppose enemies and empires that try to rule Korea during the age of imperialism. Her choice leads her to forge a legend that will endure far beyond her lifetime.

The more Nate discovers, the more he comes to realize that Queen Min's story is still relevant today. Now the choice is up to him: be submissive and accepting... or change the world.

On bookshelves March, 2018.

THE DIRTY TRUTH
A Novel by William Andrews

NAN SMITH, THE STATE campaign manager for Democratic presidential Election Reform hopeful George Bloomfield discovers a dirty secret about Bloomfield's opponent, Senator William Howard when an old woman tells her, "He murdered my daughter." The revelation thrusts Nan into the center of a massive conspiracy led by Sheldon Hanrahan who will do anything to get his man the presidency. Along the way, Nan learns how poorly regulated U.S. elections are and what candidates are able to get away with. In the end, she finds the smoking gun to expose the conspiracy but powerful forces from all sides threaten her life to prevent it.

The Dirty Truth is about bravery, commitment and one woman's resolve to do what's right for her country and family. And, it will educate the reader on how elections in the United States are run – legally *and* illegally.

Available soon through major on-line booksellers.

For updates visit: www.williamandrewsbooks.com

Printed in Great Britain
by Amazon

50560342R00182